DISNEY · SQUARE ENIX

KINGDOM HEARTS 3D
Dream Drop Distance
THE NOVEL

Disney | SQUARE ENIX

KINGDOM HEARTS 3D
Dream Drop Distance
THE NOVEL

Tomoco Kanemaki

Original Concept
Tetsuya Nomura
Masaru Oka

Illustrations
Shiro Amano

YEN ON

NEW YORK

KINGDOM HEARTS 3D: DREAM DROP DISTANCE THE NOVEL
TOMOCO KANEMAKI,
ILLUSTRATIONS: SHIRO AMANO,
ORIGINAL CONCEPT: TETSUYA NOMURA, MASARU OKA

Translation by Luke Baker
Cover art by Shiro Amano

Yen On
150 West 30th Street, 19th Floor
New York, NY 10001

Visit us at yenpress.com
facebook.com/yenpress
twitter.com/yenpress
yenpress.tumblr.com
instagram.com/yenpress

First Yen On Edition: October 2019

Yen On is an imprint of Yen Press, LLC.
The Yen On name and logo are trademarks of Yen Press, LLC.

Library of Congress Cataloging-in-Publication Data
Names: Kanemaki, Tomoko, 1975- author. | Amano, Shiro, illustrator. |
Nomura, Tetsuya, author. | Oka, Masaru, author. | Amano, Shiro, illustrator. |
Baker, Luke, translator.
Title: Kingdom Hearts 3D : dream drop distance / Tomoco Kanemaki ; original concept,
Tetsuya Nomura, Masaru Oka ; illustration by Shiro Amano ;
translation by Luke Baker.
Description: First Yen On edition. | New York, NY : Yen On, 2019. |
Identifiers: LCCN 2019032112 | ISBN 9781975358617 (trade paperback) |
ISBN 9781975358723 (ebook)
Subjects: CYAC: Fantasy. | Secret societies—Fiction.
Classification: LCC PZ7.1.K256 Kef 2019 | DDC [Fic]—dc23
LC record available at https://lccn.loc.gov/2019032112

ISBNs: 978-1-9753-5861-7 (paperback)
978-1-9753-5872-3 (ebook)

1 3 5 7 9 10 8 6 4 2

LSC-C

Printed in the United States of America

DISNEY ✦ SQUARE ENIX

KINGDOM HEARTS
3D
Dream Drop Distance
THE NOVEL

CONTENTS

Sora's Side

Prologue—Destiny Islands......3

CHAPTER 1
Traverse Town.......11

CHAPTER 2
La Cité des Cloches.......31

CHAPTER 3
Prankster's Paradise.......49

Lea's Side.......63

CHAPTER 4
The Grid.......69

CHAPTER 5
Again.......85

CHAPTER 6
Country of the Musketeers.......99

CHAPTER 7
Symphony of Sorcery.......123

CHAPTER 8
The World That Never Was.......133

Riku's Side

Prologue—Radiant Garden.......155

CHAPTER 1
Traverse Town.......157

CHAPTER 2
La Cité des Cloches.......175

CHAPTER 3
Prankster's Paradise.......189

CHAPTER 4
The Grid.......199

CHAPTER 5
Again.......213

CHAPTER 6
Country of the Musketeers.......223

CHAPTER 7
Symphony of Sorcery.......233

Mickey & Lea's Side.......241

CHAPTER 8
The World That Never Was.......259

FINAL CHAPTER
Mysterious Tower.......281

Coda.......295

PROLOGUE
DESTINY ISLANDS

IN THE MYSTERIOUS TOWER, MICKEY FACED HIS teacher, the great sorcerer Yen Sid. This spire was where the king had once trained to become a Keyblade Master and one of the first places Sora had visited before his journey to fight against Xemnas. A certain other trio had spent some time here before, too.

Sora's two journeys had ended, and so had another adventure that connected memories of the past to the memories he had now.

But Yen Sid's expression was grim.

"Yen Sid, I think we're finally close to figuring out where Ven's heart is," said the king.

"Is that so?" the sorcerer replied. "Then that leaves only Terra."

"Right. And we've gotta save all three of them," Mickey declared.

"Hmm... The question is: What does Xehanort intend to do next?"

"Xehanort?" Mickey was surprised. That name was a thing of the past, wasn't it? "But his two halves are gone. There was Ansem, who commanded the Heartless...and Xemnas, who commanded the Nobodies. Didn't Sora defeat them both?"

That battle was over, or so he thought. But Yen Sid closed his owlish eyes and rose to his feet, standing beside the window. "Correct, those two met their end. However, therein lies exactly our problem. Their destruction now guarantees the original Xehanort's reconstruction."

"Huh?" Mickey gulped.

"Xehanort's heart, once seized by his Heartless half, is now free. And his body, which had become his Nobody, has been vanquished. Both halves will now be returned to the whole. In short...this means Master Xehanort will return."

Master Xehanort—the man who had once sought to cover the world in darkness.

"And you think…you think that maybe he's gonna try something?"

"A man like Xehanort will have left many roads open."

"Well, it doesn't matter what he cooks up. Me and Sora, we'll be ready. And Riku, too!" the king confidently announced.

However, the sorcerer turned back to Mickey and shook his head quietly. "Yes, they are indeed strong, but not true Keyblade Masters, like you. Tell me…would a single one of you suffice if what you faced was not a single one of him?"

"What? What do you mean?"

Yen Sid opened his eyes, but he didn't answer the question. "Mickey, please summon Sora hither. Riku as well."

"Of course, but…why?"

"To show us the Mark of Mastery."

A new conflict was about to begin—and the future would finally link to the past.

Next to Riku, Sora waited a little uncomfortably for Yen Sid to start explaining what exactly they were doing here. Receiving a summons to the Mysterious Tower from King Mickey was all fine and dandy, but he hadn't seen Donald, Goofy, and the king in ages, and instead of doing something interesting, they were all standing here at attention. Riku was waiting silently for the sorcerer to speak, too. He seemed nervous, or maybe he just had something on his mind again.

"Hey…" Sora started to say something to him, but Yen Sid chose that moment to speak at last.

"As a Keyblade Master, Xehanort had a gift like few others."

Sora thought back on the man they knew as Xehanort. That used to be Xemnas's name back when he was human, before he became the boss of Organization XIII. Xehanort had tried to cast the world into darkness before, too, by assuming the identity of Ansem the

Wise. Still, the Xehanort Sora knew didn't have a Keyblade. Was this a different person? If so, then Sora had no idea who Yen Sid was talking about.

Sora's questions went unanswered as Yen Sid continued.

"But such great minds are often plagued by a single great question. What is the essence of the human heart that weakens us or empowers us? The answer, he believed, would be found in the Keyblade War."

More words he didn't know. The Keyblade War... So all the Keyblade wielders were fighting one another? That was strange, Sora thought as he listened to the sorcerer.

"What if the challenges of our past, in fact, were a map to the light and darkness that battles within us all? Xehanort had to know, so he renounced his duties as master and chose the seeker's life. Since then, in many a guise, he has clashed with protectors of the light—Keyblade wielders like yourselves."

Uhhh, so this Master Xehanort guy tried to start some big fight between light and darkness called the Keyblade War, and it was so he could learn about light and darkness in people's hearts? And he did it under different identities, so...um...?

Sora was already lost. He stole a glance at Riku, who was listening solemnly to Yen Sid's speech. *I bet* Riku *actually understands all this, huh?*

"And mark my words—he will trouble us yet again. We must be ready."

Okay, so this Master Xehanort is still up to no good, and they called us in to take him on! Now that I can get my head around.

"Which is why you, Sora and Riku, are to be tested for the mark of a true Keyblade Master."

The Mark of Mastery exam...!

At those words from the sorcerer, Sora finally snapped to attention like everyone else.

The word *exam* made him a little nervous, but it wouldn't be like a math test or anything. Probably. What if they made him study the history of Keyblades, though? The idea didn't exactly thrill him.

"No doubt you fancy yourselves masters already. But it takes years of training. Only a true master can teach you the proper way. Both of you are self-taught Keyblade wielders—an impressive feat."

Sora had never considered the proper way to wield a Keyblade before. He could use one just fine, after all, and he'd taken down both Heartless and Nobodies. What more did he need to learn?

Now he was getting nervous as he waited for Yen Sid to continue.

"However, the time has come for you to let go of preconceived notions, forget what you know about the Keyblade, and begin your training again with a clean slate."

A clean slate...?! I have to go from hero to zero again after coming all this way?!

Sora couldn't stop himself. "But that's a formality, right?" he complained, leaning forward. "I've already proved myself. Me and the king and Riku—we can take on anything. Right, Riku?" He looked up at his friend beside him.

But Riku's expression remained firm. "I don't know. I think that in my heart, darkness still has a hold." He summoned Soul Eater into his hand. "Walking that path changed me. I'm not sure if I'm ready to wield a Keyblade. Maybe I do need to be tested."

"Riku..." Sora lowered his gaze.

I had no idea that stuff was still bothering him. He really feels that way? Well, if that's the case—

"Then count me in. Put me through the test! Just watch—me and Riku will pass with flying colors!"

At Sora's confident declaration, the barest hint of a smile appeared on Riku's face. The king, Donald, and Goofy all shared a relieved glance, too.

"Very well, then," the sorcerer announced. "Sora and Riku, let your examination begin."

＊　　＊　　＊

A comforting and familiar sound reached Sora's ears. It was the sound of waves—the sound of the Destiny Islands.

Sora and Riku called these islands home—and so had someone else, long ago.

The two boys were gazing out at the horizon from the shoreline. Their clothes had changed—instead of what they'd been wearing back with Yen Sid, their garments were now what they'd worn when they first left the islands a year ago.

So this was what the sorcerer had meant by "forget what you know about the Keyblade and begin your training again with a clean slate." Yen Sid had told them plenty of other things, too, but most of that had gone over Sora's head.

I guess maybe we need to fight...and if we win, we pass?

"But how far could a raft take us?" Sora asked Riku, his eyes still on the horizon.

"Who knows? If we have to, we'll think of something else," Riku replied as he began walking over to the raft they had made just that day.

"If there are any other worlds out there, why did we end up on this one?"

That's what Riku had said back then. They'd seen many worlds and made many friends since. Unlike Riku, Sora had never wondered why they ended up here, but it seemed the thought had always been on his friend's mind.

Sora followed after Riku and boarded the raft—apparently, their only option for getting to other worlds.

The waters around the Destiny Islands were generally calm, but the open seas were another story. About an hour out, the skies darkened, and the ocean began to get choppy.

"Riku, a storm's coming," Sora called over to his friend, a bit perturbed. There was a chill on the wind. Thunderclaps rumbled through the air.

"I know. The waves are getting steep." Riku approached the mast. "Furl the sail."

"Right." Just as Sora headed over to take care of it, a powerful gust filled the sail and snapped the mast in two. "Whoa!"

While Sora hurriedly ducked down, Riku was knocked through the air and into the sea along with the mast. He would've gone under if he hadn't managed to grab hold of the log.

"Riku!"

"I'm fine!"

Sora held out his hand to him, but at that moment, the ocean heaved ominously, forming a whirlpool that swallowed the sea itself. Its center was a pitch-black abyss.

"What's that?" Riku whispered, and a moment later, huge purple tentacles shot toward the surface. Then, with a splash, a great sea monster rose from the water, cackling—no, it wasn't a monster; it was Ursula, the witch who had tried to trick Ariel in Atlantica.

"Oh, he was right. Those wretched guppies are here. Well, it's about time we settled the score!" Ursula shouted at the two boys, her tentacles writhing.

"Ursula? But how—? Is this the test?" Sora brandished his Keyblade.

"Come on!" Riku called. "You can work it out later!"

"All right!" Sora replied.

Using Ursula's tentacles as a series of platforms, Riku made his way back to the raft.

"Sorry, dearies, but you don't stand a chance!" The witch's tentacles lifted the raft. With a cackle, she called down lightning on Sora and Riku. "It's high time you were punished!"

She was gigantic; her face alone was five times as tall as Sora. She spit bubbles at him, but he still knocked them back at her with ease. He may have forgotten the ins and outs of how to use his Keyblade, but not how to fight. Plus, he had Riku by his side now.

"All right, let's do this!"

Sora and Riku dashed across the raft in unison and delivered a blow to Ursula with everything they had. The witch vanished with a shriek—and a shock wave that tossed the two friends into the sea.

As Sora and Riku sank into the briny depths and began to lose consciousness, they could barely make out a light in the distance.

Is that a Keyhole...?

A beam of light shot from each boy's Keyblade and opened the Keyhole. A powerful gleam radiated from it, swallowing both of them up.

And then there was someone else, watching them.

A man wearing a brown robe.

"This world has been connected."

Sora gazed at the man as if in a trance, but he was already on the brink of unconsciousness.

He and Riku slowly drifted off to sleep.

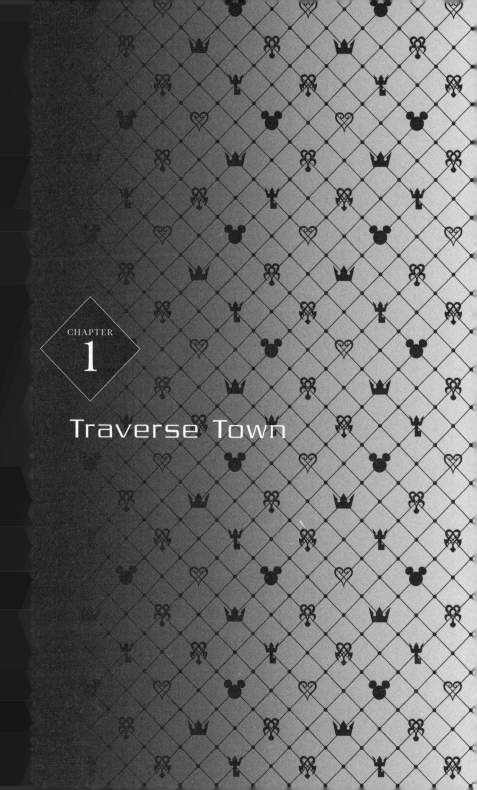

CHAPTER

1

Traverse Town

WHEN SORA CAME TO, HE WAS STANDING ABOVE A street he recognized, surrounded by dusky bricks and several neon signs. A city that felt familiar to anyone who visited it—this was Traverse Town. His very first journey had begun here, he remembered. He was pretty sure he had woken up in an alley that time. *Now, uh, I guess I'm in a building across from the Third District gate? Or out on the veranda...?*

This was the First District, and the shop at the top of the steps in that plaza was Cid's. This was where he had met Cid and Yuffie, Leon and Aerith, and then Donald and Goofy, too. Cid and the others were in Radiant Garden, though, so he didn't expect to see them around. *Plus, I'm in the middle of the Mark of Mastery exam, so...um...*

"Hey, what's with my clothes?"

Somewhere along the way, Sora's outfit had changed to one he had never seen. When he left the Destiny Islands, he'd been wearing his outfit from when he left home for the first time, so maybe this was more of Master Yen Sid's magic? There was a large X on the front of Sora's shirt, and his jacket had also turned black, but his pants were still red like before.

And speaking of things that were different from before, Riku was gone, too.

"Riku! Hellooo? Riku!" Sora called out in a loud voice. He could've sworn they were together at least up until they fell off the raft. *Then we sank into the water, and...then what?*

"Shut it. Talk about noise..."

"Huh?!"

Sora heard a voice come from overhead and leaned forward. He could see someone sitting on the roof, but he had leaned out a bit too far and tumbled right off the balcony and into the plaza.

"Ouch..."

When Sora managed to get to his feet, a teenage boy was standing next to him. He was wearing headphones over his spiky orange hair and looking intently at Sora's face.

"Sora, right?"

"Yeah, but, uh…how do you know that?"

Instead of answering the question, the boy grabbed Sora's hand and examined his palm.

"Looks like you're not a Player."

The comment made no sense. "A Player?" Sora asked. *What's a Player? I'm guessing he's not talking about the Mark of Mastery exam.*

"C'mon, keep up. In the Game."

The boy showed his own palm to the obviously puzzled Sora. There were numbers on it—apparently a time stamp of some sort. *It's going down, so…a countdown?*

"Players get marked with the time limit. And this Game, I can't afford to lose. I need my Game Partner."

Sora had no idea what this "Game" was or who the "Players" were, but he linked his hands behind his head like always did and smiled. "Okay… I don't know about any Game, but how can I help?"

"What? Time out."

Now it was the boy's turn to reply with a question. But if someone was in trouble, helping them was just what you did. That had been Sora's MO the whole time, and he didn't plan on changing it anytime soon.

"Do you trust every total stranger you meet?" asked the boy, his eyes slightly downcast. Then he continued, "Look—sorry, you're no good. You're not a Player. And my pact's with someone else."

Well, there was only one reply to that.

"Okay, so we can't be partners. Why don't I help you out as your friend?"

"Now we're friends? It's not that easy," the boy snapped as he abruptly turned away.

"Not saying it is…but you could make it easier," Sora pressed with a grin. He had made a lot of friends up till now, and he didn't intend to stop at this point. Even if this world wasn't real, there was no reason they couldn't become friends.

"Yeah, sounds great. Whatever."

And with that, the boy ran off, leaving Sora behind.

"Cool! Lead the way," Sora called after him. *If he doesn't care, I'll do what I want, then.* And what he wanted was to make a friend and help him with this Game or whatever. After all, he didn't seem like a bad guy.

Sora took off after the boy. He had the layout of Traverse Town pretty much memorized. The strength he'd gained over the course of his journeys might have been lost, but that didn't mean his memories had been wiped.

He ran up the steps in front of Cid's shop, then circled around back toward the big doors of the Second District.

It was in the Second District that Sora finally caught up. The other boy turned around once he noticed Sora's arrival.

"Hey, I didn't catch your name," Sora said.

The boy paused for a moment, then started to reply—but then a circle of very strange-looking creatures appeared around the two of them. They didn't appear to be Heartless or even Nobodies.

"Dream Eaters!" the boy cried, bracing for a fight as another weird little creature appeared by him, too.

This one felt different from the others—something about its eyes. It resembled the ones hemming them in, but unlike them, there was nothing menacing about it.

"That's a weird name," Sora muttered in reply.

"Not me," the boy snapped. "Them."

"Right. I knew that!"

Oh, so these guys are the "Dream Eaters," not him. Now that you mention it, I feel like I've heard that name before. But from where?

The Dream Eaters edged toward Sora and the boy, closing the distance. These must be the baddies they would be facing this time.

"Don't let 'em surround us! Let's split up!" the boy called.

"Got it!" Sora summoned his Keyblade.

"Oh, uh, and…it's Neku."

"Huh?" Sora asked, unsure what he meant.

"Neku Sakuraba. You asked," the youth explained, avoiding Sora's eyes.

"Neku Sakuraba. That's a mouthful!" Sora replied honestly.

"No. It's really not," Neku shot back.

"C'mon, Neku," Sora called. "Let's take 'em!"

At Sora's signal, Neku charged, and not wanting to be left out, Sora held up his weapon and rushed toward the pack of Dream Eaters. Keyblade whirling and spells flying, Sora took down the creatures. They weren't Heartless or Nobodies, but they still seemed to be tough customers.

Once the last of them had been dealt with, Neku returned with the Dream Eater he had summoned before the battle. This one seemed to be his friend.

"These things with you—they're Dream Eaters, too?"

"Yeah." Neku nodded.

That must mean some Dream Eaters are friendly, and some will try to attack us.

"If I'm gonna survive the Game, I'm gonna need some extra help. Think you could control them?"

Finally, Sora remembered what Yen Sid had said.

After he had finished going over the Mark of Mastery exam, the sorcerer had had more to say to Sora and Riku.

"If we are ever to strike down Xehanort, we need the individuals King Mickey spoke of in his letter. We must lead them out of sorrow and slumber, back to our world."

Who exactly were these people in "sorrow and slumber"? Sora didn't know why, but he felt a pang in his chest, a wistful sort of loneliness.

"To do so, seven Sleeping Keyholes must be found and unlocked, and a great power retrieved. As you know, every world is walled off from the next, preventing travel between them. In the past, you could bridge these gaps because the walls were broken or because you could open special Lanes with your Keyblades. But your new goals, the 'Sleeping Keyholes,' are harder to reach."

Seven Keyholes— That number makes me think of the Princesses of Heart: Alice, Snow White, Aurora, Cinderella, Jasmine, Belle, and then Kairi. Maybe the Keyholes and the princesses are connected somehow?

"You'll recall, in your first journey, that you brought many worlds back from the darkness—but some never returned completely. They still sleep, cut off from all outside channels. Not even the Heartless can enter."

Yen Sid was always long-winded, but unlike the teachers at school, he was lecturing about worlds Sora had never been to before. It was pretty interesting, even to him.

"But these Sleeping Worlds are said to have their own manner of darkness. They are called Dream Eaters, and there are two kinds—"

Sora wasn't sure what eating dreams entailed exactly, but he guessed Dream Eaters were like the Heartless or the Nobodies.

"'Nightmares,' which devour happy dreams—and benevolent 'Spirits,' which consume the Nightmares."

So there's good ones and bad ones. Sora found his own way of understanding.

"The Dream Eaters will guide you, just as the Heartless once guided you, to the Keyhole you seek at the heart of each world."

And with that, Yen Sid's explanation of Dream Eaters came to an end.

"So the little guy must be a Spirit."

The Dream Eater next to Neku was rubbing up against his legs affectionately.

"You can make Dream Eaters from Dream Pieces, and you get those by taking out Dream Eaters."

"Gotcha. I'll give it a shot." Sora collected the scattered Dream Pieces left behind after the battle, then put them together according to a recipe Neku handed him.

The light around the pieces swelled as they came together—and something appeared within the brilliant glow.

"…Is this…a dog?" Sora tilted his head to one side curiously.

"Nah, I'd say it's more of a cat."

Neku gave the Dream Eater a close look with his arms crossed, too. The Dream Eater—a strange, pudgy creature with a single horn on its head—was a Spirit that wasn't quite cat or dog. It was called a Meow Wow, and he was apparently already a big fan of Sora. He rolled over in front of him, belly up.

"Well, I guess it doesn't really matter. Nice to meetcha."

Sora rubbed the soft tummy, and Meow Wow let out a happy snort. After the two of them had introduced themselves in their own way, Neku eventually looked away from Sora. "Follow me," he said.

"Okay," Sora replied, then followed the boy along with Meow Wow.

They proceeded through the backstreets, dispatching Dream Eaters along the way. Neku didn't say anything.

Eventually, they arrived at the Third District, and the moment they did, Neku suddenly shouted.

"I brought you Sora! We had a bargain!" he yelled toward the door to the First District.

"What's the matter, Neku?"

What was this about a bargain? Did Neku make a deal with someone?

Without a moment's notice, the man who Neku had called to appeared. The man was wearing one of those oh-so-familiar black coats—the uniform of choice for Organization XIII, Sora's enemies during his second adventure.

Sora wasted no time readying his Keyblade.

"No way!"

The gleam of magic began to build in the man's raised hand. He then moved as if to bring down his arm.

"Hey! That wasn't the deal! You said you wouldn't hurt him!" Neku cried out in a panic. He ran in front of the man, spreading his arms to shield Sora.

"Don't! Neku! They're too dangerous!" Sora shouted—and a moment later, a heavy sensation he couldn't quite place washed over him.

He was suddenly very, very drowsy.

"What? Why am I so...sleepy?"

He crumpled to the ground, fast asleep.

"...Mm, agh..."

When he awoke, Sora was lying in the Third District, right where he'd lost consciousness. The stones were cool against his cheek. He rubbed his eyes as he stood up. Neither the man in the black coat nor Neku were there.

That didn't happen because I got hit with some attack or spell, thought Sora. *I was just too sleepy to stay awake. What's going on here? Yen Sid said we're in the "Sleeping Worlds"—does it have something to do with that? I'm not dreaming, though. Probably.*

Sora was worried about Neku, too. He had told the creep in the coat that they had a deal. What did that mean? Well, one thing was for sure—Neku and the guy in black knew each other.

"I guess I should just take a look around."

Sora decided to stop thinking and start doing. For starters, he would search the area nearby. The door across from the small fountain led back to the First District, he remembered.

He hadn't caught sight of Neku, not to mention his partner, so he'd just try to find Neku for now.

Sora opened the door to the First District to start his search there this time around.

I wonder if there's anywhere I haven't gone yet?

As Sora thought this over, Meow Wow finally left his side and waddled off on his own.

"Hey, where're you going?!"

Meow Wow led him to a door that Sora had never opened in any of his previous journeys.

"Hey, I'm not sure it actually opens…"

But Meow Wow simply pushed the door ajar with his small body.

"Oh, it does?"

Standing behind Meow Wow, Sora took a peek through the crack. Beyond it was an alley that he had never set foot in before. It was kind of nice to know that Traverse Town still had places to explore.

Sora decided to go on ahead with Meow Wow. He followed the winding lane and passed through what looked like an underground waterway, and beyond it was a great fountain. *Hey, Traverse Town has another smaller fountain in the Second District, too.*

Dispatching Dream Eaters, Sora reached the next door and stepped through.

"Wow! Never been this way before!"

This was the Fourth District, a brightly lit block with chains of glittering lamps strung across its streets. Farther ahead stood a single building with glaring neon. Several of the item-selling Moogles Sora knew so well were there.

He slid down the rails of a stairway leading to the bright structure only to spy a boy…no, a girl, standing beside the Moogles. Dressed in a hat and slightly baggy clothes, the girl looked to be younger than him. Her outfit reminded Sora of Neku's. Maybe this was who Neku was looking for.

"Hey, um…," Sora called to her. "Any chance you're Neku's partner?"

"Umm…I'm not really sure. All I know is that my name is Rhyme," said the girl.

"You mean…you've lost your memory?"

"Yep."

"Oh. Sorry…"

Sora had lost his memory before, too, so he could kind of relate. It was sad to have those precious memories and feelings vanish. And yet, Rhyme flashed a happy smile.

"Aw, it's no big deal. You know what they always say—'Sometimes memories just need a little help getting out.'"

"Yeah…that's true." Sora returned Rhyme's smile.

"Yeah!"

Still, it had to be tough not being able to remember anything. How could they restore Rhyme's memory?

"Huh, 'a little help'… I know! Maybe Neku can jog your memory! C'mon, Rhyme. Let's go find him!"

"Right!"

That said, Sora had already scoured every last inch of the way here. The only place he hadn't checked was whatever lay beyond the Fourth District. He took a look around and spotted a large door next to the Moogles selling items. He and Rhyme opened it together to find the Fifth District. There was a bridge over some babbling water.

The two of them crossed the bridge and found another big building with a sign that said FLOWERS & PLANTS. Probably a botanical garden or something. The door was shut at the moment, though, so they couldn't get inside.

Neku was on top of the glass roof.

"Hey, Neku! It's you!" Sora ran up to him, calling out. He'd been worried ever since he woke up in the Third District that Neku might still be in trouble, especially when he couldn't find him or the man in the black coat.

Something seemed off, though. "Sora…," Neku said without turning around. "What? You actually still trust me?"

"Of course I do." Sora's intuition said Neku wasn't a bad guy, and he was confident it was right.

"But you know that I tricked you, right? That guy in the black coat, he said that he could send me home—me and my partner—but I had to bring you to him first."

Neku fell silent for a moment. Sora waited for him to continue.

"Sorry."

See? He wasn't bad at all.

"No big deal. When it really mattered, you stood up for me. And besides—we're friends, right?"

"Friends..." Neku turned back and finally showed a hint of a smile.

Sora tried asking him about Rhyme, the girl standing next to him. "Oh, hey, Neku—this here is Rhyme. Is she your Game partner?"

"No," Neku replied. "Sorry. I'm teamed up with somebody else."

Just then, Rhyme was swallowed into a burst of orange light.

"What? Rhyme!"

"Huh?!"

And then, as if to take her place, the man in the black coat appeared before the startled duo. Sora immediately readied his Keyblade, but Neku was the first to launch himself at the mysterious figure. However, a black wind swirled around the man and blasted Neku away.

"Neku!" Sora called out in shock as the man raised his hands overhead. An inky glow swirled together to form a bizarre-looking creature—something best described as a box with the head and limbs of a monkey.

Sora had never seen a Dream Eater this big before. The enormous Hockomonkey roared, shaking the air itself.

As for the man, he simply melted away into the Corridor of Darkness that opened behind him.

"Huh? Hey, wait!" Sora tried to go after him, but the Dream Eater barred his path. "Out of my way!"

Keyblade in hand, Sora faced the Hockomonkey alongside Meow Wow, and the battle began.

Hockomonkey's hands, which appeared to be in boxing gloves, detached from its body and began to fly around and launch attacks on their own.

This was a real headache.

Sora avoided them, drew a bead on Hockomonkey's body, and

attempted an overhead strike only to be batted right off the edge of the building. Meow Wow followed and looked up at Sora worriedly.

"What? That was nothing."

"Mrarf?"

The creature turned its back to Sora and wagged its round tail, almost like it was telling Sora to hop aboard.

"You sure?"

"Mrarf."

As soon as Sora was astride, Meow Wow started bouncing around like a ball.

"Wow!"

Boinging high into the air, the chubby Meow Wow came crashing down on Hockomonkey and flattened it.

"Groooooh!" the Dream Eater howled and fell still.

"Hey, not bad. Now let's do this!" Now that Hockomonkey was down for the count, Sora leaped off Meow Wow's back and delivered the finishing blow.

The Dream Eater's body was enveloped in a blinding light and rose into the sky, where it burst into shards of light.

One of those shards drifted down and projected the forms of two people—Riku and a girl Sora didn't recognize. The image was hazy enough that he could instantly tell they weren't actually there.

"Riku!"

Sora was about to run toward the projection of his best friend when someone called out to stop him.

"Hold on, Sora."

Sora turned around to see a boy he didn't know. He had wavy, shoulder-length, ash-gray hair and was wearing a pale violet shirt that was open at the chest. He seemed amused by something.

Behind him, a small, indistinct orb displayed a city that resembled Traverse Town.

Wait, if I'm in Traverse Town right now, then what's that place in the sphere? Sora was getting confused.

The girl dashed out from the image and ran right past him, with Riku close behind her. It seemed they couldn't see him.

Though they were all in Traverse Town, Riku and the girl must have been in some other area.

"Joshua," Neku said to the boy who had stopped Sora.

"Hello, Neku. How long the days without you have felt," replied Joshua. The orb behind Joshua flashed, and when the light faded, Rhyme was standing beside him.

"Rhyme! I'm glad you're okay," Sora said.

The girl simply smiled back at him.

Actually, thinking about it now that things had settled down for the time being, this Joshua guy was starting to look really fishy. They'd never even met, but somehow Joshua knew his name. Sora had trusted his own intuition when it said Neku wasn't a bad person, and he also generally listened to his gut when it said someone could be bad news.

Just because he was suspicious, it didn't mean he was bad, but Sora wasn't ready to trust Joshua yet.

"Neku, do you know this guy?"

"Yeah. Joshua. He's my…friend," Neku said as he stepped toward Sora and the others.

"Okay…," Sora said, folding his arms. If Neku said Joshua was cool, then maybe he wasn't all bad. Still, something felt off about him. "Are you the one who took Rhyme away? And…why do you know my name?"

"If you'd like to settle down for a sec, I'll field your questions one at a time," Joshua replied with a smile, brushing his hair back with a hand. "Let's start with Rhyme. I'm hanging on to her dreams for her. They're my Portal," he explained.

Sora was confused. *What does he mean by "Portal"?*

"Let's just say her dreams are a gateway between worlds."

Now that was something Sora understood. He had opened plenty of gateways in the past and gone through to the worlds beyond them, so a Portal must be something similar. While he was lost in thought, Neku walked up beside him.

"Next question—how could I possibly know your name, right? This town has a little secret. It only appears when someone out there has need of shelter."

Sora knew that. Traverse Town was a special place where people came to live after their worlds were lost to darkness. That's why Leon and the gang used to be here.

"I'll spare you the details, but right now it's made up of my dreams. So of course I know you—I dreamed you up."

And now Joshua had lost him. *His dreams...? Does he mean this world comes from his mind...? So is this Traverse Town not the same one as before?*

"I know your best friend, Riku, too."

"Really? You know Riku?" Sora asked. That wasn't a name he was expecting to hear.

Joshua grinned at his reaction. "Well, yeah," he said. "I'm kind of omniscient."

"Then where is he?" Sora couldn't help but take a step forward.

Joshua turned back to the floating image of Riku. It looked like Riku was squaring off against someone. "He's right inside this projection, in another imagining of this world."

Sora considered what Joshua was telling him. So Riku's world, the one in the image, was a different version of this one? Joshua's clarification didn't really clear anything up.

"You mean...another Traverse Town? Can I get there with your Portal thing?" Sora asked Joshua. He wanted to get back to Riku right away.

"Sad to say, it won't work for you. My 'Portal thing' only opens for the one with Rhyme's dreams." He looked toward Riku again. "In this projection, you're seeing another chain of events, in another world trapped by the Dream Eaters. As for how the world got split in two...I have a feeling you'll need to ask this guy."

Riku's opponent stepped into view.

"Him again," Sora murmured. It was the man in the black coat.

In the same instant, two more figures appeared behind Sora, Neku, Rhyme, and Joshua.

There was a boy wearing a hat with a skull patch on it, and a girl in a pink cap. The boy was desperately shouting something at Riku.

The man in the black coat slowly removed his hood. He was young, with silver hair.

"Who's...that?" Sora whispered reflexively. He was sure he'd never seen this guy before—and he wasn't a member of Organization XIII. He felt familiar somehow, though. Within the image, the man vanished with a flash of light.

The boy in the skull hat disappeared next. "Beat...," Rhyme said.

Next, the girl in the pink hat faded from view, and Neku said her name, too. "Shiki..."

Sora and Riku faced each other across the boundary between worlds. But Sora's counterpart didn't vanish.

"Riku..."

The light swallowed Neku and Rhyme next, as if to take them instead.

As Sora and Riku stood together across two different worlds, Joshua softly began to speak. "In their world, something happened that brought their existence to an end. To keep them from fading altogether, I gathered up the very last remnants of their dreams and looked for a place to give them refuge."

Joshua turned away from Sora and Riku and walked a short distance away, then stopped and shoved his hands into his pockets. Sora didn't know anything about the world Neku and his friends came from. But what did it mean to have "their existence brought to an end"? Whatever it was, it sounded awful.

"It was then this world appeared to answer my call, and Rhyme's dreams allowed us to reach it. Here, I thought they might have a chance—that the pieces of their dreams could make them whole again." Joshua turned back to face Sora and Riku. "Imagine my surprise when I realized dreams take bodily form in this world. It struck me—by linking their dream pieces back together, maybe I could make them exist again. Maybe I could give them another chance."

Next to Sora, Riku seemed to ask Joshua something. Sora's voice couldn't reach Riku, and Sora couldn't hear his. But apparently Joshua could hear them both.

"Well, why can't it? By ourselves, we're no one. It's when other people look at us and see someone—that's the moment we each start to exist. All they needed was for someone to see them, to connect with them. And the two of you were a big part of making it happen."

If Sora had learned anything on his journeys so far, it was that strength of heart came from the bonds between people, from how much friends cared for one another. And those feelings made each other stronger, too. Power came from your friends—for him, for everyone.

"Joshua, just...who are you?" Sora asked. This was what had felt strange about Joshua when they first met. What made him so special? Why could he jump back and forth between his world and Riku's?

Joshua smiled at the question. "Let's say...a friend," he said, and white, angelic wings appeared behind him.

"Whoa!"

As Sora yelped in surprise, Joshua flapped his wings and flew off into the heavens.

Back down on the ground, a Keyhole floated up before Sora and Riku. Sora looked at Riku, who was here with him, just in a different world. Riku was looking back.

Even if they couldn't touch or talk to each other, Riku was here at Sora's side. That was proof enough that these worlds were connected.

Sora remembered something Yen Sid had said.

"One dream is connected to another, which means we must choose in which Sleeping World you will begin. I will return you to the

Destiny Islands just before they were swallowed by the darkness and plunged into sleep. Once dreams take you, you must let them guide you to the Sleeping Worlds. As there are seven pure lights, there are seven Sleeping Keyholes. Unlocking these will both grant you new powers and free the worlds from their wakelessness. Complete the task and return here safely, and I will name you both…true masters."

So these Keyholes would free the worlds from being trapped in slumber, and once Sora and Riku had unlocked all seven, they would become Keyblade Masters.

With a nod at each other across the divide between their realms, the two friends held up their Keyblades to the Keyhole. Light shot from their weapons into the opening, and the Keyhole of the second world yawned wide.

Sora took one more look at Riku beside him, and Riku did the same. With another nod, Riku vanished.

"All right, let's keep at it!"

With that, Sora departed for the third world.

CHAPTER
2

La Cité des Cloches

SORA LANDED ON A STREET PAVED WITH STONE AND
lined with brick houses. This looked like a pretty big city.

He was always excited to visit a new world for the first time. *I wonder what the people are like around here?*

Across the way, Sora spotted an older man dressed in striking black-and-purple robes walking toward him. There was an unpleasant look in his eyes, and he scared Sora a little.

Sensing that the man's nasty glare was directed at him, Sora tensed up as they walked by each other.

"Stop," the man called a moment later, bringing Sora to a halt.

"What? Who, me?"

"I've never seen you before. Your name?"

"I'm Sora," he replied with a grin, his arms crossed behind his head as usual.

There's no problem. I haven't done anything wrong, so there's no need to be nervous.

"Such disgusting attire," the man sneered. "I know what you are. A gypsy."

A gypsy? What's that?

"Judge Frollo. Sir!" A golden-haired, bearded man in armor hurried over to them. He seemed like a decent guy, at least.

"What is the matter, Captain Phoebus?" the judge asked coldly, turning around. "Can't you see I'm interrogating this gypsy?"

So this man must be Phoebus, and the older guy was called Frollo.

"This kid here? But, sir, he's just a boy."

Sora wasn't just any old boy, naturally, but it seemed like the best course of action here was to keep his mouth shut. Instead, he listened to their conversation.

"I shall be the judge of that. Now, Captain, did you have something to report to me or did you not?"

"Yes sir. Monsters—they've invaded the square," Phoebus reported.

At the word *monsters*, Sora reacted. They had to be Dream Eaters. "Monsters? I'll take care of it!" He summoned his Keyblade into his hand, then ran off toward the square Phoebus had come from.

"Hey, wait! It's not safe!" The captain took off after him.

Frollo clenched his ringed fingers into a fist as he watched them go.

"This city is overrun! For decades, I've worked to purge the city of those wretched gypsies, and now the streets teem with even more disgusting vermin that threaten law and order."

A dark aura coiled around Frollo's body, invisible to everyone—and especially to him.

Sora rushed into the square to find that he was right about the Dream Eaters.

There was a single human, too, sitting astride one Dream Eater that looked like a big elephant. He was waving his hands around happily. *Um, that Dream Eater seems more like a Nightmare than a Spirit...* There was also confetti in the air for some reason.

"What are you doing? You need to run!" Sora shouted a warning at the young man, who was far from handsome with his stooped back and asymmetrical features. He looked at Sora.

"Oh no, I couldn't. Today's the festival. And look, I'm the King of Fools!"

A festival? He does seem to be enjoying himself, but still...

As Sora wondered, one of the Dream Eaters broke from the pack and flew off. Phoebus had just arrived and slashed at the creature's back with his sword.

Behind him, Frollo walked into the square.

"Quasimodo!" he barked at the young man sitting on the elephant.

"It's my master." Quasimodo cradled his head fearfully.

Suddenly, the eyes of the elephant Dream Eater underneath him flashed red, revealing its true violent nature. It bucked the boy off its back and boxed him in with the help of the other Nightmares.

"No! Oh, please stop!" Quasimodo desperately pleaded with the Dream Eaters, hoping to get them to listen, but they were already well past that point. "Why doesn't anything ever go the way I want it to?"

Sora darted in between Quasimodo and the Dream Eaters, then shouted over his shoulder. "Get to safety!"

But Quasimodo didn't budge. Just then, a woman hurried over.

"Let me help," she said. She had voluminous black hair and determined eyebrows.

"Huh? Who are you?"

"Esmeralda. I'm a gypsy." She introduced herself in a calm tone.

"Thank you. I'm Sora."

Sora stood ready to face the Dream Eaters while behind him Esmeralda held out her hand to Quasimodo. Though he didn't take her hand, he did hurry after her to the cathedral on the other side of the square. Phoebus smiled after the two, but Frollo regarded them with a resentful glare.

"Gypsy witch!" he snarled.

Completely oblivious to their reactions, Sora charged into the throng of Dream Eaters. *Time to get to work!*

He knew how to fight thanks to his battles in Traverse Town, and while he may not have had Donald and Goofy at his side, he did have his Spirit friend. Meow Wow rammed one of the monsters to stun it, and Sora hit it with a downward strike.

The other Dream Eaters were really going crazy, and some of them had even climbed up the tents scattered around the square. Sora sprang into the air, spinning once around a tentpole to gather momentum, and dropped onto a Dream Eater with a downward thrust.

"Piece of cake!"

Once he had dealt with all the monsters, Sora paused for a breath and looked up at the cathedral where Quasimodo and Esmeralda had fled.

Sora had been to all kinds of worlds by this point, but he was pretty sure this was his first time seeing a huge stone building like this one. It kind of reminded him of the big clocktower from Peter Pan's world.

Concerned about Quasimodo and Esmeralda, he ran up the stone steps to a pair of enormous doors. Sora peered through the entryway

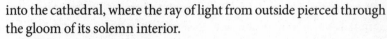

into the cathedral, where the ray of light from outside pierced through the gloom of its solemn interior.

"Hey!"

There was no one inside. Sora stepped through the doors and walked all the way to the back of the huge chapel, but aside from a few Dream Eaters that popped out, there was no sign of Quasimodo and Esmeralda.

"Where could they have gotten off to?" Sora tilted his head to one side. Meow Wow was rolling around idly in one of the beams of light near the entrance.

"Havin' a good time?"

"Mewoof."

As Sora knelt down and rubbed the Spirit's belly, he noticed the light was coming from an opening for a spiral staircase leading up to the floor above.

"Guess we should try upstairs. C'mon, let's go."

Sora and Meow Wow climbed the stairs to the roof of the cathedral.

"Wow, it feels great up here!"

The top of the structure offered a view of the city. This place was pretty big.

"Huh?"

When he looked down at the square, Sora noticed something—a group of what seemed to be soldiers were peering into the building. He had a feeling something really bad was happening.

"Where did those two go anyway?"

Sora spotted a small door as he walked around the roof. It was the only one ajar; maybe that was where Quasimodo and Esmeralda had gone. He stepped inside to find a place that looked to be a garret among the wooden crossbeams of the frame. There were three stone statues, and above him, Quasimodo and Esmeralda were standing next to a giant bell. This must be a bell tower.

"This is Big Marie."

Quasimodo pointed out the huge bell to Esmeralda. It looked big enough to fit ten people inside. Esmeralda peeked into it. "Hellooo!" As her voice echoed, the bell answered with a tiny, timorous ring.

"She likes you," Quasimodo told her warmly.

"Looks like Quasi's gonna be just fine," Sora whispered, watching them talk together with peaceful smiles.

"Indisputably."

"He's tough."

"We may be hard as stone, but Quasi's stronger."

At the sound of voices from behind him, Sora turned around. "I know... WHOA! Talking gargoyles?!" he yelped.

He'd met all kinds of people by now, but never talking gargoyles. All the moving statues he knew attacked people—although there were talking teapots back there, too.

"Excuse us for havin' personality!" retorted the smallest of the gargoyles, the one in the middle.

Just then, Sora felt someone come up behind him. It was Esmeralda, watching the square uneasily from a window. "...It looks like they've got the place surrounded," she said. She must have spotted the soldiers Sora saw earlier.

"You could stay here forever," Quasimodo offered.

"No, I couldn't." Her response was firm.

"Oh yes. You have sanctuary," the boy said, somewhat confused.

"But not freedom. Gypsies don't do well inside stone walls," she told him, starting to walk away.

"You helped me. Now I will help you," Quasimodo declared after a moment's thought.

"But there's no way out. There're soldiers at every door."

So those soldiers I saw before were after Esmeralda...! Sora resolved himself to help her out, too, if he could.

"We won't use a door," Quasimodo said to Esmeralda, picking her up. "It's all right. Are you ready?" A moment later, he jumped out of the window.

"Didn't expect that." Apparently, there was no need for Sora to take the stage here. He turned back to the gargoyles. "So how come you and Quasimodo are so close?"

One by one, the statues told him the story.

"We've been friends for years," began the brownish gargoyle in the center. Her name was Laverne. She sounded like an old woman.

"More than a decade of camaraderie," added Victor, the tall, bluish gargoyle on the right. He talked a little more confidently than the others.

"Breakfast, lunch, and dinner!" said Hugo, the chubby green member of the trio. All the gargoyles had horns on their heads.

"He never leaves?" Sora asked.

"Oh, he's not allowed to leave," said Laverne. "Judge Frollo forbids it."

That was a strange rule—really strange. Sora decided to ask the three statues. "Why?"

"Care to pull up a stool?" muttered Victor.

"The short version is, Frollo thinks he's doing Quasi a favor by keeping folks from seeing that mug of his," Hugo explained.

"After a lifetime of watching from the nosebleed seats, Quasi just wanted to go to the Feast of Fools," said Laverne. "And we're so proud of him for finally working up the courage to do it."

The three of them seemed to be worried about Quasimodo's welfare.

No one would ever describe him as handsome, not even to be polite, but that was no reason to bar him from leaving this place.

"'Tis a shame those creatures dashed his hopes," Victor lamented.

"You should talk," Hugo jeered. "When was the last time you looked in a mirror?"

"Well, you broke it!" Victor barked, rounding on Hugo.

"Oh, a wise guy, eh?"

"Knock it off! Ya couple of blockheads!" Laverne shut them down before Hugo could do any more taunting, then returned to the topic at hand. "I just hope this one failure doesn't cause Quasi to give up. He was so close."

Quasimodo had finally broken free into the outside world; it would be awful if he let his heart become his new prison.

"Don't worry. I'll go talk to him!"

Sora turned away from the gargoyles and dashed out of the bell tower after Quasimodo.

Sora ran down the spiral staircase and out of the chapel, then sprinted through the square. Then a voice called for him to stop.

"Oh. Hello again. Sora, was it?"

That's the guy who was with Frollo earlier. I'm pretty sure his name was Phoebus. He doesn't look quite as imposing without his armor on. His white shirt and pants weren't very captain-like at all.

Still, Sora was bracing himself for conflict. Frollo had locked Quasimodo up, and if this guy was friends with him, that meant he was up to no good.

But Phoebus spread his arms and smiled. "Easy. I'm not looking for any sort of fight." He sure didn't seem like a bad person, especially when he was trying to calm Sora down.

Sora relaxed a little and dropped out of his fighting stance.

"Finally, someone sensible. I'm Phoebus." After introducing himself, the man looked up at the great stone facade. "Tell me, is she still safe at the cathedral?"

He must be talking about Esmeralda. "If 'she' is Esmeralda, then Quasimodo helped her escape."

Phoebus's expression clouded over. "Blast."

"What's wrong?" Sora asked the pensive captain.

"It's Judge Frollo. He's obsessed with destroying the gypsies, and his mind is in a dark place. When I objected to his barbarous actions, he banished me from the guards."

"What? That's not fair."

"Don't worry about me. Frollo said he'd found the 'Court of Miracles'—the gypsies' haven within the city. Esmeralda and her friends are in danger. We have to find them and warn them before Frollo gets there."

That was when they heard someone behind them. It was Quasimodo.

Sora and Phoebus rushed over to him and saw a small pendant lying at his feet.

"Quasimodo, Esmeralda's in trouble!" Sora told him, but the young man was still staring at the ground.

"Where did she go?" asked Phoebus.

"I don't know. She…she just vanished into the streets," Quasimodo said sadly, then scooped up the pendant. So Esmeralda had taken off without even telling him where she was headed. "She… gave me this pendant. Esmeralda said this would help us find her. 'When you wear this woven band, you hold the city in your hand.'"

Quasimodo gazed at the pendant, a small, round wooden frame crisscrossed with a lattice of thread. There was a tiny cross in the center and a miniature gem decorating the pattern.

"It's the city! It's a map, see?" Quasimodo cried out in excitement. "Here's the cathedral and the river. Go this way, cross the bridge, and—the Court of Miracles!"

As someone who spent nearly all his time looking out over the city from the rooftop, it didn't take long at all for Quasimodo to solve the puzzle. Sora certainly couldn't have done it.

"Well done, Quasimodo!" Phoebus gave him a pat on the back.

"Yeah, Quasi. Nice!" Sora took him by the arm happily.

"Yes, I'm going to save her."

The trio hurried to the Court of Miracles, the hidden bastion of the gypsies.

"This way!"

Sora and Phoebus followed Quasimodo over a bridge.

"Hey, Quasimodo, I thought you'd never been out in the city before."

"W-well, I've always been looking at it, so I know everything there is to know about its streets," he replied, looking back at Sora.

"I'm not surprised. I'm new around here, so I don't know my way around like you do… Whoa!"

The trio's path was barred by Dream Eaters, prompting Phoebus to immediately draw his sword.

"Leave this to me! You take cover, Quasimodo!" Sora readied his Keyblade as well, then dropped into his fighting stance.

"Allow me to lend a hand." Phoebus attacked them with his steel, and as might be expected from a captain of the guard, his skills with a blade were impressive.

"Here we go!"

Together, Sora, Phoebus, and Meow Wow dispatched the Dream Eaters. Once all their foes were gone, Sora called out to Quasimodo, who was cowering behind some boxes.

"The coast is clear, Quasi."

He lowered his hands from his face and got to his feet. "…You two are incredible," he said sadly with a look between them.

"Don't sweat it!" Sora reassured him. "We never would have figured out the pendant without you, and plus, you're the one who knows the lay of the land. Right?"

"…I-if you say so." Quasimodo didn't seem convinced.

"He's right, Quasimodo. We're going to need your guidance from here on out, too," Phoebus said, placing a hand on Quasimodo's back.

"…Okay."

Sora and Phoebus shared a look once the boy began to walk off.

"He's really locked himself away, hasn't he?"

"All of Frollo's commands are like chains around him," Phoebus said gravely. Quasimodo had never known anything except the inside of the cathedral, and he'd had hardly anyone to talk to except Frollo and the gargoyles. What would it take to restore his faith in himself?

"We just need the right chance…," Sora mused.

Quasimodo turned back toward them. "O-over here!" he called, beckoning them into a dimly lit cemetery. "I think this is the entrance."

One of the gravestones had been shifted aside, revealing a dark stairwell that led underground.

"We're going in here?" Sora peered nervously into the gloom beyond the stairs.

"These are the catacombs," said Phoebus.

"The what?" Sora asked.

"This city has had an enormous burial ground beneath it since long ago. That's why they say the streets are built over graves."

But the city was so beautiful; Sora had never imagined he might meet a ghost underneath it.

"W-we'd better hurry," Quasimodo urged.

"Right!" Sora mustered his courage and descended the steps. "Oh man…"

The catacombs were steeped in a musty stench and murky light, with skulls piled along the walls. Quasimodo stood in the center, turning his head this way and that.

"What's the matter, Quasimodo?"

"I—I don't know which way to go…," the youth said anxiously as he looked at Sora.

"Oh yeah, I guess you can't see what's underground from the roof." Sora crossed his arms.

"We'll just have to keep moving forward, then," Phoebus said. Still, they didn't know the right path.

That was when Meow Wow took off running ahead of them.

"Huh, where're you going?!"

Sora hurried after him and found him wagging his tail by the wall. Sora recalled how Meow Wow had showed him the way back in Traverse Town and the cathedral.

"…I think there's a cave on the other side. There's a breeze," Phoebus said with an ear pressed to the wall.

"Which means…"

Sora gave the wall a good whack with his Keyblade—and it crumbled.

"Let's go!"

He entered the tunnel beyond the wall and pressed onward. Up a set of stairs at the far end was the Court of Miracles, full of colorful tents and groups of wagons.

"Esmeralda!"

The three had found her at last.

"Quasimodo? What are you doing here?" Esmeralda looked at them curiously.

"Phoebus and I came to warn you," said Quasimodo. "Frollo's on the way!"

Phoebus nodded. "Take what you can and flee!"

Esmeralda's skirt fluttered about her ankles as she whirled to make her preparations—when a deep voice rang out.

"Well done, Captain Phoebus."

Sora and the others turned toward the one who had spoken.

"Thankfully, you are every bit as predictable as I had hoped." It was Frollo, flanked by a gang of Dream Eaters. The judge smirked. "Dear Quasimodo. I always knew you would someday be of use to me," he murmured as he approached his ward.

Quasimodo was frozen.

"I have you at last, you witch," Frollo said to Esmeralda. "There'll be a bonfire in the square."

"Let go of me!"

Frollo seized Esmeralda's arms, but the Dream Eaters kept Sora and Phoebus from getting any closer.

"No. Please, Master!"

Though Quasimodo tried desperately to pursue them, Frollo fixed him with an icy, imperious gaze. Quasimodo froze again, like a frog caught in the eyes of a snake.

"Frollo, I won't let you do this!" shouted Sora, but he couldn't go after the judge with the Dream Eaters in his way.

"I'll leave them to you! We'll go on ahead! Come on, Quasimodo!" Phoebus dashed off, but Quasimodo remained with his eyes lowered.

"You have to go, Quasi!" Sora shouted as he hammered the Dream Eaters that tried to go after Phoebus.

However, the young man nervously turned away from Sora.

"You can't give up!" Sora cried out again, and Quasimodo finally ran after Phoebus. It was like he was running away.

After he had finally mopped up the Dream Eaters, Sora went after Quasimodo. Unfortunately, by the time he got back to the square, it was already a sea of flames with Esmeralda at the center, bound to a stake. Frollo stood before the gallows, watching her with a look of satisfaction. Esmeralda herself was limp, possibly unconscious.

"Esmeralda!"

Just as Sora made to rush over to her, someone swung down from the cathedral on a rope.

It was Quasimodo. Using the rope, he kicked off the wall and made his way down to Esmeralda, then swiftly untied her and took her in his arms.

"Way to go, Quasi!" Sora cheered as Quasimodo made his ascent back up the rope with the girl.

The young man clambered up the wall of the cathedral, and once he was back on the rooftop, he shouted, "Sanctuary!"

Frollo had watched the whole thing with his head craned upward, and when he heard the cry, he stomped his foot with fury and set out for the cathedral. Sora started after him, only to find a colossal shadow bearing down on him.

"A Dream Eater!"

The towering beast, Wargoyle, smashed the gallows platform and stood in Sora's way.

The giant Dream Eater was similar to the Hockomonkey he had faced in Traverse Town, but this one was wilder and more violent with its enormous firearms attached to both arms. Wargoyle fired off round after round into the sky at terrifying speed, where the shots rained down on Sora all at once.

Dodging and weaving his way between them, Sora glanced to the top of the cathedral.

You got this, Quasimodo.

Quasimodo and Frollo were glaring angrily at each other on the rooftop. The judge's hat had fallen off, and he gripped a blade in his hand. Esmeralda watched the scene anxiously from where she had fallen to the stone roof.

"I should have known you'd risk your life to save that gypsy witch—just as your own mother died in her pitiful attempt to save you," said Frollo.

"What?" Then Quasimodo remembered what Frollo had said to him so long ago.

"Oh, my dear Quasimodo, you don't know what it's like out there. The world is cruel, and you are deformed and ugly. You will be shown little pity. You must believe me. I am your only friend. And how can I protect you, my dear boy, unless you stay in here? Remember, Quasimodo. This is your sanctuary."

That was why he had lived within the cathedral all this time. Why he had never taken a step outside of it until recently. Then there was what Esmeralda had said, about how she couldn't live without freedom. But what did freedom really mean? He had forsaken Frollo's instructions in order to save her—maybe that was what it meant.

"Now...I'm going to do what I should have done twenty years ago!"

Frollo slashed with his blade at Quasimodo. Quasimodo ducked out of the way, but the force of the swing knocked both of them off-balance and sent them over the edge of the roof.

Suddenly, Esmeralda took ahold of Quasimodo's hand.

"Hold on! Hold on..."

Beside him, Frollo had somehow managed to grab and climb onto one of the gargoyle sculptures sticking out from the roof. He bellowed with laughter. "And He shall smite the wicked and plunge them into the fiery pit forever!"

The judge was poised to strike Esmeralda down with his sword as she desperately struggled to haul Quasimodo up. She was helpless to stop him.

However, suddenly his footing shifted. The gargoyle adorning the church appeared to move, just like its fellows from before. Frollo slipped and caught hold of the figure's neck.

"Urgh…"

As he tried to hoist himself up again, the gargoyle slowly opened its mouth and bared its fangs.

The cathedral was Quasimodo's sanctuary, and all the statues around it were his friends. The gargoyle broke off, as if its base had crumbled, and dropped both itself and Frollo into the lake of fire in the square.

"Ahhh!!!"

Esmeralda was too busy trying to pull Quasimodo onto the roof to even see what had become of Frollo after his fall.

"Quasimodo!"

But she wasn't strong enough to do it on her own. Her arms couldn't take much more, and her strength was about to give out.

"Quasi, no!"

When Quasimodo began to slip out of her grip, Phoebus's powerful hand grabbed the young man and drew him up onto the roof.

Once he had regained consciousness on the cathedral roof, Quasimodo took Phoebus into an embrace. The captain and Esmeralda had never once laughed at him because he was ugly. Neither had Sora.

Esmeralda and Phoebus eventually shared a long look. Quasimodo got to his feet, took both of their hands and placed one on top of the other, then enfolded their hands between his own large ones.

By the time Sora reached the cathedral roof, it was all said and done. Quasimodo was quietly watching Esmeralda and Phoebus as they walked away. The three statues had arrived behind him, and they were watching him. Sora noticed the sorrow in the set of his shoulders.

"Quasimodo," he said. "You can't let your heart be a—"

"I know." Quasimodo cut Sora off mid-sentence and turned around. "I can't blame Frollo for putting walls around me," he said, brimming with confidence. "It wasn't the walls that were holding me back." He gazed intently at what lay beyond the doors of the cathedral. "But my heart is free now. I'm ready to really see what's out there."

With that resolute declaration, Quasimodo stepped toward the light.

"Looks like we don't have a thing to worry about," commented Laverne, and the gargoyles went back to their customary spots.

Sora turned back toward the gloomy chapel and looked at the statue in the center.

All that time, Quasimodo let himself be trapped inside the nightmares Frollo gave him. He thought about what it really meant to let your heart be a prison and to let it live free. *I can't imagine how painful and sad it must be to go through life with your heart locked away. You can't follow your heart and live the way you want.*

"Hypocrite. You are the one who has made your heart a prison…"

Sora spun around at the unexpected voice.

It was the silver-haired young man who had been speaking to Riku back in Traverse Town.

"You again. What are you talking about?"

Just then, for the barest sliver of a second, the man's form shifted into a near perfect doppelgänger of Sora himself, wearing a black suit for battle. Sora had never even seen him before, much less met him. *So why do I feel like I know him?*

"Even if you are not the prisoner."

The young man and the boy condemned Sora in unison.

"What?!" Sora replied in utter confusion, but the man walked away and vanished into a Corridor of Darkness.

Someone else is a prisoner in my heart? What does that mean? Is someone trapped in my heart? My heart's just mine, isn't it? Or

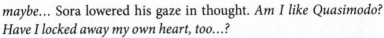

maybe... Sora lowered his gaze in thought. *Am I like Quasimodo? Have I locked away my own heart, too...?*

At that moment, a light began to shine from the stained glass ceiling of the chapel. And at its center was a Keyhole.

Sora quietly raised his Keyblade. As always, the light it fired disappeared into the Keyhole and opened the way.

As he regarded the open gateway, Sora felt uncertainty spreading through his chest. *My heart's...a prison?*

Worried, Meow Wow nestled up against Sora's legs where he stood lost in thought.

CHAPTER
3

Prankster's Paradise

"WOW!" SORA EXCLAIMED AS SOON AS HE ARRIVED IN the next world. *An amusement park!*

Beneath the night sky, there was a Ferris wheel, a merry-go-round, a roller coaster racing by directly overhead, and strings of flags and little sparkling lights decorating the grounds. He saw plenty of other things that looked fun, too.

Sora had been to all kinds of worlds, but this was his first time in a bona fide amusement park. Suddenly, he wanted to just run around the whole place. He started to take off, but he was stopped by a familiar voice.

"That Pinocchio—he must have his poor father worried sick."

Hey, is that...Jiminy?

He looked around and finally spotted Jiminy's diminutive figure in his trademark silk hat, sitting on some steps. The palm-sized cricket had stayed in Sora's pocket on his previous travels and provided all sorts of advice.

"Still, that little fella's some miracle. Imagine...Mr. Geppetto's wooden puppet brought to life by the Blue Fairy! She made his wish for a son come true because he's given so much happiness to others. Now Pinocchio needs me to guide him and be his conscience, so maybe one day he can be a real— Well now, let's not get ahead of ourselves, Jiminy. First, you gotta go find Pinoke."

Jiminy mumbled to himself as he got to his feet.

"Hey, Jiminy!" Sora called to him. "What's up?"

The cricket spun around at the voice, looked up at Sora, then cocked his head to one side in confusion. "Hmm? Who are you? You shouldn't be here, young man!"

"What?"

Jiminy didn't seem to recognize Sora at all.

"Are you okay, Jiminy?" Sora asked, startled.

The cricket placed a hand under his chin and thought for a moment. "Huh? You mean you've heard of me? Well, I'll be. The name Jiminy Cricket's already spread far and wide."

Sora had no idea his real name was Jiminy *Cricket.* "Really, you feeling all right? It's me, Sora!"

A bit exasperated, Sora bent over and peered into Jiminy's face.

The cricket was still baffled. "Sora, you say? Gosh, I don't think I recognize ya, but the name does have a familiar ring."

Both Jiminy and Sora fell into thought. *Now that I think about it, Yen Sid did say something about this…*

"In the Sleeping Worlds, real time does not flow. Unless one restores the world by waking it from its slumber, it will stay locked in a dream forever. Thus, you may encounter familiar faces…but they are just figments of the dream. In actuality, they are sound asleep— trapped within a world that is also sleeping. What's more, whilst someone may no longer dwell in the real version of a world, dreams may paint a fuller picture and restore what seems to be missing."

When Yen Sid was explaining, Sora didn't really get it, but this was probably the type of situation he was referring to.

The real Jiminy wasn't trapped in this world; he should be with the king and the others. Meaning the Jiminy here now was a figment of the world's dream, not the Jiminy he knew.

"Oh! Okay."

"What's that? I can't hear ya."

"Right… It's very nice to meet you, Jiminy."

Sora greeted the Jiminy of this world again. When he did, Jiminy theatrically swept his silk hat off his head and bowed. "Well, sure. The feeling's mutual, Sora."

Though they were just meeting for the first time, the two of them shared a smile like they had known each other for ages.

"You can't fool me," Jiminy said with a smile. "You still think we know each other. And you've just about got me thinkin' it, too." He replaced his hat. Perhaps some of the links in his chain of memories remained within him even in this dream world.

That reminded Sora that there was something he was curious about. "Oh yeah. So how come you said I need to get out of here?"

"Oh yes, this is a terrible place! Boys here are allowed to wreck things and loaf around and make jackamules of themselves!" Jiminy said as he turned to face the amusement park.

"Jackamules?!" But this place looked like so much fun—did Jiminy really mean that?

"And poor, lost Pinocchio, he wandered in here on my watch," the cricket stated dejectedly. But then he clapped his hands as he made a realization. "That's right! That's where I musta heard your name, Sora—from my friend Pinoke!"

"He knows me? But how?" Sora asked.

Jiminy elaborated. "He said that a fella in black clothes told him to play a trick on you."

Black clothes? Bet it's that guy with the silver hair.

"If I don't find Pinoke, he'll turn into a donkey like the rest of the boys."

"Right. Then let me help you find him, Jiminy." Sora couldn't let Pinocchio transform into a donkey.

"Really? I'd be grateful. But how in the world do you know Pinocchio?" the cricket asked curiously. If Sora and Jiminy didn't know each other in this world, it was strange for him to be able to recognize Pinocchio.

Sora couldn't come up with a good response. "Oh, um…" Just then, he spotted Pinocchio walking through the amusement park. "Hey! Over there, I see him!"

Jiminy leaned in where Sora was pointing and confirmed that he was right. "Gosh! That is Pinoke!"

"All aboard, Jiminy!" Sora prompted, and the cricket sprang onto his shoulder like always. At least that hadn't changed between the normal world and this one.

"Take it away!"

"Roger that!"

With Jiminy atop his shoulder, Sora raced down the steps, but—

"Dream Eaters!"

His path was blocked by monsters.

"Well, I'll be. I've never seen anything like these fellas before."

"They're dangerous, so you'd better hide, Jiminy."

"If you insist!" The cricket dove into Sora's pocket.

"Okay, here we go!"

His Keyblade in hand, Sora charged toward the Dream Eaters. Meow Wow was alongside him, of course.

Fighting among all the rides and buildings of the amusement park was a bit difficult, but Sora kicked off the walls to give his attacks some extra punch.

"Mrarf!" Meow Wow ran around fighting off the Nightmares as well.

"Gosh, you're pretty strong, Sora." Jiminy poked his head out of the pocket, holding down his silk hat so it didn't get knocked loose.

"Hey, I told you it's dangerous, Jiminy!" Sora ran toward the center of the amusement park where Pinocchio was, defeating Dream Eaters along the way.

"Pinocchio!"

"There you are!" Sora and Jiminy exclaimed together.

Pinocchio turned around toward them curiously.

"Pinocchio, it's not safe for you here. Listen to Jiminy and go back to—"

Before Sora could finish, Pinocchio transformed into a Dream Eater.

"Oh my!" Jiminy cried as Sora looked around.

Another group of Dream Eaters had them completely surrounded. "Pinocchio" had really been a Nightmare in disguise.

"Only one way to solve this problem! You'd better keep out of sight, Jiminy!"

"But...Pinocchio..."

"Don't worry!" Sora rushed into the pack of Dream Eaters yet again.

Once he had finished off the last one, Jiminy leaped down from his pocket. "...Where could that Pinocchio have gone off to...?" He walked around the nearby area again. "Pinoke! I'm not angry with ya, honest, so just come on out!"

"Up there!" Sora spied Pinocchio on top of a tall tower.

"All the way up there?" Jiminy sighed.

"...How're we even supposed to reach him?"

"We'll have to take the roller coaster, I suppose." Jiminy didn't sound thrilled by the idea, but Sora certainly was.

"Can we?!"

He'd ridden trains and the Gummi Ship before, but never a roller coaster!

"If we don't, we won't be able to reach Pinocchio...," said Jiminy as he looked up at the tower.

Sora did have one concern, though. "You think riding the roller coaster will turn me into a donkey, too?"

"Well, you aren't goofin' around, so I doubt it."

"Yeah, I guess I'm not, huh?!" Sora remarked happily, marching over to the roller coaster platform.

"Wait for me, Sora!"

"Oops! Sorry, Jiminy!"

Once the cricket had climbed inside his pocket, Sora took off running with glee.

"Remember, we aren't playing around here, Sora," Jiminy admonished him from his jacket.

"I know! We're doing this to save Pinocchio."

"...I sure hope you're gonna be all right..."

"Huh? Did you say something, Jiminy?"

"No, it's nothing!"

Sora ran up the steps to the roller coaster platform. "Okay, here we go!" he cried, jumping aboard. "Yahoo!"

They could see the sea from the roller coaster and the big, round moon overhead. The night breeze felt nice.

"S-Sora! If you don't remember what you have to do..." Jiminy stuck his head out from the pocket, holding down his hat to keep it from getting blown away.

"Huh?"

"You'll turn into a donkey!"

"Don't worry! Look, there's Pinocchio!"

With a big jump from the roller coaster, Sora landed atop the tower where Pinocchio was, while Jiminy hopped out of his pocket.

"Gee, Pinoke, how'd you manage to get up here?" Jiminy worriedly hopped over to Pinocchio.

"C'mon, let's go home," Sora urged, but at that very moment, Pinocchio transformed into a Dream Eater again.

"Another impostor," Jiminy lamented with a sigh. But by the time Sora had his Keyblade ready, the Dream Eater had disappeared.

"There! See him walking?"

"What?!"

Sora ran over to the edge of the tower, then pointed out Pinocchio, who was heading toward a big tent with a clown's face on it.

"Well sure, if that's really him."

"Don't give up, Jiminy," Sora chided. "Come on, let's go!" Sora picked up the weary cricket on his palm, then put him in his pocket again and jumped down from the tower.

Full of energy, he set off after Pinocchio's trail and looked up at the tent. "Huh, maybe there's something going on inside?"

There were several brightly colored posters on the poles in front of the tent. *Maybe it's a circus? I've never seen one of those before, either!*

"That Pinocchio, worryin' me so...," mumbled Jiminy from his pocket.

"Let's go, Jiminy!" Sora stepped into the tent.

The interior was covered in colorful fabric, and huge nets around the big, round trampoline in the center stretched all the way up to the ceiling.

"Pinocchio!" Sora and Jiminy cried out in unison as they spotted the wooden boy clinging to the netting.

"Jiminy! Help me, Jiminy!"

He'd noticed Sora and Jiminy from his perch on a platform near the top of the net. And he'd been cornered by Dream Eaters!

"Oh, my stars above!" Jiminy cried. "We've got to do something!"

"Okay, I got it covered."

Sora jumped onto the trampoline and arrived next to Pinocchio on the platform in a single bounce.

"You're okay now!" Sora reassured the trembling little boy, picking him up and jumping back down to Jiminy.

"Oh, Pinoke! Look at ya!" Jiminy exclaimed when he saw what had happened to Pinocchio.

He had the ears of a donkey, and there was a tail sprouting from his rear end.

"I think, for now, you two better get out of here," Sora advised them, and Pinocchio and Jiminy quickly ran toward the exit of the tent. "All right, bring it on!"

The Dream Eaters were bouncing around on the trampoline, and Sora jumped in with them to take them out one after the other. Fighting on a trampoline was kinda fun. There was even a swing overhead. Sora took hold of the swing with one hand, then dropped down on a Dream Eater on a platform to hit it from above.

"Is that all you got?"

Once the last Dream Eater was gone, Sora ran off after Pinocchio and Jiminy.

But a Corridor of Darkness opened in front of him, and the silver-haired youth in the black coat stepped out.

"You again?" Sora shouted.

The young man didn't react in the slightest. Behind him, another black portal opened, and the one who emerged from it was—

"Xemnas? This is impossible!"

It was Xemnas, the leader of Organization XIII that Sora had once fought and defeated—or so he thought.

The silver-haired youth and Xemnas felt similar somehow. Maybe it was the black coats, or maybe it was the color of their hair.

"My, my, a hollow puppet that's managed to grow a heart. Just imagine that."

A hollow puppet—was Xemnas talking about Pinocchio?

"Pinocchio isn't anything like you Nobodies!" Sora couldn't keep himself from shouting—but there was a question forming in his heart, and he asked it only a second later. "But if Pinocchio could be given one—shouldn't you be able to have a heart inside you, too?"

Xemnas burst into laughter. "Maybe so." He turned away from Sora. "However…do not forget that you yourself are not so very different from us," he said, looking back for a few seconds before he vanished back into the dark corridors. The silver-haired boy went with him.

Sora pondered Xemnas's words for a moment, staring at the spot where the two had disappeared.

I'm not so different from them? Is he trying to say that I'm like a Nobody? Or does it mean something more…? I don't get it.

"Hypocrite. You are the one who has made your heart a prison… even if you are not the prisoner."

Sora recalled what the silver-haired boy had said back in Quasimodo's world.

I'm like the guys from the Organization? Other prisoners in my heart? What does all this mean? And hollow puppets…

"Oh yeah, Pinocchio!"

Sora went back to tracking him and Jiminy down.

When he stepped out of the tent, he didn't see any sign of them.

"Hello?" he called, and that moment, one of the stars overhead began to shine brighter and brighter, until it was almost blinding.

Sora shut his eyes against the brilliant light. When he eventually reopened them, standing before him was a winged pixie wearing a blue dress—the Blue Fairy.

"You must be Sora."

"Oh. Yes, ma'am." Sora couldn't help but stand up straighter as he replied.

"I'm afraid that I have grave news. Good Geppetto went off to look for Pinocchio, and he was swallowed by a whale named Monstro."

"What?" Sora had met Geppetto once before. He even knew about Monstro. Geppetto had been swallowed by the great whale in the past, too, but that didn't mean he wasn't still worried. "Have you told Pinocchio and Jiminy about it yet?"

"Yes, and when I told them Geppetto was still alive inside the whale and at the bottom of the sea, those two little ones ran off at once. They're very determined to save him."

"But that's crazy! I've gotta find them!" Sora turned away from the Blue Fairy and hurried for the cape.

When he reached the promontory at the end of a cave, he saw the sea illuminated by the big moon. *I'll be fine; I'm a good swimmer.* Sora took a deep breath and dove into the water.

While it was quite dark beneath the waves, a little bit of moonlight still filtered through the water.

Sora remembered how he used to swim in the sea practically every day back on the Destiny Islands. *I wonder what Riku's up to now...?*

Just then, a sudden, powerful ocean current started pulling him along.

"Pinocchio!"

He saw Pinocchio running desperately on the seabed, along with Monstro bearing down on him.

Wait, that isn't right. Is something chasing Monstro, too...? Monstro overcame Pinocchio and slapped one of the cliff walls with his huge tail.

Then he saw the gigantic Dream Eater shaped like a crayfish closing in on the whale from behind.

"Pinocchio! Jiminy!"

Sora tried his hardest to swim over to his friends, but in the next instant, Monstro swallowed the two of them down.

Meanwhile, the big crayfish, Chill Clawbster, cast a spell from the propeller-like tip of its claw. The spell froze the surface of the water with Monstro inside.

Looks like I have to take care of this guy first.

Sora swam over to the ice-encased whale and climbed atop him to face off with Chill Clawbster.

If it uses ice magic, then it must be weak to fire…

Sora enchanted his Keyblade with flames and hurled it at Chill Clawbster, but the Keyblade just bounced off its hard carapace and returned to him.

"…It's too tough!"

Sora caught his Keyblade and ran beneath the Dream Eater's abdomen for another attack. A Fire spell this time.

Unfortunately, Chill Clawbster jumped out of the way.

"Whoa!"

Sora scrambled out of the way to keep from getting crushed, but he ended up tumbling right off Monstro's back. Before he could hit the icy surface of the ocean, though, Meow Wow gave him a soft landing.

"Growr!"

Sora hurriedly jumped to his feet and scooped up Meow Wow in his arms. "You okay?!"

The limp Spirit wagged his tail feebly.

"I think we're gonna have to change it up…"

Sora gently set Meow Wow on the ground, then glared at the Chill Clawbster, which was now hovering in the air.

If they wanted to put a dent in that sturdy shell, they couldn't use just any old attack.

If that's how it's gonna be—! Sora cast Fire not on Chill Clawbster, but instead the frozen Monstro.

The ice around the whale melted a bit. Next, Sora tried chopping at it with his Keyblade.

"Groooooh!"

Monstro regained consciousness and starting wriggling free. Salty water shot out of the hole on his head and scored a direct hit on Chill Clawbster.

"Meow Wow!"

Sora hopped onto his Spirit, who then jumped up and slammed down onto the crayfish. The great splash woke Monstro completely, enough to smash the ice around him and swallow down the Dream Eater.

Sora and Meow Wow hit the surface of the water at about the same time.

That very moment, Monstro let out a big sneeze. After all, Chill Clawbster had made for a very strange meal.

"Wh-whooooooooaaa!"

Sora and Meow Wow were flung out into the sea.

He could hear the waves—it was such a familiar sound.

Someone's licking my cheek. Pluto? No…this is…

"Meow Wow!"

Sora had been lying unconscious on the shore until his Spirit finally woke him up.

He leaped to his feet, ready to hurry back into the sea, when he stopped.

This was a dream world, not the real one. Soon, this world would be consumed by the darkness, and Monstro would be sent into the Ocean Between with Pinocchio and the others. Sora would meet Pinocchio in Traverse Town, and after that, he would find him along with Geppetto inside the whale's belly.

This was a never-ending dream. If Sora didn't wake up, he wouldn't be able to return to the real world.

When Sora gazed up at the moon hanging above the sea, a big Keyhole arose there.

He undid the lock and moved on to the next world.

Lea's Side

I'M...DREAMING.

I'm in the usual spot on top of the clocktower in Twilight Town, watching the sunset in the distance. In my hand is a cold, salty-sweet bar of sea-salt ice cream. I'm eating it by myself, wearing my usual black coat.

"Hey, Axel. You haven't forgotten?"

Suddenly, my best friend, Roxas, is beside me.

"Hmm? What?"

Roxas is eating ice cream, too. "You made us a promise."

A promise? What kind of promise?

"I did?"

"That you'd always be there...to bring us back," says Roxas.

"Yeah...," I reply. Each reply makes me nervous. Roxas should be watching the sunset with me, but I can't tell where he's looking. It's unsettling.

"Got it memorized?" Roxas points at his temple, mimicking me.

"Best friends forever," I answer.

No one's beside me anymore.

The dream is short, but it feels so long—and then I wake up.

Axel opened his eyes in the laboratory of Radiant Garden, a room with computers in the back of what was once an office. He wasn't sure what was going on. He'd saved Sora, but what about after that?

How did I end up here? Axel sat up slowly. His head was groggy. *What happened?*

"Roxas?"

He wasn't there, but Axel could see himself reflected in the glass of the lab.

"That's me..."

He spotted a few others collapsed in the same room. The ones in white lab coats were Even and Ienzo, and then there was Dilan and Aeleus still in their former uniforms. Aeleus was starting to get to his feet with a groan.

Why aren't they wearing the black coats? Wait, don't tell me—

Axel checked his reflection in the glass again and looked for the marks. They were gone. The marks under his eyes were missing.

"We're people again."

Oddly enough, he found the fact easy to accept. All four of the men behind had joined the Organization here. Xehanort didn't count, so there were only two missing: Braig and one other.

"Isa?" Axel—now Lea—softly said the name of his old friend.

"What the devil...?" said Aeleus, the first to wake up. He was holding his head.

"Beats me," Lea replied with a smile as Ienzo also unsteadily got to his feet.

"What...happened...?" Ienzo asked.

"If you don't know, then I don't, either," Lea answered in his usual teasing manner.

Ienzo frowned, clearly unsatisfied.

Ienzo wouldn't have known about any of the events following his visit to Castle Oblivion as a member of the Organization. Explaining it all would be a pain—although if he had retained his memories from the castle, things might get a little complicated. *Ienzo's Nobody, Zexion, was destroyed because of me. I need some time to myself to think before we get into all that.*

"I'm gonna go look for the others. I'll leave things here to you."

Lea left the other four and walked to the room Ansem the Wise had once used as his office, but the wall was decorated with a portrait of Xehanort. It was littered with books, just as he remembered from when he'd snuck in here before. No one else was there.

Lea stepped into the hallway and found a skateboard, covered with dust and seemingly abandoned for some time.

"Don't go leavin' this here," he muttered, then gave the board a small kick as he thought of its owner before walking off.

No, really, what happened? I mean, I know I'm human again. I always thought when a Nobody fades away, that's when they really and truly cease to exist, but I must've been wrong about that. I'm the human I used to be; I can tell. We didn't have separate personalities like Roxas and Sora.

Why was that? I guess because Roxas was special—or Sora was anyway. But special how, exactly? "You've lost your hearts," *they told us, over and over, but I wasn't buying it. Not completely, at least. If I didn't have a heart, then what was that ache in my chest?*

Lea kept walking until the side entrance was up ahead. He could feel a faint breeze from outside. *I doubt the other two are gonna wake up anywhere outside the castle.*

He stopped.

Suddenly, he recalled a certain memory. *It was back when I was a kid—yeah, back before they called this place Hollow Bastion. The first time they called it Radiant Garden. I met someone, and we kinda ended up friends. I hung out with him because I wanted to be remembered by as many people as possible and live forever. What was his name?*

Lea couldn't recall, but the guy reminded him of someone else. Who was it? Memories from deep in Lea's heart were resurfacing. Maybe turning human again was why he was suddenly remembering things from his childhood? No, he should've been able to remember all along.

At the same time, the doubts he'd been holding ever since he became human again were beginning to come into focus.

Why did we go back to being human? Did something change us back?

What is Xemnas up to this time? No, he must be Xehanort now.

"Sheesh, what a mess..." Lea scratched his head.

What am I supposed to do? He needed time to think it over. Lea slowly made his way back to the laboratory.

"Where are they? I've turned this castle upside down."

Aeleus was putting books back in their former places on the shelves in the lab. Lea had to wonder if that was really necessary right now, but maybe it was just a soothing task for him at the moment. Ienzo was also organizing the desk. He seemed to be searching for something, but Lea couldn't quite tell. The other two were missing.

"Hey. Are the other two out cold?"

"Dilan and Even are conscious again but still unstable. They're resting inside," stated Aeleus as he reshelved books.

"Gotcha. Well, I guess I'll give the castle grounds a sweep."

Lea made to retrace his steps and leave, but Aeleus stopped him. "Don't. If they were back, we would have found them by now."

Lea scratched his head again and let out a little sigh. "So do ya think they were blasted off to some other world or what?"

Ienzo spoke up from in front of the desk. "I highly doubt it. When someone who has lost their heart is recompleted, they should return to the place where it happened. And if that world is unavailable for whatever reason, a refuge is made for them in the realm between—a world called Traverse Town. They would be sent there."

As Ienzo explained, Lea walked the interior of the lab and looked up at the likeness of Xehanort.

"Or perhaps—"

"No, look, okay," Lea interrupted before Ienzo could elaborate. "The fact is—we're here. We've been recompleted, right? So they should be here, too, plain and simple."

"I agree, it is strange," Ienzo affirmed in a strained voice. What could their absence possibly mean?

"What a drag," Lea said with a big sigh, then turned to Ienzo and offered the only answer he'd found. "Could they not have been recompleted at all?"

It wasn't completely beyond the realm of possibility; in fact, it actually made the most sense. Even if Ienzo did explain further, they'd still arrive at the same answer. *The question is, what do I need to do now?*

"Well, you see—"

"Ah! Forget it." Lea interrupted Ienzo before he could say any more, then, after another look at the portrait of Xehanort, shifted his attention to some scribbled notes on the wall. Secrets of the worlds, secrets of the soul, and secrets of Kingdom Hearts, along with some faded words that had to be a password.

DOOR TO DARKNESS.

The Door to Darkness, huh?

"You know what? I'll bring 'em back myself," he said.

"Huh? How exactly?" Ienzo exclaimed, which prompted Aeleus to slowly stand up and look at him, too.

"Why do I always get stuck with the icky jobs?" Lea complained, although he didn't sound particularly upset by the idea. He slowly made his way out of the room.

CHAPTER
4

The Grid

THIS WORLD WAS STRANGE; EVERYTHING WAS PALE blue.

Threads of light raced by all around him, like they were in a hurry to get somewhere. *What was this place again? It looks kinda familiar.* Sora looked around.

"Oh!" he exclaimed as he noticed that his clothing had changed into a tight bodysuit with conspicuous blue-white lines on it. He was even wearing a helmet.

Hey, this reminds me of how I looked that other time, when we went on our adventure with Tron. The scenery's similar, too. Everything's all geometrical. Maybe I'll be able to see him again.

Aw, but this is a Sleeping World. Even if I do run into him, he might not be like the real Tron.

Sora was still having trouble getting his head around the ins and outs of these Sleeping Worlds he was visiting for the Mark of Mastery exam.

Then a shadow fell over him as something passed by overhead.

"Whoa! What is that?"

A large bridge-shaped transport ship, a Recognizer, was flying above Sora. Just seeing all these huge machines sure was exciting.

Sora hurried after the Recognizer, only to find the way obstructed by Dream Eaters.

So even this world was infested with them. The Dream Eaters still looked more or less like the ones he'd met in the previous worlds, so they really stuck out like a sore thumb here.

Sora kept glancing up at the Recognizer as he battled the creatures. Was it some sort of vehicle?

When Sora took care of the last Dream Eater and resumed his pursuit, the upper part of the bridge portion of the Recognizer slid downward.

"Whoa! Oh man!" Sora marveled as he looked up at it. *I guess people really do ride in the top part.*

There were also several people wearing pitch-black suits—Black

Guards. Their outfits had orange lines on them, and they carried long staves of the same color. Noticing Sora, the guards approached him warily.

"Identify."

"State your handle, program."

Their voices were distorted and mechanical.

What do handles have to do with this? "I, uh…don't have any handles, but the name's Sora!"

The Black Guards paused for a moment at Sora's response.

"Verifying handle 'Sora'…," said one of them. "Handle not found. Stray program recognized." The guard took Sora by the shoulder.

"Huh?"

The other one seized him by his other shoulder.

What's a "stray program"?! Are they talking about me?

"Isolating for quarantine," said the guard impassively.

Sora shook off his grasp and jumped back. The guards leveled their orange staves at him.

"Whoa there! That is so unfriendly!" Sora shouted as he edged backward, but his words were having no apparent effect. Just as he realized that the Recognizer was hovering directly above him, an orange beam shot down at him.

"Hey!"

Sora turned from the Black Guards and ran for it. Now instead of Dream Eaters, he was in a struggle against a seemingly endless succession of Black Guards. With the ability to fly through the air and hurl grenades, they were nothing to sneeze at. And that wasn't even counting the Recognizer on his tail.

"C'mon, guys, I'm not a stray program!"

Talking wasn't getting him anywhere with the Black Guards, though. Sora arrived in an area with several platforms on different levels, and he fought his way up to the wide roadway on the highest one.

Unfortunately, there was an enemy waiting for him there, too.

Though he looked a lot like the Black Guards, especially with the orange lines on his body, he just felt different.

This new foe removed round discs from his back and brandished them in Sora's direction. Sora had managed to get through the Black Guards, but running wasn't going to be an option here, he could tell. This new enemy was much more intense than his predecessors.

And the battle began.

In the shadows, three people observed the scene.

"Tron... He's alive," muttered Kevin—a bearded man dressed in a robe-like coat that obviously didn't mesh with the rest of the style on this world. Next to him was a beautiful woman with short black hair and another man with his brown hair neatly trimmed. The two of them wore suits similar to Sora's.

"Look at that boy's weapon. It's different," murmured the woman, Quorra, as she watched the conflict.

"But it's something you programmed, right, Dad?" asked the man, Sam.

Kevin and Sam were father and son, but Kevin was so focused on the one Sora was fighting that he initially didn't appear to have heard his son's question at all.

"Dad?"

"Huh? No, Sam... No, I've never seen it," he eventually answered.

The trio followed the battle between Sora and his foe, when the man wielding the discs, Tron, suddenly went still.

He holstered the discs on his back, leaped over Sora, and ran away.

"What was that about?" Sora wondered.

That was weird. Sora was still puzzling it over when he heard a feminine voice behind him.

"Hey, that weapon. Can I see it?"

"Huh?!"

Sora spun around at the sudden question to see a woman staring

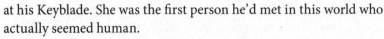

at his Keyblade. She was the first person he'd met in this world who actually seemed human.

"This is just incredible. What a program—the weapon and the wielder."

"Program? Not me!" Sora said back. *I'm a person, not a program!*

But that reminded him where he'd heard about this stuff before—Tron had also talked about programs.

In his world, Tron was a security program—does that mean I'm back?

That was when two more people, Kevin and Sam, appeared from the shadows.

"I'm Sam. The one who just spoke to you is Quorra. And this is Kevin."

"This is called a Keyblade, and I'm Sora." Since they had provided their names, Sora introduced himself as well. And hey, maybe they'd have the answer to his question, too. Sora surveyed the area again. "So this is, like, Tron's world, right?"

"You know Tron?" Kevin suddenly asked, a little forcefully.

He's freaking me out a little. Maybe I shouldn't have mentioned Tron. "I, uh…yeah, I've met him…and stuff."

Sora hedged, unsure of how to explain, when Kevin stated, "Listen, that program you fought *was* Tron."

"What? That was Tron?"

Sora couldn't possibly imagine the one he had just fought was Tron. Tron had been kind—there was no reason for him to attack out of the blue like that.

"Tron used to be a good friend. Together, we created this place, the Grid. It was something, man…but then CLU staged a coup. I was exiled, and…Tron wound up getting de-rezzed. Or so I thought. CLU made him into a new program called Rinzler."

What? That Rinzler guy was like the complete opposite of Tron! I can't let that CLU creep get away with this! Plus, if Tron was in trouble, Sora wanted to help him any way he could.

"That's the thing about programs. Mess with the code a little, and their whole nature and memory can change."

"But that's…horrible!"

Kevin was just explaining it as cold hard fact, and that saddened Sora even more. He didn't know about programs or any of that, but it seemed this place wasn't quite the same as the world where Tron had once lived. That didn't make Sora any less determined to save him.

"Still, if that's really the Tron I know, then we should change him back."

"Bingo. And now you're up to speed," Kevin replied, smiling at Sora's firm declaration. He closed his eyes, perhaps thinking of something, and then opened them again. "If we're lucky, CLU kept a backup of Tron's source code. He's a program, after all. He'd be methodical like that," the older man said with a chuckle. Sora wasn't sure what was so funny, but he did get the idea that they were going to need this "source code" to save Tron.

Sora then asked Kevin a question. "So if we get Tron's 'source code' back from CLU, we can put him back to normal, right?"

"That's the idea." Kevin nodded.

"Great! Thanks, mister!" With that, Sora turned on his heel.

"Where are you going?" Kevin asked.

"I'm going after CLU," Sora replied. *Where else?*

"Do you even know where he is?"

"Nope, no idea."

At the second question, Sora realized that maybe he didn't know where he was going after all and turned back around.

Quorra laughed. "What a strange user," she said. "You're nothing like Flynn or Sam. Come on, Sora. I'll show you the way." She gave Sora an encouraging pat on the shoulder.

"Quorra, we have to keep moving," Kevin said to stop her.

"Yeah, what are you gonna do if Rinzler attacks again?" Sam added.

"If we're in a hurry, we have to take care of Rinzler first," Quorra replied, then looked intently at Sora's face.

"The two of us can handle him!" Sora assured them, and Kevin finally smiled.

"All right. Do what you can. Maybe you and Sora can help Tron."

"Dad, no." Sam still had his doubts, though.

"Relax, Sam," Kevin admonished him. "Sora is someone I have a feeling we can trust. Now you and me need to press on."

"Okay." Reluctantly, Sam acquiesced.

Sora smiled up at Kevin, happy to see how much faith the older man placed in him.

"Quorra, be careful."

"You too."

As Sam and Quorra reminded each other to stay safe, Sora wondered, *It's pretty obvious that Kevin and Sam are father and son, but where does she fit in?*

With that, Sam and Kevin left on their own mission.

"All right, it's you and me. You ready, Sora?"

"Yeah. Let's do this, Quorra."

She and Sora shared a smile, but there was something mysterious about her expression. Sora couldn't put his finger on what exactly it was. Unlike the other two, she just seemed…special.

"CLU should be at the helm of his battleship, the Rectifier. We can get there with a Solar Sailer from the underground docks."

Together, Sora and Quorra set out for the battleship.

Right around that same time, CLU was in the command vessel of the Rectifier, inspecting an image projected from the disc in his hands. Beside him stood Rinzler. The projection depicted Sora fighting with his Keyblade.

"What's this? A 'Keyblade'…," CLU said softly, then tossed the disc back to Rinzler. The program caught the disc and attached it to his back.

"And it can open any lock—"

CLU gazed out at the world unfolding overhead from the window—the Grid. His face was the spitting image of Kevin's.

Sora and Quorra snuck through the linked carriages of the Solar Sailer to the enormous battleship, and from there, they hopped onto the Throneship, CLU's command vessel.

Unlike everywhere else they had been, the walls and floors of these chambers were traced with geometric patterns of orange light. The color was the same as on Rinzler's—Tron's—suit.

"You sure we'll find Tron's source code here?"

Sora took in the area. *First off, I'd like to have some sort of lead to help us find this code. What is it like? What shape is it? What color?*

Quorra passed him by and strode to the back of the room, where she placed a hand on the glowing wall and slowly walked beside it, tracing her fingers across its surface.

Sora watched her attentively. He could tell from her focused expression that she was searching for the source code.

"It's not here. Maybe CLU has it with him. Sora, let's look elsewhere."

"All right," Sora replied, but Quorra stopped in front of him and turned her full attention to the door. Sora was on guard, too, but his senses weren't picking up anything.

Until the door opened to reveal Rinzler.

Quorra immediately took the disc from her back and stood ready to fight him, but Sora caught hold of her hand.

"Wait, Quorra! Let me talk to Rinzler. A little heart-to-heart might jog his memory."

"He's a program, Sora. Programs don't have hearts."

"Programs don't have hearts"—Sora felt like he'd heard someone say that once before.

"That's not true. The Tron I knew, he had something." After persuading Quorra, Sora stepped toward Rinzler—slowly, so as not to provoke him. "Hey, you used to be called Tron, right? CLU did something to you to mess with your memory. You're a little confused, but that's okay."

The armored, pitch-black helmet around Tron's head completely obscured his face.

Sora drew even closer. "C'mon, remember, Tron!"

But Rinzler removed the discs from his back, dropped into a fighting stance, and hurled them with all his strength at Sora. Quorra sprang forward to protect the boy and managed to knock the discs away, but the recoil still sent them both sprawling. Rinzler kicked off the wall and caught the discs as they came flying back to him through the air.

"I don't think Rinzler is quite the friend you remember," Quorra told him, before she took her own disc in hand and charged at Rinzler. Quorra had protected Sora, but not completely, he realized. His arm hurt, but the ache in his heart was even worse. Clutching his arm, Sora stood up and hung his head.

Tron would remember him; he had to. But a cry from Quorra brought him back to reality.

"Quorra!" Sora shouted and rushed forward. Quorra had fallen, and Rinzler was about to bring his discs down on her. "Tron, don't!"

But before he could reach them, the door shut in his face.

Sora was separated from the two combatants. There was a mechanical sound from beyond the door, and Sora could hear something moving.

Tron hadn't responded to any of his entreaties. How could this happen?

"Tron...why?" Sora whispered to himself.

Behind him, someone replied, "That's what we do. Put the most precious memories in the back of our minds where they're safe." Sora whirled around to see the silver-haired guy in the black coat. "Or in your case, the most precious...hearts?" the young man said with a smirk as he placed a hand on his chest.

"Not you again!"

As Sora braced for a fight, another man emerged from a Corridor of Darkness. "The memory and heart are tightly linked."

The man's name was...

"Xemnas!" Sora yelled. Xemnas himself was standing right in front of him. This was the second time he had encountered him on this test.

"Rub a few memories together, and you get a spark of emotion, a feeling. But in a digital world, memory does not work like that. Nothing is ever felt. You can hold a thousand, a million times the information, but there is still no heart with which to parse it." Xemnas's long speech continued. "Once, my master, Ansem, found an old system and made a copy of its Master Control Program...and used it to serve his own ends."

Sora remembered hearing something about that once. Tron was a security program of Radiant Garden—well, Hollow Bastion at the time—and he was part of the system that managed the town. Tron had said that the massive computer system originally designed by ENCOM had been repurposed by a new user—namely Ansem—and named the Hollow Bastion OS.

"This is the original data of that system. Here, data can be copied. Memory can be changed and easily manipulated."

The world around Sora suddenly went dark, and a copy of himself appeared. More and more Soras popped into existence around him, until he found himself surrounded. He was startled, but Xemnas just kept talking.

"Tron is a digital entity, so why would he be any different? He obeys the rules of this world. Sora—what about you?"

"Me?"

Sora didn't know what Xemnas was getting at.

"Your heart, memories, your data, and your dreams. The bits and bytes that have made up your life so far—can you say for sure they are not just copies of someone else's?"

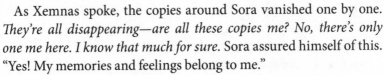

As Xemnas spoke, the copies around Sora vanished one by one. *They're all disappearing—are all these copies me? No, there's only one me here. I know that much for sure.* Sora assured himself of this. "Yes! My memories and feelings belong to me."

The darkness finally disappeared at Sora's forceful response.

"You had better check. Make certain the box's contents match what's on the label...since you have been chosen."

Xemnas turned his back on Sora and vanished yet again into a Corridor of Darkness.

Sora didn't understand. Chosen for what? Chosen by the Keyblade? Or maybe...

"You think this is the realm of dreams, but there you are mistaken. Data does not dream, cannot dream. This world is real," said the silver-haired youth, who had not left with Xemnas, and the door behind Sora suddenly slid open. The howling wind battered him. "You haven't the slightest idea where you are—that you have already wandered off the path."

"What do you mean?" Sora shouted, but the young man merely smiled before fading into a dark passageway just as Xemnas had.

Off the path— Where was he?

Sora shut his eyes against the lashing wind—and when he reopened them, he was in a completely different place.

"Disc wars! Disc wars! Disc wars!"

Sora could hear crowds of people shouting this. Around him was what looked like a big fighting ring racing with blue light. Was this a stadium...?

"What in the world?" Sora couldn't help but whisper.

A robotic mechanical female voice announced, "Combatant thirteen versus Rinzler."

At that, the cheering turned into the chanting of a name. "Rinzler! Rinzler! Rinzler!"

What is going on here?

Two people appeared before Sora: a man and Rinzler...Tron.

"Greetings, Sora," said the man. "I've been waiting." His suit was covered in orange light just like the Black Guards'. His face was visible, though, and he wasn't carrying an orange staff.

"Who are you?"

"I am CLU," the man replied. His face resembled Kevin's. Rinzler stood motionless behind him.

"So it was you! You're the guy who turned Tron into Rinzler!"

"Correct. I had to repurpose his code."

"Well, un-repurpose it!" Sora yelled, but the response was not what he expected.

"Yes. Under the right parameters, I might."

"Huh?"

"You have a little item called a Keyblade. It can open any lock, isn't that right? Hand it over, and I'll change Rinzler back into Tron," said CLU, an unnerving smile rising to his lips. Rinzler slowly advanced toward Sora.

"The Keyblade? I…I can't." Sora summoned the weapon in question and gripped it tightly. "This is what lights the darkness. A chance to make everyone happy!"

CLU snorted derisively. "Ha! Flawed reasoning. I'll have to take it by force."

No sooner had CLU declared his intent than Rinzler sprang into the air and hurled his discs at Sora. Sora halted the attack with his Keyblade, deflecting the discs.

"Tron, why can't I get through to you?"

Rinzler just snatched his discs from the air and poised to strike Sora again.

"Fight, Sora!" Quorra called, and Sora looked up to see her standing on an upper level of the stadium—no, she was actually on the Throneship.

"Quorra! You're okay! I can't believe it!" As Rinzler's discs came at him again, Sora smiled and knocked them away.

"Yes. I think Tron heard you. Long enough for me to escape. You can do it. You can get through to him!"

Yes! I'm getting through to Tron…!

Quorra had more to say. "Sora, you have to fight him!"

"But Quorra! How can I—?" Sora didn't want to fight Rinzler—his friend, Tron.

"You have that key. It will bring him to his senses," Quorra shouted as Rinzler came after him again. Sora blocked the attack with his Keyblade, then looked up into Rinzler's black face guard.

The Keyblade should be able to bring Tron around...!

"I'll try!" Sora pushed away Rinzler's blow and readied his Keyblade. "Let's go, Tron!" Shouting his friend's true name, Sora charged toward him.

Tron moved completely unlike anyone he had ever fought before. One second, he was leaping into the air and the next he was spinning on one leg or bouncing off the walls; Tron was so quick it was hard to keep track of him.

Meow Wow pursued him alongside Sora, but there was just no keeping up with his speed. Amid this fierce battle, Sora was at last able to briefly stop Tron in his tracks by throwing his Keyblade.

It was only for a second, though, as Tron soon got to his feet and whipped his discs at Sora. The two discs approached from both the right and left, and Sora brought his Keyblade up before his face to knock them away.

How could he get Tron to stop? He thought back on the time they fought together in Hollow Bastion.

"Tron!"

His friend stopped short at his call. Tron edged back, still poised to fight with his discs.

He was listening, but his heart was definitely still bound by the Rinzler program.

Where is that program anyway? Well, if it's a program, it has to be— Right! It should be on those discs. Which means...

"Meow Wow!" The two of them had fought alongside each other for so long that they were in perfect sync. The Dream Eater dashed ahead at the same time as Sora, and while Sora kept Tron busy, Meow Wow slammed into his side.

The impact knocked a disc from his hand, and Sora knocked it far away using his Keyblade. It collided with the wall and fell to the ground.

Tron hurled his one remaining disc, but Sora stopped it dead-on—not with his Keyblade but with his right hand. The spinning disc was hurting his palm, but he didn't mind. Anything to help bring Tron back.

Sora held the disc until it stopped spinning, and it fell to the floor.

Tron lunged for him, but Sora held out his Keyblade toward Tron's chest.

Reprogram.

That was what it was called—the move he could only use with Tron. It could overwrite programs and cause damage.

The light from the Keyblade caught Tron and held him in mid-air. Sora could sense that the eyes behind the helmet were staring at him. Eventually, Tron dropped slowly to the floor and fell still.

"Tron…"

Would it be enough to remove Rinzler and restore Tron to normal?

Just then, an orange disc flew at Sora from another direction.

It belonged to CLU. But before it could strike—

Tron leaped up to protect Sora from the disc, but when he knocked it away, it shattered a part of the floor, opening a large hole. The stadium was floating in the air exactly like the ships. It was a long way down to the ground—and Tron fell through. Sora desperately reached out to help him.

"Tron!"

His friend responded to his call and reached back—but it was too far. Tron plummeted from the stadium.

"I'll deal with you later. I have to retrieve Rinzler," CLU grumbled before boarding his Throneship and departing the stadium.

Sora couldn't care less about CLU, though. He remembered Tron's hand, inches from his. Tron had tried to take his hand.

Quorra quietly walked up to him.

"Tron is still in there." Sora looked pleadingly up at her. He knew it. He just knew it.

"You and that key have a special power," Quorra told him with a smile.

"So do you—the power to make me see it." Sora wouldn't have fought Tron if she hadn't called out to him back then.

"So does that mean we're friends?"

"Of course," Sora replied happily.

"Well then, Sora. I have to go meet Sam and Kevin."

"Okay, I'm sure we'll see each other again somewhere."

"I'm sure we will. I'll see you and Tron again." Quorra walked away, slowly.

Once he was alone, Sora fell into thought.

"What if my memories aren't my own?"

That shouldn't be possible. My memories belong to me and no one else. But what if they don't?

Aren't there some memories that I've forgotten? I was asleep for a whole year, and I know I lost some of my memories along the way. But my heart remembers. The chain of memories may come undone, but the links are still there. That's why the memory of my promise will always be inside me somewhere.

It was the same for Tron. Whether his program was the original or a copy wasn't the issue. The Tron he had once fought alongside and the Tron of this world might have technically been two separate beings, but that didn't change anything. That's what Sora believed had brought him back to normal.

Even if he was walking the wrong path, Sora had no doubt his heart would lead him to the truth.

A Keyhole chose that moment to rise up before him. When he opened it, another world would await him.

Sora held out his Keyblade.

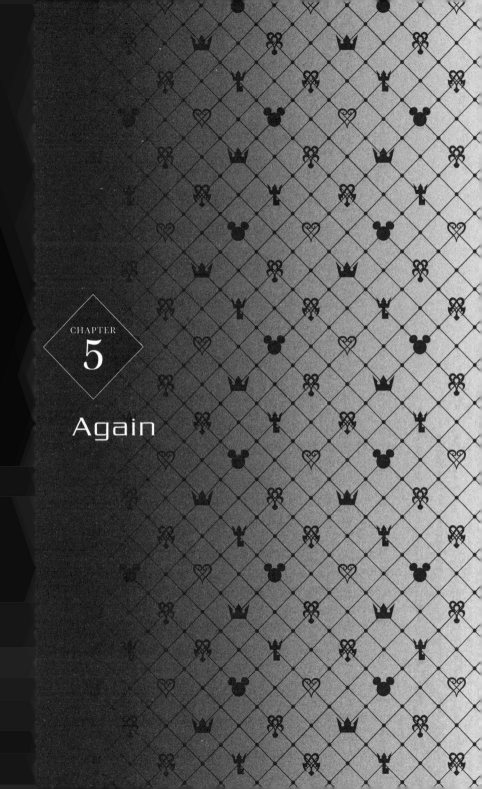

CHAPTER
5

Again

AFTER SORA OPENED THE KEYHOLE, HE FOUND himself in—

"Huh? I'm back in Traverse Town," Sora commented as he looked around. He was standing on the glass roof of the botanical garden in the Fifth District.

Behind him, he heard a familiar voice. "Why, hello down there, Sora. I've been waiting."

When Sora turned around, he saw Joshua sitting with his legs crossed on the highest point of the roof.

"You do know you can wait on the ground, right? Come down so we can talk."

"Now?" Apparently, that was too much trouble for Joshua. He lazily brushed away his long hair from his face.

"'Now?' What do you mean, *now*? You're the one who said you were waiting!"

For a guy who was just complaining about Sora's timing, Joshua didn't seem to be in much of a hurry. "Oh, well." He reluctantly hopped down to Sora and ambled over toward him. "You know you're turning more into Neku every day."

Sora cocked his head at Joshua's remark. *I'm like Neku? Really?*

"But listen, I'm glad you two showed up because—"

"You 'two'? Does that mean Riku's here?" Sora cut off Joshua mid-sentence with a question of his own.

"Yes. But you and he are still a world apart. He didn't seem especially worried, though. He knows he'll find you."

"Yeah." The news made Sora happy. Both that Riku was safe and sound and that they both believed they would find each other.

"Just look at Neku. He and the others all found their Game partners."

"Oh, they're back home safe now?"

Joshua shook his head. *Does that mean they didn't make it back...?*

"Remember what I told you. Their existence is on the line—and the Reapers are dead set on erasing them for good. But they found refuge in this world—and luckily each other, too."

"'Reapers'?"

Joshua started strolling off, and Sora followed.

"Right. If Neku and the others want to get back to where they came from, they need to win the Reapers' Game. It's like a series of missions. Those are the rules of their home ground. Except…this time the mission is a tough one." Joshua stopped at the edge of the roof and turned to face Sora. "They're pitted against a Dream Eater that can summon a hundred more like it. So I was sort of hoping you and Riku could help us out. You have your Keyblades, and with those, we might still have a chance."

"Well, I'm glad he's here with me." *Maybe I'll actually get to see him this time.*

"If he is, Riku's on one side of the Portal, and you're on the other. He might be by your side—he might be a million miles away. You can't measure the distance in time or space. Even without the wall between you, it's hard to say."

What does that mean, you can't measure the distance in time or space? And we're in opposite halves of the world… Either way, Riku is definitely over there, and he met Joshua.

Joshua seemed a little concerned, Sora noticed. "Don't worry," Sora assured him with a smile. "He's with me—even when it might seem like he's not."

"Then you two are lucky," Joshua said almost to himself, looking away from Sora for a moment.

Joshua had volunteered a lot of information, but he had yet to reveal much of anything about himself. *He said we're "lucky." Does that mean he wants a connection like ours? Maybe there's someone, but he hasn't been able to bridge that gap.*

But times like these, he knew exactly what to say. Sora took an unconscious step forward. After all, this was really important. "You and your friend are lucky, too, Joshua."

Joshua snorted. "I appreciate you saying that with conviction, even though you have no idea what you're talking about."

"Hey!"

I do know, too, what I'm talking about! Or...maybe I don't, but he still didn't have to laugh at me!

"Anyway...Neku and his partner are pinned down in the Fountain Plaza. I can count on you, right?" Once his laughter had run its course, Joshua looked toward the Fourth District.

"Always!"

Without further ado, Sora leaped down from the roof of the botanical garden with Meow Wow—and Dream Eaters arrived almost as if they had been waiting for him.

"We're in a hurry here!"

As Sora swung his Keyblade, he noticed the Nightmares were much stronger than they had been during his last visit. Maybe that was because of that Dream Eater that could summon more of them? Neku and his partner could really be having a tough go of it.

"There's no end to them!"

Sora dashed through the pack of Dream Eaters and hurried to find Neku.

Right about that same time, Neku and Shiki were squaring off with Dream Eaters in Fountain Plaza.

"This is starting to wear me down," said Neku's partner, Shiki, to the black cat plushie in her arms. "Can we get a time-out?"

As Neku turned to Shiki, the huge, birdlike Spellican flying around them raised its staff and called lightning down right where he was standing.

Shiki was sent flying and slammed headfirst into the fountain. To make matters worse, more Nightmares were pouring out from the ground where the bolt had struck and attacking her with magic. Neku recovered his balance and jumped in to protect Shiki, but he didn't have time to repel the magic. He closed his eyes instinctively—but there was no impact.

Cautiously, he cracked open an eye...

"Miss me?"

"Sora?"

"I'll take it from here!"

Several more Dream Eaters appeared in front of Sora and shuffled this way and that, as if they were figuring out the right time to strike.

"No. I don't need your help."

"'Course you do! Where are your Dream Eaters? How else can you fight?" Sora countered.

"I don't need them anymore."

Oh, so Neku found his partner. But that just means he needs my help more than ever.

"Oh, right, your partner. Well, don't you want to make it out of the Game? Who's gonna help her if you get hurt?" Sora offered his opinion.

The tension finally left Neku's shoulders. "Okay, you win. I'll let you do the sweating."

Once Sora was sure that the two had gotten away safely, he turned back to the Dream Eaters and got his Keyblade back into position. Overhead, Spellican brought down its staff again, and the blast of magic struck the ground and created an arcane square that brought with it a fresh wave of Dream Eaters.

"Bring it on!"

Sora started with the newly summoned creatures, then dashed around the Fountain Plaza with Meow Wow and wiped out the rest.

"Is that it?" Sora asked, catching his breath.

"Mrarf!" Next to him, Meow Wow barked (or maybe meowed?) at the sky.

Spellican had been watching Sora's battle, and now it was disappearing into the glowing Portal it had summoned.

"He got away!" Sora said with chagrin, just as Neku and Shiki returned.

"Sora," Neku called.

Sora turned around and recognized the girl next to him.

"So you must be Neku's partner."

She was the girl who had been with Riku in the other side of this world, back during his last visit to Traverse Town.

"Yeah. I'm Shiki. Nice to meet you. Neku told me all about you."

"Cool. But you should have seen him. He looked everywhere for you."

Sora recalled how worried Neku had been when he was searching for Shiki after they first met. He'd been determined to go back to his world with his partner.

But Neku hurriedly stopped him short. "Hey, Sora, stop talking!"

"What? Why? You said you need her," Sora replied. "That's a good thing."

Shiki laughed at Neku's mild panic. "That's sweet, Neku," she said.

"I need you to stop annoying me." Neku looked away and played with his bangs. Was he blushing?

"Mm-hmm. Well, I still think it's sweet. It's nice to be needed," the girl said as she tenderly cradled a stuffed plushie named Mr. Mew.

"I'm sorry, is this a bad time?" Joshua arrived in the plaza, and he was speaking a bit more quickly than usual. "Because that Dream Eater we're after has retreated to the other imagining of this world."

"'Other imagining'?" Sora asked back. "You mean...where Riku is."

"Yes. He and our other friends will do what they can."

Well, if Riku's handling it, there's nothing to worry about, Sora thought.

However, Joshua's expression remained gloomy. "But we'll just run ourselves in circles at this rate. We need to trap that thing in one place, and then we can finish it."

In other words, they needed to work together with Riku to defeat Spellican for good. "Trap it where?" he asked.

"The Third District," Joshua responded immediately.

"Okay." *We'd better hurry, then.* Sora took off running with Neku and Shiki.

But then Neku came to a halt. "Joshua," he said without turning around.

"Yes, Neku?" Joshua regarded him curiously.

"Tell me—are we really gonna make it home?" He sounded uncertain.

"But, Neku, I thought you couldn't afford to lose. Give up on yourself and you give up on the world," Joshua said to Neku's back, as airy as always.

"Right… So I'll see you there?"

Joshua's breath caught in his throat. Stunned, he asked, "Me?"

Neku finally turned around to face Joshua directly. "Yeah. You're my friend. It's your home, too."

Joshua closed his mouth, then smiled. "Maybe it's you that's turning into Sora." He walked slowly toward Neku.

"Huh?"

"Thanks."

With that, Joshua set off in a different direction from Sora and Shiki, while Neku took off running after his friends.

Neku caught up to Sora and Shiki in the First District, where the two of them had just finished off a group of Dream Eaters.

"Where were you, Neku?"

"Don't worry about it…" He averted his eyes at Shiki's question.

"What would you do if I got hurt after you left me all alone?" she complained.

"…Sora's here, isn't he?"

"Yeah, leave it to me!"

Shiki was clearly upset with Neku, but she couldn't hold back a giggle at Sora's eager reply. "You're funny, Sora."

"Huh? How so?" Sora tilted his head, unsure what was so funny.

She giggled again and hugged Mr. Mew. "You're Riku's friend, right?" she said, eyeing him.

"Oh yeah, you were with him." Sora remembered how he'd seen Riku with Shiki and the man in the black coat in the Fifth District.

"Mm-hmm. He saved me. But you two are nothing alike." Shiki leaned in close to Sora's ear and whispered, "You know, Neku and Riku are really similar."

"Huh?" Surprised, Sora looked at Neku.

Now that you mention it, I can see it. They're both a little prickly sometimes, but they have a heart of gold underneath.

"Wh-why are you staring at me...?" Neku returned Sora's gaze a bit uneasily.

"Yeah, you may be on to something."

"Right?"

Sora and Shiki shared a grin.

"What're you two talking about?" Neku grumbled.

Shiki laughed again. "Our secret. Right, Sora?"

"Yep, it's just between us." Sora laughed, too.

Neku was a little miffed at being left out, but after a short silence, he began walking to the door to the Third District. "Let's get moving, you two."

"Okay!" Sora and Shiki both shouted before dashing past Neku.

"Hurry up, slowpoke!"

"H-hey, wait for me!"

No sooner had the trio opened the door to the Third District than a glowing orb appeared in the middle of the street.

It was a Portal.

Sora jumped ahead of his companions and into the center of the district, adjusting his grip on his Keyblade as soon as he landed.

Spellican emerged from the sphere. If it was showing up here, that meant Riku must've been successful on the other side.

"I got it, Riku!" Sora shouted.

Then Joshua, who had arrived in the Third District at some point, called down from the roof of a building.

"It's working! He pulled through for us!"

Spellican waved downward with its staff, causing several magic squares to appear on the ground where Dream Eaters emerged.

Neku shouted, "We'll handle things here. You take care of the boss!"

"Will do!"

Shiki and Neku dashed off, leading the other Dream Eaters away until Sora was facing Spellican one-on-one.

But the Dream Eater waved its staff yet again, and this time, an even larger magic square arose.

What appeared from it was Hockomonkey, the massive, simian Dream Eater Sora had faced in Traverse Town before.

"You can summon *that*, too?!" Sora exclaimed in surprise, but he didn't stop moving. He gripped his Keyblade tightly and charged toward Hockomonkey. *I know his tricks, so this guy should be way easier than a brand-new Nightmare—as long as he hasn't gotten any stronger.*

Sora swung his Keyblade up from near Hockomonkey's feet and landed a blow. As it stumbled back, he hopped onto the Dream Eater's big knee and sprang up high in the air. His Keyblade extended, he dropped straight onto the monster's head.

"I've gotten stronger, too!"

Sora had opened the Keyholes of three worlds since the last time he fought Hockomonkey. He was much more formidable than back then. He wasn't going to lose.

Hockomonkey fell with a howl.

But before Sora could even take a breath, Spellican reappeared in the center of the plaza. Sora closed in to attack it, but the barrier around it made attacks impossible. Probably a Protect spell.

With its defenses impenetrable, Spellican raised its staff aloft. The next magic square called forth Wargoyle, the Dream Eater Sora had fought in Quasimodo's world.

"Let's do this!"

Sora hopped onto Meow Wow, ever by his side, and bounded high into the air to take care of Wargoyle from above.

"Next!"

Having finished off Wargoyle in a single go, Sora readied himself for the next Dream Eater.

Spellican had been summoning boss-tier Nightmares from each of the worlds, so it was easy to imagine what the last one would be.

Unfortunately, Sora's expectations were off.

What arose from Spellican's magic square was Char Clawbster, a huge Dream Eater that resembled a red crayfish.

Hey, I was expecting the guy who froze Monstro!

Char Clawbster was similar enough to Chill Clawbster that they could be twins, except for their different colors. Chill Clawbster had a blue shell and icy spells powerful enough to freeze Monstro solid. Char Clawbster was red.

"Which means—Blizzara!"

Sora sprang upward and tried casting Blizzara, an ice spell, from the air.

The ice from his Keyblade hit the Char Clawbster near its face, causing it to raise its pincers in rage. Ice magic worked just as well as he'd expected.

The Nightmare slammed its claws into the ground, but Sora rolled out of the way, enchanted his Keyblade with an ice spell, and then threw it. A Keyblade bolstered with the element of ice proved more effective on its tough shell than a regular attack. The Keyblade struck home, and part of Char Clawbster's red face turned blue.

The instant his Keyblade returned to him, Sora leaped and broke the creature's shell. Char Clawbster fell still and eventually faded away.

"Okay, next!"

Sora landed and waited for his next foe to arrive, but instead, a Keyhole to one of the doors of sleep rose in the air. Spellican soared upward and fled into it.

"Not again!"

Neku, Shiki, and Joshua ran over to the disappointed Sora.

"Hey, Josh, where'd it go?" Neku asked Joshua.

"Somewhere else. Out of Traverse Town and out of my reach. We'll just have to let it go."

"Great...," Neku replied with disappointment.

"So we failed the mission?" Shiki nervously asked.

"Mm..." Joshua lowered his eyes.

"I'll go after it!" Sora announced without hesitation. "C'mon, I'm not an actual Player. Can't I bend the rules?" He grinned, causing Neku and Shiki to both smile.

"Well, I guess the rules of the world don't apply if your hearts are connected—right, Sora? That's how you roll."

"Right! Then it's settled," Sora answered, holding out his Keyblade to the Keyhole.

Behind him, Neku called his name. "Sora."

"Huh?" Sora glanced back at him.

"Thanks. It wasn't easy, but you made it easier."

"Yeah."

See? Making friends isn't hard at all. Anyone can do it.

"Wow, Neku," Shiki said with a smile. "You've changed."

"Huh? You think?" Neku asked.

"Yeah, you're less dorky."

"What?" Neku wasn't ready for that.

With a giggle at her friend, Shiki turned to Sora. "Once you find your friends, Sora, you should come hang out in our town!"

"Definitely. See you in Shibuya," Neku added.

"Sure. It's a deal," Sora replied to them both.

Shibuya—a town he'd never heard of before, in a world he'd never visited.

Of course I wanna go if you guys are there!

Sora held out his hand toward the other three. Shiki was the first to take it, and then Neku placed his own hand on top of them both. Joshua was standing on his own with his hands in his pockets, but he looked at Sora and then slowly added his hand to the pile.

"Anything I should pass on to Riku?" Joshua asked Sora.

But Sora had only one answer for him. He shook his head. "Nah. I'll see him soon."

"Okay."

The four of them smiled together.

"Well then, guess I'll be on my way."

Sora turned away from the other three and raised his Keyblade once more. The beam lanced into the Keyhole, opening the door to another new adventure.

Okay, on to the next world!

CHAPTER
6

Country
of the Musketeers

PETE, THE HEAD MUSKETEER, STOOD IMPERIOUSLY AT the top of the steps in the yard the Musketeers normally used for training and surveyed the three new recruits.

"Congratulations, boys," he announced. "In light of your lacklustrious potential, I dub you Royal Musketeers! Just look at yas—all dressed up and goin' nowheres."

This Pete had a beard and mustache and a peg leg of some sort, and he was wearing a matching black feathered hat and cape. Beside him stood Minnie in a pink dress, a crown of glimmering gold on her head. Mickey and Donald saluted the captain, while Goofy stared off into space as if his mind had wandered somewhere else.

Yes, the three in the red uniforms and brown feathered caps of the Royal Musketeers had recently been appointed to their new post. Mickey's ears were too big for his hat, so his sat at an angle with one ear sticking out.

"Now then, let's get right down to your inaugurary mission— bodyguards to…Princess Minnie! Some nefarious nincompoop has got it out for her, see? And it's your job to personally keep her safe."

The princess was in peril! The trio were thrown into an uproar.

"Somebody's after the princess? Count on us!"

Their first job as Musketeers was a highly motivating one, and Mickey's heart stirred with courage.

But beside him, Donald didn't seem so sure.

"What? So soon?" he asked, lowering his head. "Don't we get to practice?"

Meanwhile, Goofy was counting something on his fingers. "Why? The one, two…three of us are ready for anything!" he told them blithely.

Pete turned away and smirked.

"Don't worry, Donald's real brave, and Goofy's clever. And while I may be small, I've got the heart of a Musketeer!" declared Mickey earnestly, unaware of Pete's sinister expression. He held his sword aloft. "All for one…"

As he began the credo of the Musketeers, Donald and Goofy put the tips of their own blades together with his.

"...And one for all!" the trio cried in unison. Their first mission would be to escort Princess Minnie's carriage.

The princess gracefully took her leave into the building.

"All right guys, assemble in front of the gates in ten minutes!" After issuing the order, Pete followed Minnie inside.

When he was gone, the remaining three jumped together in a group hug, unable to contain their joy.

"We did it! We're finally Musketeers!"

"All that hard work paid off!" Donald dramatically pretended to weep.

The three of them had been sweating away at the castle all this time so they could become Musketeers. Though they had made mistakes left and right, their efforts had finally been recognized.

"Now we'll get to do real missions!" Mickey cheered.

"Leave it to me!" Goofy thumped himself in the chest a little too hard and choked a bit.

"C'mon, fellas! We can't be late for our first mission! Let's get over to the gate!"

The three descended into the yard and walked toward the meeting point—and met a group of Dream Eaters.

"...Monsters!" Mickey brought his sword into position. But Donald was frozen in fear at the sudden arrival of enemies. "Donald!"

The creatures edged closer and closer to the trio.

"We're doomed!" Donald screamed, running off without even drawing his blade.

"Donald! Where ya goin'?" Mickey called out desperately to his friend.

Beside him Goofy squeezed his eyes shut and barreled ahead, slashing about wildly with his weapon. "Stand back! Here goes nothin'!"

"Hey, Goofy, that's the wrong way!"

His eyes still closed, Goofy charged off into an empty corner of the yard, leaving Mickey on his own.

"All right. I'll show ya what a Musketeer can do!" Mickey squared off against the monsters with his blade at the ready—only to be swatted away.

That was when Sora arrived.

The boy dispatched the Dream Eater in a flash. "King Mickey, are you okay?" he called.

"Huh? Have we met before?" Mickey asked curiously as he pushed himself to his feet.

Wait, maybe it's like with Jiminy and Tron, and this isn't the Mickey I know. This isn't Disney Castle, and the castle never went to sleep anyway.

But if so, then who's this Mickey?

Sora fell into thought.

"You okay? What's wrong?" Mickey hurried over.

"Oh, um… I was wondering…where I was?" Sora asked.

"Hmm? Where'd you get that key?" Seeing Sora's Keyblade, Mickey seemed to realize something.

"This? It's a Keyb—"

"Shh!" Mickey placed a finger to his lips before Sora could finish saying the word, and his expression grew serious. "I know. You came from another world, right?"

"Huh? Uh, yeah," Sora replied.

Mickey glanced around cautiously. "My name's Mickey. I'm workin' on a problem. That's why I'm in this world bein' a Musketeer," he explained, although that only gave Sora more questions.

He came here from another world? So was he in a world the king visited before they met, and that world was trapped in sleep?

"You seem confused," Mickey said with a smile.

Just then, another wave of Dream Eaters showed up.

"Look out!" Mickey got his sword ready.

"I'm Sora. Let me handle 'em," Sora said, then rushed into the fight. If what he saw earlier was anything to go by, the Mickey in this world wasn't that strong. After he'd dealt with the Dream Eaters as he always did, he took a moment to catch his breath.

"Thanks. I sure owe ya one," Mickey said. "Some Musketeer I turned out to be."

Meanwhile, Goofy came blundering along, his eyes still shut. "Where's the bad guys?"

"Goofy!" Sora cried out happily. Mickey was unexpected enough; he never thought he'd get to see Goofy here, too. Did that mean Donald was here as well?

"Everything's under control, Goof!" Mickey called, and Goofy finally opened his eyes and looked around.

"Really? You mean we clobbered 'em?"

Donald timidly tiptoed over to them, looking around. "Are they… gone?"

"Hey, Donald!" *I can't believe I get to see my friends from our journeys before! Even if it is just a dream.*

Donald inclined his head, puzzled by Sora's elation. "What? Who are you?"

"Gawrsh, do I know you from somewhere?"

Beside him, Goofy had his arms crossed and head to one side, too. So in this world, they really didn't know Sora.

"No… Nice to meet you."

He got why, but saying those words to Donald and Goofy still stung a little.

But that was when Mickey piped up cheerfully.

"Say, fellas, this is Sora. And it doesn't matter when we met. Once we make a friend, we're friends for life."

The words filled Sora with joy. Yeah—they already were friends, and they always would be.

"Hi. I'm Donald."

"And I'm Goofy."

Just hearing them say their names made Sora even happier. Not that he didn't already know, though.

"Friends for life." Sora nodded with a smile.

"Now, we've gotta go protect the princess! Donald, Goofy, follow me!" Mickey called before marching off.

"Hey, wait! You're not gonna let me come along?"

The Donald he knew would never run from a foe, and Goofy wasn't one to fight with his eyes closed. Mickey didn't even have his Keyblade. Sora knew they could use a hand.

"But you're not a Musketeer," Mickey replied. "And this mission is fraught with danger."

"All the more reason I should help. When the going gets tough, the tough call their friends."

"Hmm…" Mickey gave it a bit of thought, then smiled. "Well, all right. Thank you!"

"Great! Should we do the thing?" Goofy asked.

"The 'thing'?"

Sora didn't know what that meant. Goofy leaned in toward Sora's ear and quietly told him what he wanted to do.

When Sora nodded, Mickey held his sword into the sky. "All for one…," he cried gallantly, prompting Donald and Goofy to also hold their blades aloft. Sora was a little late, but he raised his Keyblade along with the others.

"…And one for all!" four voices said in unison.

All for one and one for all—that was how they'd always been. The credo lifted Sora's spirits.

"Okay, let's go!"

With that, the four of them headed for the gate.

Princess Minnie stepped into her carriage.

"So Minnie's the princess they were talking about…," Sora commented quietly.

"Huh? Did you say something?" Mickey asked.

"No, just talking to myself."

Mickey and Minnie, and then Donald and Goofy… That meant there might be even more of his friends from Disney Castle here in this world.

"Let's get moving!"

Goofy took the driver's seat, while Sora, Mickey, and Donald

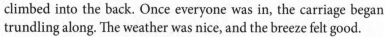

climbed into the back. Once everyone was in, the carriage began trundling along. The weather was nice, and the breeze felt good.

"Where's this carriage headed anyway?"

"She's going to the opera house!" Donald replied in his usual quacking voice.

"This is our first ever mission, so we have to keep her safe and sound."

But before Mickey's explanation even finished, a strange rumbling reached their ears—and it wasn't coming from the carriage.

"What's that?"

Sora turned back to find—

"A Dream Eater!"

A huge, dinosaur-like Dream Eater—a Tyranto Rex—was charging in their direction.

Sora and Mickey quickly drew their blades, while Donald tumbled back in surprise.

"Gawrsh, it's a bad guy!"

Goofy tightened his grip on the reins and sped the carriage up, but Tyranto Rex plowed right into it. The carriage shuddered violently, and Mickey, Donald, and even Goofy went tumbling right off the side.

"Guys!"

Sora clung to the roof with all his strength, then climbed back up and turned to face the monster with his Keyblade at the ready. While he was worried about the three who fell off, his biggest concern right now was keeping the carriage and Minnie safe.

"Roooooooh!!"

Tyranto Rex spit out a ball of fire, but Sora immediately swatted it back with his Keyblade and gave the dinosaur a taste of its own medicine.

"C'mon, big guy, try that again!"

Unfortunately, Tyranto Rex caught up to them in a flash, then snapped at Sora and got a chunk of carriage, too.

"Whoa!"

Though he was almost knocked off the roof again, Sora desperately maintained his grip. Minnie was watching nervously from the window.

"Don't worry, Minnie!" he called.

She gave a small nod.

"Okay, come and get me!"

Tyranto Rex belched out more fire, which Sora knocked back. When the Dream Eater got close again, he swatted it on the snout with his Keyblade to drive it away. Tyranto Rex spat another ball of flames, but Sora was already casting a spell.

"Blizzaga!"

The cluster of ice canceled the Dream Eater's fire and went on to connect with its head. Finally, the Tyranto Rex slowly collapsed and faded away.

But this was no time to relax. When Sora turned around, he found three suspicious characters in brown cloaks behind him.

"Huh?"

As Sora froze briefly in shock, the three Beagle Boys drew their swords.

"We'll be lightenin' your load by one princess," said the first.

"Now, make like those Musketeers and scram," jeered the second.

"Au revoir!" called the third, and then he threw his sword.

"Whoa!" Sora leaned back to get out of the way, but he lost his balance and fell right off the roof.

The carriage sped away in a cloud of dust, leaving Minnie alone with the Beagle Boys.

What do I do now...?!

Meanwhile, Mickey, Donald, and Goofy were trudging up the road.

"Your Majest— Ah, I mean, Mickey!" Sora called.

Mickey raised his head. "Sora!"

"I'm sorry. They got away with the princess."

Sora ran up to Mickey, then apologized.

"Don't be," Mickey consoled him. "It's not your fault."

"As long as we all stick together, I know we can get the princess back!" Goofy added.

But Donald was still staring at the ground. "It's hopeless…," he moaned anxiously.

"Goofy's right. As a team, we can anything!"

Mickey's confidence seemed to lift even Donald's spirits.

"Yeah!" Sora cried. "Come on!"

They all nodded at one another.

"But where?" wondered Goofy.

"After the carriage! See?" Mickey pointed out the tracks. "Those'll take us right to it."

"Let's hurry!"

The four of them raced off.

…That said, it was looking like they had a long road ahead of them.

"Gawrsh, fellas! Wait for me!"

"Hang in there, Goofy!" Sora called over his shoulder as the clumsy Musketeer began to fall behind.

"We're just gonna have to leave you!" Donald's feet were slapping the ground in his familiar waddling run, but he was running out of steam, too.

"Guess it's time for a break." Sora slowed to a walk. Unlike the counterparts he knew, these two weren't used to fighting or getting this much exercise at once.

"Maybe we aren't cut out to be Musketeers after all…," Donald said weakly.

"That's not true! Isn't being Musketeers what we always wanted?" Mickey reassured him.

"He's right, a-hyuck! We finally made our dream come true, so we can't give up without tryin'."

"I'll show *you* who's giving up!"

Goofy started running again, and Donald began to catch up to him.

Sora and Mickey shared a smile, then hurried after them.

"Hey, look, Mickey! There's the carriage!" Goofy called back, a step ahead of the others. The four of them rushed over to the carriage, but Minnie did not appear to be inside.

"But there's no sign of the princess," Goofy worried.

"Then that means…"

"Yep. She's out there somewhere, counting on us to come to the rescue." Mickey finished Donald's sentence.

"Yeah, 'cause we're Musketeers!" Donald said to rally the others, then set off at a run.

"And we're gonna be the ones to save her!" Mickey went after him with Goofy in tow.

"Hey, aren't you forgetting someone?" Suddenly alone, Sora rushed after them.

The three crossed over a bridge and headed for a tower standing next to a single enormous tree on a sandbar in the middle of a big river. Minnie had to be confined somewhere inside.

"Are we sure about this…?" Donald peered into the tower from the doorway.

"Let's go, fellas!" Goofy flung the door open.

The tower was quiet, with no signs of anyone inside.

"Maybe she's upstairs?" Donald cautiously stepped onto the circular staircase winding around the inside of the walls. Sora and the others followed his lead.

Partway up, they heard a suspicious noise getting louder and louder above them. They looked up the stairs.

A large barrel was rolling right toward them.

"Look out!"

Sora charged up the steps and knocked the barrel away with his Keyblade, but it was far too big. It merely shifted to the side and kept tumbling down the stairs.

"Wa-wa-wak!" Panicked, Donald tried to flee, but the barrel rolled right over him. "Wak…"

"You okay, Donald?"

"Yeah…" Donald stood up and rubbed his tail.

"That settles it, though. The princess is definitely here!" Mickey asserted, looking sternly into the upper reaches of the tower.

"We better hurry!"

Goofy started back up the stairs straightaway. Another barrel came rolling by, but he neatly hopped out of the way.

"Don't forget me!" Donald followed after him.

The barrels kept coming, but the four of them managed to steer clear and make it all the way to the top, where they found Minnie in a birdcage and the Beagle Boys waiting for them.

"Heh-heh."

"This oughta be fun, eh?"

"You, defeat us? *Mais non!*" the Beagle Boys taunted.

"I'll take care of you!" Sora got his Keyblade ready, but then Mickey called out to him from behind.

"Wait, Sora."

"Huh?" Sora turned around to see Mickey looking at Goofy.

"Got any suggestions, Goofy?"

Goofy thought for a moment—and then seemed to have a flash of insight.

"You've got an idea?"

"And it might even be a good one, too! Hold on."

"Sure, take your time."

With that, Goofy snatched up Mickey and dove right out the window. "Charge!"

The two of them hit a branch on the tree standing outside, which bent down so far that the recoil flung them right back through the window and into the Beagle Boys. They didn't stand a chance.

"Ack!"

"Urgh!"

"Oof!"

The villains were knocked out the window on the far side, tumbling one by one into the river below.

"How'd I do?" Goofy grinned, and Mickey leaped into the air.

"Yeah, we did it!" he cheered. "Hooray for the Musketeers!"

Donald poked his head around the barrel where he'd been hiding. "We did it?"

Sora and Mickey shared a look and burst out in laughter at the stunned expression on his face.

After savoring their triumph for a brief moment, Mickey respectfully opened the door of Minnie's cage.

"Sora! Thank you. Princess Minnie is safe. We couldn't have done it without ya!"

"Sure. Happy to help."

Minnie smiled, but she couldn't take her eyes off Mickey. "Oh, my hero!" she cried.

A little embarrassed, Mickey held his sword skyward. "All for one…"

Sora, Donald, and Goofy followed his lead.

"…And one for all!"

Swords and Keyblade came together as the Musketeers' motto filled the air.

"…Huh?" Sora lowered his Keyblade, confused.

"What's wrong?" Mickey gave Sora a curious look.

This should've wrapped things up here, but the Keyhole isn't showing up. Maybe that means this world hasn't woken up yet.

"It's nothing." Sora shook his head at Mickey's concern.

"Okay, then let's go back to the castle!" Mickey offered his arm to Minnie and started down the stairs.

"Yeah, let's head back!"

Sora joined Donald and the others heading down.

That night, Sora was joining Goofy on patrol in the yard.

"Man, I'm full." They had eaten dinner together, too, so Sora did a big stretch to keep from getting too drowsy. "Huaaaah."

"We didn't even get a fancy dinner. And we worked so hard…"

Saving the princess did seem like a feat worthy of a reward, but no such luck. Now that he thought about it, they hadn't seen the princess at all after they got back to the castle. The meal they had all shared was just soup and bread. It was still more than enough, though.

"Huh? D'ya see that?" Goofy squinted his eyes, spying something in the distance.

"Hmm? What's up?" Sora asked, but his friend ran off. "Goofy! Where are you going?"

Sora started after him, but then Mickey called for him to stop. Pluto was with him. "What's the matter, Sora? Hold on!"

"Oh, Mickey. Goofy just sort of…took off."

"Goofy's gone? But why would he leave his post?" Mickey seemed troubled.

Then Donald came running toward them. "HELP!" he wailed, zooming right by.

"Not you, too, Donald?"

Donald skidded to a halt, then turned around and came rushing back in a panic. "What do we do? It's a disaster!"

"Calm down, Donald!" Mickey scolded. "Start from the beginning."

"The captain's gonna kidnap Princess Minnie!" Donald cried.

"What? But he's the one who made us Musketeers."

Mickey immediately shot down the idea. Why would the very captain who had named them Musketeers be after the princess?

"It was all a big lie."

"A lie? Well…lie or no lie, Musketeers never run from danger!"

"Then it's time for me to get a new job!" Donald snapped angrily, then turned away from Mickey and waddled off.

"Donald, wait!" Mickey pleaded.

Donald stopped and turned back, but he didn't seem to have any courage in the face of danger. At least, not when that danger was the captain.

"Together we can stop Captain Pete," Mickey said.

"Yeah," Sora added. "We're in this together!"

"C'mon, we'll be right beside you, 'cause we're friends."

But the duck shook his head at Mickey's entreaty. "I just can't do it. I'm sorry." And with that, he ran out of the yard.

"Donald!" Mickey took a step forward, but then stopped when his friend didn't even look back. "Donald…"

Pluto rubbed up against the dejected Mickey to help cheer him up. "He'll be back," said Sora. "I know it."

Donald had never left for good, not even when Sora lost his Keyblade. He was sure the Donald of this world would do the same.

"Aw, thanks, Sora." Mickey still seemed saddened, though.

"So this captain guy's the culprit. I wonder what he's up to," Sora murmured.

At that moment, a familiar voice rang out. If there was any troublemaker in Mickey's world, it was—

"Ee-heh-heh-heh… Bwa-ha-ha-ha! What am I up to?"

Sora turned around.

"I'm up to plenty!"

Someone had emerged on the highest level of the yard.

"Pete?" Sora summoned his Keyblade.

"Whozzat? A stranger lookin' to be endangered… You, mangle these yardsticks!"

At Pete's command, Dream Eaters appeared around Sora and Mickey. Mickey weaved between the monsters and jumped up to the top of the steps, sword in hand.

"Captain Pete, by the power vested in me as a Musketeer, I arrest you, mister!"

"Bah-ha-ha!" Pete burst out in laughter, as if it was the funniest thing he'd ever heard. "That's a good one. Wah-ha-ha-ha! Well, how's about this? By the power invested in my fist, I clobber you!" He threw a punch at Mickey with all his power behind it.

"Mickey!" Sora tried to hurry over to his friend, but a Dream Eater took his moment of distraction to launch an attack. "Mickey…"

With that, Sora lost consciousness.

"Sora?"

"Sora?"

Donald and Goofy were peering into his face with concern.

"Donald…Goofy…"

I messed up! Sora quickly scrambled to his feet as he regained

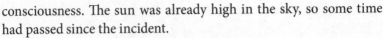

consciousness. The sun was already high in the sky, so some time had passed since the incident.

"Where's Mickey?" he asked.

His two friends shared a momentary troubled look.

"Captain Pete and his guys took Mickey to Mont Saint-Michel," Goofy told him, despondent. "And that means he's in big trouble! Once the tide comes in, the dungeon'll fill up with water!"

"And so will Mickey," said Donald, refusing to look up from the ground.

"Well, come on. We gotta save him!"

Donald and Goofy didn't seem to be quite as ready to go as Sora.

"Oh…but how?"

Sora gave the two a long look. "What are you saying? You and Goofy wouldn't have come back if you weren't ready to save him! We're friends—friends for life, remember?"

Yeah, we're friends for life. In this world and in all the rest. We'll always, always be friends. That will never change.

"Yeah!" Donald agreed.

"Best of friends to the very end!" Goofy chimed in, too.

Sora had finally gotten through. Even here in this different time and place, maybe somewhere in their hearts they still remembered what really mattered.

"Good. Let's go!"

"Okay!" Goofy and Donald answered Sora's call in unison, and the courageous trio sallied forth for Mont Saint-Michel.

Until Sora suddenly stopped. "Uh, where's Mont Saint-Michel again?"

"Wak!"

"Yipe!"

Donald and Goofy crashed into Sora's back.

"Don't stop out of the blue like that!" Donald shouted as he rubbed his bill.

"Heh, sorry."

"Mont Saint-Michel's a prison. You can take a boat from the shore, or if the tide's out, you can walk. But if it's in…" Goofy shuddered.

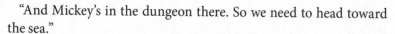

"And Mickey's in the dungeon there. So we need to head toward the sea."

"Yeah! We gotta hurry!" Donald cried.

"Okay, let's get moving."

Sora and his friends started running again.

As the sun began to set, Sora and the others set out for Mont Saint-Michel on a small boat from the sea. Goofy was rowing.

"I'm scared!" Donald shivered as thunder started to rumble.

"We'll be fine with the three of us," Sora said encouragingly.

"Almost there," Goofy announced, and shortly after, the boat arrived at Mont Saint-Michel.

From the word *prison*, Sora had imagined something cramped and confined, but the place was almost the size of a small city that covered the island.

"Let's go!" Sora vaulted out of the boat and broke into a run with Donald and Goofy close behind. But the inside of Mont Saint-Michel was infested with Dream Eaters.

"Why are there so many monsters?!" Donald ran around, trying to get away from them. Apparently, the Donald of this world couldn't use magic.

"Donald! Hey!" Sora cried. Next to him, Goofy had once again starting waving his sword around with his eyes clamped shut. "Yikes! Careful, Goofy!"

Sora fought off the Dream Eaters, but he was also trying to stay out of the way of Goofy's flailing sword. They weren't going to get anywhere at this rate.

"Meow Wow!" Sora called the Spirit over so they could fight alongside each other. "Goofy! Stop waving your sword! Just open your eyes!"

"Huh?"

"Donald, get it together! We're gonna make a run for it!"

"Wak!"

Sora grabbed Donald's hand and sprinted, calling to Goofy. Meow Wow bounded along behind them, keeping them covered.

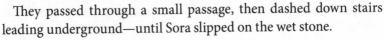

They passed through a small passage, then dashed down stairs leading underground—until Sora slipped on the wet stone.

"Whoa!"

"Gwak!"

"Wahoo!"

When Sora tripped and fell onto his stomach, Donald landed on top of him tailfirst, and Goofy dropped onto them both headfirst.

"Ow!"

"Wak! Get off me!"

"Gawrsh…"

Just as Goofy was about to climb off Donald, Meow Wow came bouncing down onto them and delivered the finishing blow.

"Urgh!" Sora grunted from the bottom of the pile. Still, this wasn't the first time this had happened, he remembered, and he was a little glad for the sense of familiarity.

"You surprised me!" said Goofy. He was the first to stand, moving Meow Wow aside and rubbing his back.

"You sure are heavy!" Donald grumbled as he stood, and then Goofy helped Sora to his feet.

"…Huh?" Goofy cocked his head to one side and put a hand behind his ear. He must've heard something.

"That sounds like water!" When Sora strained his ears, too, he caught the rush of water coming in. The sun had almost set, and the tide was flowing into the dungeon.

"There's no time to lose!" With a sudden burst of newfound energy, Donald ran ahead. "Wak!"

But it wasn't long before he was backpedaling again.

A group of Dream Eaters approached him with threatening growls.

"Let me take point; you guys stay behind me!"

Sora quickly slid in front of Donald and made short work of them with his Keyblade. So the underground passages were rank with Dream Eaters, too.

He fought off several packs of the monsters alongside Meow Wow, taking care not to slip in the water, but never once did he think of Donald and Goofy as a burden. After all, they had always been a big help to him. Once he had finished with the last of the Dream Eaters, Sora headed deeper into the dungeon with his friends.

"Mickey!"

In the deepest depths of the dungeon, there was an entrance that led down into yet another underground chamber. Water was pouring into it, and it was almost full.

"Hold on!"

Sora took the biggest breath he could and plunged into the water. He wasn't only a good swimmer; he was a good diver, too.

Underwater, he furiously removed Mickey's chains, took his friend in his arms, and kicked up to the surface. Donald and Goofy pulled them out.

"Aw, I hope he's okay..." Donald looked into Mickey's face with concern.

"He'll be fine," Goofy said, but he looked worried, too.

"Mickey!"

Donald shook his unconscious friend, which helped Mickey finally spit up water straight into the duck's face.

"Wak!"

With that, Mickey was finally awake.

"Donald? Goofy? You too, Sora? You came back," Mickey said happily as he got to his feet, still sopping wet.

"C'mon, men! We gotta save the princess!" Donald set off with no further ado.

But Mickey's gaze was still lowered. "Aw, fellas. We're not even real Musketeers."

"Wrong. You are real Musketeers! And don't let anybody else tell you you're not," Sora said to cheer him up. This wasn't like Mickey at all.

"It doesn't matter what you wear," stated Donald, his chest puffed out proudly.

"Only what kind of heart it is that beats inside of ya!" Goofy added.

"...Yeah." Mickey smiled at last, then stood. "You know what? You're right, pals. When the bunch of us stick together, we can accomplish anything!"

Everyone grinned. Their hearts were connected—that was what made them friends and what gave them courage.

"Pete said he was headed for the opera house. And that's where we'll find Her Majesty! C'mon, Musketeers. We've got a princess to rescue."

The team of four set out for the opera house.

The opera house was a humongous theater for a sizable audience. Even at night, it was brightly lit, like preparations were underway for a party.

"Hey. Over there!"

As soon as they arrived, they spotted the Beagle Boys lugging around a large chest.

"Oy! Those nitwits!"

"The boss is gonna be mad."

"Hurry!"

The trio hurriedly picked the box back up and carried it inside.

"Help!" Inside the chest, they heard a faint but familiar voice...

"Princess!" Mickey shouted. Minnie was definitely locked up inside of that container.

Mickey drew his sword, and Donald and Goofy followed suit. Without a moment to lose, the four of them ran into the opera house, passed through the lobby, and made for the auditorium.

Waiting for them there was Pete and Minnie, who was somehow free.

"You came to rescue me!"

Minnie ran over to Mickey. All four of them were relieved to see that someone had rescued her from the box—but there was still one foe left to defeat!

Onstage, Pete guffawed from his perch on the set of a ship. "Wah-ha-ha-ha!"

"The jig is up, Pete!" Mickey brandished his sword.

"There's no escape!"

"Yeah, it's three against one now!"

Donald and Goofy backed him up.

"Geh-heh-heh…" Even after losing his prisoner and having four new foes, Pete still seemed confident. He glanced up to the catwalks—and a big wooden crate that was about to come tumbling down onto the three Musketeers.

"Look out!" Sora cried out instinctively, only for the box to vanish in a flash. "Huh?" he said in surprise.

That light reminded him of the Portal in Traverse Town.

Hey, that means—

"Riku. Riku saved us."

Our worlds are still connected, and Riku's with us on the other side! I bet he's the one who saved Minnie, too. Sora was positive.

"Impossible!" Pete stamped his foot in frustration.

"All right!" Sora turned to face Pete and readied his Keyblade. There wasn't a doubt in his mind now that he could take care of this. "Musketeers! Get the princess to safety! I'll handle things here."

"No way! We'll fight, too!" Mickey said with his sword at the ready, as if Sora's courage had reached him as well. Donald and Goofy didn't step away, either. "Princess, please find somewhere safe!"

"All right!" Minnie lifted her skirts and hurried off the stage.

"Okay, fellas, let's go!"

"Why you…!" Pete snarled. "How dare you thwart me in the nick of time! This don't add up, I tell ya. Hey! Over here, boys!"

As the Beagle Boys revealed themselves, Sora repositioned his Keyblade and faced those three stubborn henchmen.

"Oy, don't forget about us!"

"Come on!" Goofy cried. "I'm ready for ya!"

But Sora grabbed Goofy before he could run off with his eyes closed again.

"Hold on, Goofy! Donald, Mickey, you too!" Sora gathered the trio around him and whispered his plan.

"I see! All for one!" Mickey nodded with a smile.

"Exactly!" Sora grinned back.

"You chumps cookin' up some kinda scheme? Heh, good luck!" Pete yelled from the boat onstage.

"We'll start with you!" Sora turned his Keyblade toward one of the Beagle Boys.

"Wak!" Donald rushed forward, followed by Goofy, and then Mickey until they had the Beagle Boy surrounded.

"Huh?"

The lone Beagle Boy at the center was too startled to react. Goofy suddenly rammed into him from behind, and before he could recover his balance, Donald gave him a web-footed kick hard enough to lift him up off his feet.

Before the Beagle Boy could hit the ground again, Sora grabbed his arms, and Mickey took hold of his legs.

"Heave-ho!"

Sora and Mickey swung him back for extra momentum, then hurled the henchman at Pete.

"Weeeeh!"

"Gyaaah!"

Pete and the lone Beagle Boy screamed together.

"Y-you!"

Pete shook his fist from underneath his own flunky.

"All for one—or maybe just four-on-one!" Sora stuck out his tongue at the villain.

"Two more to go!"

Donald ran over to one of the two remaining Beagle Boys and tried to tackle him. But Donald wasn't going to win a wrestling match, and the two came to a standstill.

"Donald!"

Sora joined in and grabbed the Beagle Boy from the other side, holding him in place.

"A-hyuck!"

Once their foe was trapped, the tall Goofy grabbed him by the arms.

"I've got this side!" Mickey took hold of his squirming legs, and once they were sure Mickey had him, Sora and Donald stepped away.

"Heave-ho!"

"Aaagh!"

The second Beagle Boy crashed into Pete, who was starting to get wobbly.

"Okay, that only leaves you!"

Well aware of what was happening, the final Beagle Boy edged backward as the four heroes closed in on him. When he reached the edge of the stage, he slashed about with his sword in a fit of desperation.

But Sora put a stop to that with his Keyblade, and Goofy took the opportunity to wrap his arms firmly around the Beagle Boy from behind. The rascal still tried to stab at them with his sword, so Donald reached up under his armpit and began tickling him.

"Ha-ha! Wa-hoh-hoh-hoh-hoh!"

As soon as he dropped his weapon, Sora grabbed his right leg while Mickey seized the left one. Goofy adjusted his grip on the henchman's arms. And then—

"Haaaargh!"

"Eeeagh!"

After the last of his goons crashed into him, Pete toppled over unconscious.

"We did it!"

As Sora and Mickey celebrated their victory with a high-five, they heard the sound of applause.

"What marvelous work!" Minnie cried, clapping her hands in praise.

"Princess!"

Mickey hurried over to her and knelt reverently. Sora and the others followed suit.

"In gratitude for being so brave and saving us all, I hereby officially dub thee Royal Musketeers," Minnie told them gently. "Thank you all."

"Hooray!"

"We did it!"

"A-hyuck, this is great."

The four heroes shared a smile of joy. Mickey then stood and held his sword overhead.

"Fellas?"

Everyone nodded and placed their blades together.

"All for one and one for all!"

Four voices joined together to fill the auditorium with one great call.

"You're really going?" Donald said in disappointment.

It was the next morning, and they all stood on the training ground of the Musketeers. Princess Minnie had arranged for a big meal and a good night's rest for all of them, but now he was setting off.

"Yeah, I have to."

"But we only just met…," Goofy said sadly.

"We'll see each other again. You can count on it," Sora said to the two of them with a smile.

"He's right, fellas," said Mickey. "We'll always be friends, no matter how far apart we are."

"Yeah." Sora nodded.

No distance can ever break the bond between our hearts—and not just for me and the guys here. It's the same with Riku, and with everyone else I've met in all worlds I've visited so far.

A Keyhole floated in the air, as it always did, and Sora held his Keyblade up to the sky.

"All for one and one for all!" he declared, imagining his Keyblade crossed with Riku's on the other side. Somehow, he knew Riku was doing the same with the Musketeers over there, too.

Light shot from Sora's Keyblade into the Keyhole, and the door opened.

Hey, Riku. Let's ace this exam and become Keyblade Masters together!

And Sora made his way to the next world.

CHAPTER
7

Symphony of Sorcery

WHEN HE TOUCHED DOWN IN THE NEXT WORLD, MUSIC
filled the air.

Sora looked up at the source of the sound, who was standing on a precipice over a stormy sea.

It was Mickey, wearing a wizard's robe and a pointy hat. In fact, it was a dead ringer for the one Yen Sid was always wearing.

Mickey waved his arms like a conductor directing the sound, causing the waves to swell with the music, the stars to dance, lightning to flash.

"Whoa…," Sora breathed at the terrifying beauty of the spectacle. When Mickey raised his arms up high over his head, the clouds parted.

And behind them was Spellican—the big Dream Eater that had slipped through Sora's fingers in Traverse Town. He readied his Keyblade immediately, but it just swatted him away and knocked him out cold.

"Ow…"

When Sora came to, rubbing the bump on his head, he was somewhere very familiar—a place that looked exactly like Yen Sid's room in the Mysterious Tower. But he had still only opened six doors; it was too early to come back. That, and the place felt different.

Sora looked around and saw someone in the chair where Yen Sid usually sat—the king.

"King Mickey!"

Sora hurried over to his friend, but Mickey was still wearing his robe and hat from earlier on the cliff, and he was waving his arms in the same manner. What's more, he was surrounded by a strange aura, and worst of all, he looked to be in some distress.

The room was also extremely quiet.

There were two music stands to Mickey's rear, and an uncanny aura exactly like the one around Mickey was emanating from the musical scores they held. Maybe these were what was troubling the king.

"All right… Ack!"

Sora took his Keyblade in hand and struck one of the scores, only to be knocked back, hitting the ground. As he got to his feet, he could hear Mickey's voice, as if the king was speaking directly into his mind.

"Gosh, is that a Keyblade? Who are you an apprentice to? I'm Mickey, the sorcerer's apprentice."

If Mickey is the sorcerer's apprentice… Does that mean this world is from back when Mickey was still in training here? Maybe this world went to sleep in the past, too.

"What's wrong?" Mickey spoke again to Sora, who had lapsed into thought.

"What? Oh, uh, I'm Sora—the, uh, 'prentice of…umm…" *Am I technically Yen Sid's apprentice? Maybe not…?* Sora didn't have a good answer. More importantly, there was something he wanted to ask. "Hey, listen, Your Maj— I gotta stop that. Mickey—what can I do to save you?" Sora asked the apparently sleeping king.

"Thank you, Sora, but it's no use. A monster's possessed that music. And he's releasing darkness that stops anybody from going in there to fight him. To dispel the darkness, we need a Sound Idea."

A monster possessing the music? I bet that's Spellican.

"Okay, where do I get a 'Sound Idea'?" Sora asked, stepping closer to his friend. He was sure he could wake Mickey from his bad dream with its power.

"What? You'll find one for me?"

"Of course!" Sora replied with a smile. There was no question about it.

"Thank you."

It wasn't every day he got the chance to save the king. He did help him out a bit back in the Musketeers' world, but normally it was the other way around. "So what exactly is a Sound Idea?"

"Hmm…" Another music stand appeared as Mickey replied, *"Inside this musical score should be a power that can sweep away any*

darkness. But you gotta be careful. In between those clefs and notes are monsters—not as strong as the big one, but still pretty strong."

"Got it."

Sora nodded and held his Keyblade out toward the musical score. As beautiful melodies flooded outward, he was pulled into the world of music.

"Wow!"

Sora arrived in a realm above the clouds. He had been to all kinds of places but never anywhere so high. He took off at a run across the spongy ground, which honestly felt kind of weird. He'd expected to be the only one allowed inside, but Meow Wow was there right behind him.

The world was alive with music, too—and Dream Eaters, unfortunately.

"Okay, let's get this party started!"

Normally, each hit he landed with his Keyblade resulted in a dull *thud* and an impact in his arm, but here he was surprised to hear a lovely sound like an instrument. *Let's try that again.*

"Whoa, it makes a note!"

This time, he heard the sound of a different instrument. Sora swung his Keyblade to the rhythm of the world around him as he dealt with the Dream Eaters.

He felt a little like a musician. Maybe this was how Mickey felt when he was controlling the music on that cliff before.

"Whoo-hoo!"

As Sora deftly wielded his Keyblade, the music swelled, and this time a rainbow bridge appeared.

The bridge brought him to a stormy forest. Dark clouds hung everywhere, and lightning crashed to the ground with thunderous noise—all in time to the music. The wind also whistled by his ears in tune, but it was so strong that he could barely make any progress forward.

Wielding his Keyblade in time with the rhythm had opened new paths in the clouds before. If so...

"It must be the same here," Sora said to himself, then began taking out the Dream Eaters at a good tempo. The thunder and lightning were like the beating of a drum—*flash, boom, flash, boom.* Sora added the swings of his Keyblade to the rhythm.

When he did, the rain clouds vanished all at once, and a blue sky emerged. The wind died down, too, and he could finally make some headway.

Sora ran forward until he reached the place the wind had been coming from, a beautiful pastoral landscape.

There, he spotted a musical score and hurried over to it. This had to be the Sound Idea.

"So easily you sink into the depths of slumber," someone said behind him, just before he could hold out his Keyblade.

Sora turned around, and there was that guy with the silver hair again. He brandished his Keyblade, but the man extended a hand as if to stop him.

"Beautiful world, isn't it? Almost like a dream," the man said as a cascade of flower petals drifted down around them, reflecting the light in a pleasant way.

"Why are you following me around?" Sora edged closer, unable to hide his irritation.

Why did they always run into each other wherever he went—and why did he always say a bunch of cryptic nonsense and then leave? Sora wanted to know what he was after.

"You really haven't caught on?" the man said. "Or are you just assuming it's all part of your little test?"

The melody playing through the world swelled with his second question.

The shower of petals, the music—the guy was right. This place was definitely like something out of a dream.

"I'm not part of your dream. And if you thought I was...then you're softer than they say." The man caught one of the fluttering petals and then opened his hand. The crushed remains drifted away in the breeze. "But...this will all be over soon."

He turned from Sora and began to walk away.

"Just who are you people?" Sora asked toward his back.

I know about Xemnas, the guy you showed up with before. But with you, I've got nothing. It's like we've met somewhere before, but also like we don't know each other at all.

"Sleep on and we shall meet again."

"Hey!" Sora shouted, but the man didn't turn back. A cloud of petals blew by, and when they scattered, he was gone.

I have no idea what's going on here. Wasn't this a test? If he isn't part of my dream, then what is he? I don't get it. He said to sleep on—maybe I'll find something out if I keep going. Once I open the Sleeping Keyhole in this world, that'll be the last one. Will he be waiting on the other side?

Behind him, the musical score began to glow. When he turned around, the score flew into his chest and vanished, as if it had been waiting for the chance.

So this was a Sound Idea...

As Sora closed his eyes, the music ceased.

He opened his eyes and found himself back in the room where Mickey slept. The chamber really was silent—except for the tiny melody of the Sound Idea he had just obtained.

"Thank you, Sora. I can tell you found us a Sound Idea. Well, I guess we should try and put it to work."

Sora waved his Keyblade like a conductor in front of the shining score. A mysterious and wonderful song began to play—but was something missing?

The notes transformed into light that flew into the ominous musical score behind Mickey.

"That's strange... Is one Sound Idea not enough?" said Mickey.

If one isn't enough... "Don't worry," said Sora. "I've got a friend out there who will help. He's always picking up the slack for me."

As if answering Sora's call, another new musical score flashed into being next to its shining twin.

This had to be Riku's Sound Idea. Its melody dispelled the sinister presence from the second musical score.

"Wow! *The sounds are joining together to make even more powerful music!*" Mickey cried happily.

Yeah. The melodies came together to make a song—kinda like us. With Riku and everyone else behind me, I can face anything.

"Okay. Can I get in there to fight that thing now?"

"Yes. But Sora—," Mickey started to say worriedly.

"I'll be fine! See ya in a jiff." Sora raised his Keyblade to the musical score. The ensuing light opened the music, and then Sora was standing on the precipice where he first found Mickey. Spellican lay in wait for him there.

"You won't get away this time!"

With his Keyblade in hand, Sora leaped into the air and landed on a storm cloud, then cast a Zero Graviga spell to pin Spellican in place. The orb of light around the Dream Eater rendered him completely immobile.

"No escaping now! Here I come!"

Sora jumped on Meow Wow and bounced into the air to smack Spellican around a little before the magic wore off.

I'm not alone. Riku's with me, and Meow Wow, too. So nothing will ever be too much to face. Someone will always have my back, no matter what.

After the last few hits to Spellican, Sora touched back down on the cliff, and the Dream Eater vanished in a burst of light before his eyes. The storm, the wind, and the thunder combined to make its own kind of music. Just as sounds joined to create music, these forces could come together to give rise to something even more incredible. That's what he believed.

Sora closed his eyes—and returned to the real world.

Mickey stretched himself out as he woke. He hopped from the

chair onto the desk, then checked his legs and shook himself out to make sure everything still worked.

Sora knew that Master Yen Sid would probably be furious to find his apprentice on the big desk, and the Mickey he knew would never do something like this. He couldn't help but burst out in laughter. Turns out the king wasn't quite the perfect student Sora had envisioned. Now that he thought about it, Mickey had been full of mischief in that monochrome world from the past underneath Disney Castle, too.

Mickey carefully removed Yen Sid's hat from his head before Sora and set it on the desk.

"Thanks, Sora! Don't know what I woulda done without ya."

Sora took the hand Mickey extended and shook it—or started to, until Mickey shook his hand free and jumped into the air.

"Oh no! The water! I'm in big trouble if I don't fetch it!"

Flustered, Mickey darted to the door of the room.

In trouble with Yen Sid? Yeah, I bet he's really scary when he's upset.

Mickey stopped before he reached the door and looked back. "See ya real soon, Sora!"

"Yeah. You know it."

After Mickey had left the room, a Keyhole floated above the hat on the desk.

This was the final door. The test should be finished now. And yet, Sora felt like he still had a long ways to go.

The last thing that guy had said raced through his mind.

"Sleep on, and we shall meet again."

Sora extended his Keyblade toward the Keyhole.

The final door opened, and he stepped into the world beyond.

CHAPTER

8

The World
That Never Was

SORA HAD ARRIVED.

"Wait, isn't this…?"

He looked up at a very familiar building, where neon signs lit the pitch-black sky. This was the World That Never Was, the head-quarters of the Organization. Something was different about it, though. Sora wasn't sure what, but it didn't feel the same. This world shouldn't have been trapped in sleep.

He counted the doors of sleep he had opened on his fingers. The first was in Destiny Islands, in Traverse Town, another in La Cité des Cloches with Quasimodo, Prankster's Paradise and Pinocchio, then there was the Grid with Kevin and Tron, the Country of Musketeers with Mickey and the gang, and finally the Symphony of Sorcery with another Mickey. That made seven. So…the exam should be over, and he should be back with Yen Sid.

Maybe there's one final test here…?

"Aw, what's the matter, sleepyhead?"

At the voice from nowhere, Sora got his Keyblade ready. "Who's there? Show yourself!" He'd heard this voice before—Xigbar. *Didn't I destroy him?*

"We jumped through a lot of hoops to get you here. But it looks as if it's gonna pay off."

Sora leaped to the side as a piercing bolt of red light shot out at him; then he followed its trajectory up to the top of a tall building to see that he'd been right about the voice. Xigbar jumped down to the ground with an ugly sneer.

"You're a part of this?"

"Hey. Let's hit these plot points in order, Sora…Roxas." Xigbar spread his hands theatrically and launched into his explanation. "First, you must be wondering about your revised itinerary. 'Why am I here, not back home?' The answer's simple. We brought you to this place! Hijacked your little slumber party before it started."

Sora thought back to the moment he had fallen asleep. They'd defeated Ursula at the Destiny Islands and fallen into the stormy sea.

"And ever since, we've been both your companions and your constant guides."

A hazy recollection was coming back to the surface—an image of someone in a brown robe with them in the water. Sora also remembered how he had kept bumping into the silver-haired youth and Xemnas everywhere he went.

"Before it started? And so that guy in the black coat, and Xemnas..."

"Bingo," Xigbar stated with another smirk, pointing at Sora. "You were able to go back in time to just before your home became a Sleeping World only because a past version of you already existed there. And I can see, in the past, you already met Mr. Robe Guy. Yup, he was there to make sure you ended up here now." Xigbar slowly walked toward Sora.

"That's ridiculous!" Sora yelled. *That shouldn't be possible. I met him in the past? Where? I do remember meeting some guy in brown robes way back before this exam, before I left the islands for the first time. What did he tell me, again?*

"This world has been connected."

What else?

"One who knows nothing can understand nothing."

That guy...who was he?

"It sure is. It's too perfect. Who'd ever believe it? Which is why you idiots never saw it coming."

You're telling me this moment was decided before I ever left home? No. No way.

"You thought you were off doing some kind of test, right?" Xigbar said, walking around with grandiose, affected gestures. "Well, test this—how come you're wearing the same clothes if you're already back home? You are not gonna wake up, okay? Look—there's no real versus dreams anymore. There's just you, us, and this."

When he was done, Sora stared intently at his back. "I see. Fair enough. So what? At least I know who to blame for it!" He summoned his Keyblade and gave Xigbar a glare.

"Ooh, I see you've still got that angry look down. But here is where I tag out. I got a few more hoops I gotta jump through."

Xigbar popped his neck irritably, vanished, and reappeared in midair to fire his Arrowguns at Sora. A total of twelve arrows hit the ground around him, each one transforming into someone in a black coat. The final arrow, directly in front of Sora, turned into the silver-haired boy he had encountered so many times during this journey.

"Come with me."

The young man held out his hand to Sora. It reminded him so much of the way Riku had reached out to Sora that fateful day they set out from the Destiny Islands. After a moment, Sora could sense his vision blurring.

"Ungh… What?"

His head was so heavy. He was swaying. *What in the world…?*

"Pleasant dreams, kiddo," Xigbar said to him gently.

Sora then fell into a deep sleep.

He could hear the waves rushing to the shore. The sun was blindingly bright—so bright that it woke Sora up. These were the Destiny Islands. His home. The silver-haired young man was standing at the edge of the water, but he seemed a little different. Mostly his clothes. The young man was approached by a man in a brown robe.

"Yes. This was where it started."

Sora suddenly heard a voice next to him, and he looked toward the one who had spoken. It was the young man with silver hair again, this time sitting on the sand.

"At this point, I still had no idea that I was talking to myself. He cast away his bodily form just to set me on the appointed path."

"What do you mean?" Sora asked back. *"At this point, I was talking to myself?" So the guy standing over there is the same guy sitting here next to me. And robe guy is going over there to talk to himself, too? Is it all the same person? I don't get it.*

"That is Xehanort reduced to just a heart—the being you and your friends called Ansem."

Sora raised his head to find the man in the brown robe right in front of him. He jumped, startled, and then his mind fell back into sleep.

When he came to, it was night on the Destiny Islands. The man in the brown robe was entering the secret place, and another Sora—the Sora whose journey was about to begin—was following him into the cave.

Present-day Sora had no idea what was going on anymore.

"Yes," said the youth with silver hair. "This is the point in time that Xigbar mentioned."

Sora thought about what Xigbar had said. *Was that me from right before this world was consumed by the darkness...?*

"To move through time, you must leave your body behind. Ansem first sent me on my way and then placed himself here when the time was right. That is what set all these events in motion."

"What are you saying? That he knew everything that would happen?" Sora asked again. *It was all predetermined...? My journey, and his?*

"No, not everything." The young man shook his head. "But remember, Ansem possessed Riku and saw his experiences in real time."

"So? That could only tell him so much. How did he know I would be here today?"

"Simple."

Just then, there was a *boom* from the cave so loud it shook the world around them. As Sora watched, Kairi's body was hurled out of the entrance.

"Kairi!"

He immediately opened his arms to catch her, but she passed right through him. Sora then fell into another deep sleep.

*   *   *

This time he woke up in Traverse Town. This was where it all started, and he'd been here so many times since.

Overhead, the sky was filled with twinkling stars. But one of them suddenly blinked out—and he could see several copies of himself drifting down from the sky. *Wait, am I one of the ones falling, too?* He couldn't even tell that. It really was like being inside a dream. Sora slowly landed on the ground.

He saw versions of himself walking all over town. He was wearing the same clothes as when he first set out on his travels. He walked, ran, fought, fell, and then...

"You've been here many times. Your first journey...your voyage through memories...in the datascape...in your dreams. Relived again and again...like déjà vu," remarked the boy with silver hair, who was suddenly standing next to him.

Just then, the king—Mickey—ran down the steps leading to the Second District and headed for the Third District. Shortly after, Donald and Goofy walked right through Sora's body, looking up at the sky and talking about something as they made their way toward the Second District. Pluto was following along behind them.

"Donald! Goofy!"

Sora started after them almost on instinct. When he did, Pluto came bounding from an alley and passed through Sora yet again, this time headed for the Third District.

"Pluto!"

Sora chased after the dog, but he couldn't catch him.

Sora...!

Instead, he collapsed into unconsciousness.

When he woke up again—

"Huh? Am I back?"

Yes, this was the World that Never Was, where he'd run into Xigbar and fallen asleep. The king, Donald, and Goofy ran by in front of him.

"Wait, Your Majesty! Donald! Goofy!"

Sora reached out and called to them, but the trio ran off without even looking back. Sora impulsively went after them, until a girl with golden hair in a white dress materialized in his path.

"Naminé, is that you?"

It was her. Kairi's Nobody, and the witch who controlled memories—Naminé. She lowered her gaze, and then a ghost of a smile crossed her lips as she started to run away.

"Wait! Naminé!" Sora hurried over to her and caught her hand. "I've got a message for you. I meant to tell you once this was all over."

As she looked back, though, she changed into a girl he had never seen. She had black hair and looked a lot like Naminé—a lot like *Kairi*, actually. She wore one of the Organization's black coats.

"Huh? Who are…you?" he asked, and as he did, his chest began to ache. He could feel a tear running down his cheek.

"Huh? Why am I…?"

He touched the tear on his face. *Why am I crying? This happened once before, too, back when I first left Twilight Town. I saw the sunset from the train after I said good-bye to Hayner and Pence and Olette, and I got really sad. Is this the same thing…?*

As he wondered to himself, the girl put up the hood of her black coat, shook off Sora's hand, and started to run.

"Hey, wait!"

The girl didn't stop, though. She was going to get away at this rate, but he couldn't keep up. His head weighed a ton. He was getting dizzy. No, no. He had to. He had to catch her.

He started running.

He could sense something sinister in the air of the city. Meow Wow was by his side, but he couldn't remember whether the Spirit had been with him before this or not. He couldn't even tell which way was up—whether he was running on the top of the buildings, under the buildings, or even on the walls.

Is it just me, or is the whole world warping?

His head was so heavy. Everything was heavy.

"Mrarf."

Meow Wow rubbed against Sora's legs. Even that felt wrong. He couldn't tell if this was a dream or reality anymore.

Sora took another step. Where was he now?

Someone in a black coat was standing in front of him, facing away. It was that girl. Sora called out to her.

"C'mon, wait up. Who are you?"

She looked back and removed her hood to reveal someone else.

"You're...Roxas," Sora said. A boy with golden hair. *My Nobody.*

Roxas smiled quietly at Sora.

"How can you be here? Am I dreaming?"

Roxas shook his head, still saying nothing.

"C'mon, say something."

The smile vanished. "This could have been the other way around."

"Huh?"

"But it really has to be you," Roxas continued.

"What do you mean?"

If it had to be me and not him, then—

"There are so many hearts that are connected to yours. You're me, so you can feel what I felt."

I don't think that's right. Sora shook his head. "No. Roxas, you're you. We're not the same. I wanted to tell you that. That you deserve as much as I do to be your own person."

I've been wondering since the beginning. He's not me at all, so why can't he exist outside of me?

Roxas's smile returned a bit. "Sora, see?" he said. "That's why it has to be you."

The Nobody gripped Sora tightly by both hands. In that moment, a wave of thoughts flowed into Sora. *Is this...sorrow? It's awful. My chest is aching. What do I—?*

Roxas was gone. He had vanished and left only his sadness.

Not again... Did they cause all this pain? What are you trying to show me?

I—

"What do you want me to see?!" Sora screamed.

The sound faded into the hollow sky.

Sora, don't chase the dreams. They'll lead you nowhere, just to an abyss you'll never be able to wake up from.

But Sora didn't hear the voice. He was completely alone.

He looked at the path ahead of him. *What's waiting for me up there? I have no choice but to go, though.* As he came out of his thoughts, he realized Meow Wow was beside him again.

"I'm gonna keep going."

Sora took a step. *I don't care what's up there—I'm going.*

He proceeded between some bizarre buildings. Ahead on the path—were Riku and Kairi.

"Riku, Kairi, I found you!"

Sora ran to them. But as the two of them turned around, they became strangely distorted.

"Huh?"

The pair shifted into two people he didn't know. Riku became a tall man with brown hair, while Kairi was a blue-haired woman.

"Who...?"

The two of them looked at him wordlessly, then smiled.

"Ven," said the man.

"Ven," said the woman.

He didn't know that name. *Ven? Who's that?*

They reached out to him, and Sora reached back. He had to take their hands—but the two of them distorted again as they turned away from him. As they started to leave him behind, they reverted to Riku and Kairi. Sora tried to go after them, but he could barely move. Something was weighing him down. He didn't know if it was his own body or the air itself.

"What is going on?"

Sora! Don't! You've gotta wake up! Sora!

Sora felt like he heard someone calling. That voice—he got the sense that it had been calling to him this entire time. And then the two he was trying to catch changed from Riku and Kairi back to that pair he didn't know. Everything was twisting and distorting. *I'm running and running, but I just can't reach them. What…what is this place?*

A brilliant light burst forth in front of him.

"Wait!"

The light swelled until it was all he could see—and then he was on the Destiny Islands again.

He could hear the familiar waves. The sun was setting, and a young Sora and Riku ran by. *Yeah, Riku and I always used to play tag on the beach, ever since we were kids.*

He remembered that. And yet…

The blue-haired woman that Kairi had turned into a moment ago smiled at his childhood self and at Riku's. *I don't know her. Don't remember her. My chest is aching again.*

And again, everything was warping. Someone was standing on the shore. *Is that…Ansem?!*

Just then, a swift, sudden sleep overtook him.

Sora's knees buckled and hit the ground, as if he had dropped from the sky.

"Oopsy-daisy. Wasn't easy putting you into a second sleep, and he almost woke you up."

That voice belonged to Xigbar.

Sora fought to keep from gasping against the pain in his chest. It was so hard to breathe. "So then, all that stuff I just saw—did you put that in my head?" Sora struggled to his feet and glared at Xigbar.

"No." Xigbar shrugged. "That wasn't 'stuff,' it was a dream. The falling asleep part was definitely our bad. But we can't put stuff in your head. Hey, I got an idea. Ask your heart. See if it's got a clue."

"Well…my heart was aching. That's why I kept going."

It was almost too much to bear. The sorrow—the pain, and so many other feelings. A suffering so much greater than anything he'd ever known.

Hatred, sadness, anger, jealousy, fear, resentment, anguish, envy, uncertainty, pain, despair.

Who did these feelings come from? Roxas? That woman? Those two people called me Ven—maybe him? Or someone else?

"Oh... Thank you, Sora's heart, for pushing him right into our clutches. Aren't hearts great? Steer us wrong every time," Xigbar remarked, mocking as ever.

Hearts? Steer "us" wrong? Is that really true? Actually, there's something else I've been wondering for a while now.

"You know, right, because you all have hearts!" Sora said, testing Xigbar. "Axel and Roxas and Naminé, and that other girl. I felt what Roxas felt and...they laughed together, got mad, and they grieved." The ache in his heart belonged to everyone. "You have to have a heart to cry."

Xigbar snorted derisively. "It's about time you noticed."

A Corridor of Darkness opened behind Sora, and Xemnas emerged. "Indeed. A heart is never lost for good. There may have been variances in our dispositions, but a number of us unquestionably showed signs of a burgeoning replacement."

A burgeoning replacement...

"Once born, the heart can also be nurtured. Our experiments creating Heartless were attempts to control the mind and convince it to renounce its sense of self. But understand, one can banish the heart from the body, but the body will try to replace it the first chance it gets, for as many times as it takes. And so I knew, even after we were divided into Heartless and Nobodies, it was just a temporary separation."

And the Nobodies who had regained a heart had suffered—Roxas and Axel. They couldn't be the only ones. So then why?

"Why, then? Why did you lie to them and tell them they had no hearts?" Sora shouted accusingly at Xemnas. *They went through all that pain, all that grief, because they believed they had no hearts. They thought they weren't even human. That's why they hurt so much. Why they were so...sad.*

"Xemnas and Xehanort formed the Organization for a specific reason—round up a bunch of empty husks, hook them up to Kingdom Hearts, then fill them all with the exact same heart and mind," Xigbar explained behind him.

Sora turned around. *Empty husks? Is he saying they're going to break them with sorrow and put another heart into them...? Or did they already do it?*

"Translation—they were gonna turn all the members into Xehanort."

"Make more Xehanorts?"

You're hollowing out people's hearts to put Xehanort's inside them?! "You tricked your friends to—? But you—aren't you scared of just turning into someone else?" he asked.

One corner of Xigbar's mouth twitched up in a sneer. "Me? I'm already half Xehanort."

"That's...nuts...!"

Xigbar's golden eye regarded Sora.

It doesn't make sense. What does he think he can do by throwing away his own heart and becoming Xehanort? I don't get it. And what is Xehanort after? Why's he putting his heart in other people?

"However—through weakness of body...weakness of will...or weakness of trust—most of the original members we had chosen for the Organization were inadequate. Thus, naturally, they never had a chance to attain their goal. Yet, even this was to be expected. We have learned of the heart's folly, and we have achieved our other goals. This last excursion has proven to be a worthy closing assignment for the Organization," Xemnas proclaimed calmly.

"Just stop it! You treat people's hearts like they're bottles on a shelf, but they're not!" *Hearts aren't "foolish," and other people aren't tools for you to use.* Sora faced Xemnas and summoned his Keyblade, ready to fight. "Hearts are made of the people we meet and how we feel about them—they're what ties us together even when we're apart! They're what...make me strong."

However, Xigbar laughed and pointed at Sora. "Duh!"

Sora looked back at him.

"You're strong because of the ties you have with other people. As if the Keyblade would choose a wimp like you. But no pouting. We see much bigger and better things in your future...once you side with us."

Sora's eyes shifted to his Keyblade, and he gripped it tighter. "I know the Keyblade didn't choose me, and I don't care. I'm proud to be a small part of something bigger—the people it did choose."

By now, this Keyblade has connected me to so many people—Riku, Kairi. And the king. Donald and Goofy. Roxas and all the friends of the ones who aren't me.

"My friends. They are my power!"

My power comes from the hearts connected to mine—from our feelings and our memories. Even the ones that hurt.

"Those are just words. You've lost," Xigbar sputtered, sensing a powerful force behind Sora. "Ugh. Fine. See where your power gets you here. Xemnas! He's all yours." With that, Xigbar slipped away into a Corridor of Darkness.

Xemnas spread his arms and raised them toward the sky, drawing in the nearby buildings to gather behind himself with a terrifying power. The towering structures came tumbling down at Sora's feet, but Sora held off the impact and blast wave with his Keyblade, then glared angrily at the Organization's leader.

"As your flesh bears the sigil," Xemnas intoned, "so your name shall be known as that of a recusant."

A sigil of a recusant? What's that?

No time to worry about that now. Xemnas closed the distance between them in a flash, but Sora blocked the attack. Like in their first battle, Xemnas wielded swords made of red light in both hands—Ethereal Blades. Sora knocked them away and tried to counterattack, but before he could land a hit, darkness enshrouded Xemnas's form and carried him to another part of the battlefield.

"Is that the best your heart can do?"

I'm not done yet. I'm not gonna lose, no way. Not with everyone else behind me. Meow Wow returned to Sora's side and bounced around him, healing him bit by bit. *See? I've even got this little guy; he's been by my side the whole time.* Sora launched himself straight at Xemnas's chest and swung upward with his Keyblade.

"—Fool!"

Xemnas leaped back, giving Sora some breathing room—or so he thought, before his foe took control of the buildings again, floating them over and dropping them down on him.

"Meow Wow!"

Sora hopped onto the Dream Eater and bounded between the falling buildings toward Xemnas where he hovered in midair.

"Sorry!"

Sora stood on Meow Wow's back and jumped even higher into the air, then brought his Keyblade down on Xemnas from above.

"Ngh—"

Xemnas caught the blow with his Ethereal Blades, and Sora was almost knocked away. *No, I'll be okay. I won't lose, no matter what. Not even if my own strength gives out. You can't stop me.*

"As long as my friends are with me, I'll never lose!!"

The two of them plummeted to the ground headfirst and landed hard—but soon after, Keyblade connected with Ethereal Blades once more. It was time for the final blow—Sora poured all his strength into the hand gripping his Keyblade.

"*That's* my power!"

He knocked the Ethereal Blades up and out of the way, then hammered the Keyblade into Xemnas's chest. His opponent flew into the air, and the darkness took him—but Sora was also at his limit.

He toppled backward, limbs splayed. He ached all over, and every breath was a struggle. But he beat him. He fought to get his breathing under control. He was exhausted…

That was when the silver-haired young man appeared before Sora.

"You…again." Sora, still prone and out of breath, looked at the young man.

"You just make it too easy. I know you think you've won, but you lost the moment you dived this far in. You're in the deepest pit of slumber, and you've worn yourself down to nothing. There's no returning to the world above."

"What do you mean?"

I don't know what he's saying. I'm just so tired. Sora could see a strange black smoke rising from his body. *What's happening...? I'm trying to stand up, but my body is too heavy.*

"We told you. It was not the Sleeping Keyholes that guided you. They are not the reason you are here. You've been on a path, one we laid out for you." He pointed at Sora's chest. "That sigil on your chest is the proof."

"What?" Sora looked down at his torso. He'd thought the new outfit came from Yen Sid—but the man was right. The X was there on his chest.

The youth with silver hair slowly drew an X in the air. "See? That sigil, the X, tells us where you are at all times. You had wondered aloud before—why we kept showing up where you were. It's because we need you, Sora."

Ugh... I'm just...so...tired...

"Or, to be precise, we need what will be left of you—the thirteenth dark vessel."

"Why...? I..."

Everything was warping and twisting. The man bent and blurred in his vision.

"Why was it assured you would come here today? Because I followed my destined path, and I'm here looking at you right now. You can move through time, but time itself is immovable. Today, all my selves throughout time were meant to gather here and to welcome you, Sora, as our thirteenth member. These facts cannot be changed."

The young man knelt down beside Sora and leaned in closer to his face.

"What's...gonna happen...?"

I don't even have the strength to move. I'm tired. I'm so...so tired. It's all I can do to keep him in focus. I can barely even keep my eyes open.

"I have now told you all that I know. We are all here, and what the future holds in store is beyond my sight. I will return to my own time and grow into the man who becomes all these others. While I know this future now that I have lived it, returning to my own time will erase the memories and experiences I have gained here. Still, my appointed path is now etched in my heart, which will first lead me to seek the outside world."

Sora could sense darkness enveloping his body.

What's happening to me...? Am I falling...falling into darkness... again...?

"Riku..."

Finally, Sora called out to his dear friend. Riku had always come to save him. *One more time... Riku. I'm sorry, Riku. I...*

"Your heart will sleep forever in the folds of darkness. And your body will be another vessel for me. So light gives way to darkness. Good night, Sora."

The darkness crept in at the corners of his vision, until it finally swallowed him completely.

I...

Sora was descending into the depths of a profound darkness.

And yet, a light quietly drew near, gentle and kind. It was a piece of someone's heart, of the heart sleeping within Sora.

Ventus.

The light shone out into the darkness, illuminating Sora and bursting free from the gloom dragging him down into its depths.

It became armor that encased his body.

Everything is born from sleep, and from that sleep it longs to wake.

And Sora slept on...

PROLOGUE
RADIANT GARDEN

SOME YEARS EARLIER...

Ansem the Wise had always kept peace in the beautiful world of Radiant Garden. At the center of his realm was his laboratory, where he and his apprentices carried out their research.

Now, though, an eerie silence had fallen over the lab. Two figures wearing white lab coats lay on the floor—Ienzo and Even. They had been helping Ansem with his experimentation. Before them a man with a single eye, Braig, faced a computer. He looked up as someone else entered the lab.

"Hey! Is this how you wanted it?" Braig hurried over to the man, a youth with silver hair. "Xehanort! You wanna fill me in?"

He called the young man Xehanort, but Braig had once known someone else, an old man, who went by the same name. The two looked nothing like each other. Xehanort had been defeated in battle, after which Braig had discovered this man collapsed here in Radiant Garden with no memory of his past—or at least that was how the story went. Braig was the sole person in this world who knew the truth of his identity.

His name had once been Terra. His hair was a different color now, but it was undeniably him. The unfortunate Key wielder had apparently lost his memories after his struggle with Xehanort and then assumed the name of his foe after he woke up.

There was no telling whether the name Xehanort was all that remained of Terra's scattered memory or if his body had become host to the old man's mind. Braig didn't even know if the amnesia was real.

What determined a person's identity anyway? The mind or the body?

Not that Braig really cared much either way.

"I am...," Xehanort began, and Braig noticed that something seemed off. The young man held out his right hand, and a Keyblade appeared in it.

Braig's breath caught in his throat. "Hey! Do you remember now, or...? Wait, did you never lose your memory?"

But Xehanort said, "That's not my name. I'm not 'Xehanort.'"

The denial stunned Braig. Did that mean this was Terra?

The young man thrust his Keyblade into Braig's chest so suddenly that Braig still wasn't sure what had happened as he felt consciousness slipping away from him. He crumpled to the floor, and something was shining in his chest—his heart.

"My name...is Ansem."

Braig was certain that was the name he heard, just before everything went dark.

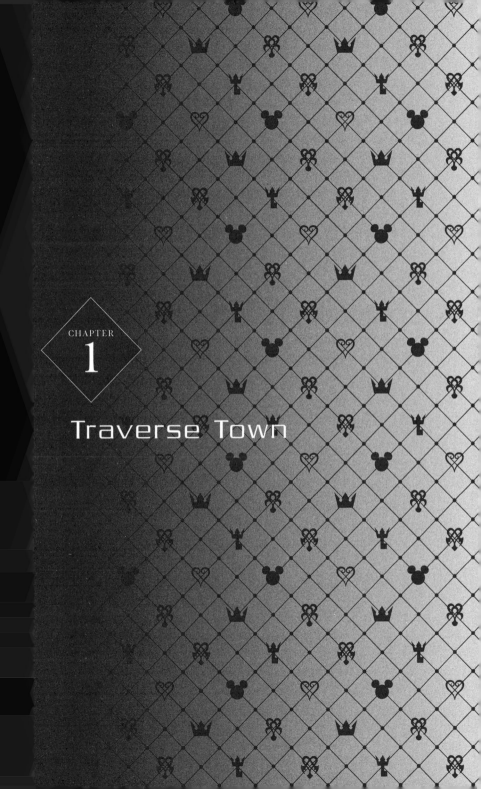

CHAPTER

1

Traverse Town

WHEN RIKU AWOKE, HE WAS IN TRAVERSE TOWN.

As he took in his surroundings, Riku spotted the familiar little fountain with a relief of a canine couple, Lady and the Tramp. This was the Third District. He'd been here before, back when Maleficent was whispering her lies in his ear. He hadn't been back since.

At the start of their test, he'd been wearing the same clothes as back then, too, but now his outfit had changed. He'd also been with Sora, who was missing now.

"Sora! Where are you?"

Riku called out his friend's name as he searched, but Sora was nowhere to be found.

They'd set out from the Destiny Islands on a raft, battled Ursula, fallen into the sea, and then opened a Keyhole. That much he knew. Meaning he was beyond the Keyhole—in one of the Sleeping Worlds. Was Traverse Town imprisoned in slumber, too?

"Wow! Where's your Portal? It takes something special to jump between grounds without one," someone said from overhead.

Riku looked up at the sudden voice. A boy around his age, with ash-gray hair in a pale violet shirt, was sitting atop the decorative arch over the fountain. He smiled at Riku.

"Who are you?" Riku asked, a little tersely. While it wasn't anything worth summoning his Keyblade over, there was something strange about this guy.

But the other boy seemed completely unbothered by Riku's suspicion. "My name is Joshua," he said, sweeping back his long hair.

"What do you mean, 'Portal'?" Riku asked another question, still watching Joshua.

The boy gave a little smile, as if he found something amusing. "Are we skipping past the part where you tell me your name?"

It was a fair point. "Riku," he said.

The boy's smile widened. "Hello there, Riku. Portals are like gateways that link up our worlds. Apparently, the world you and I are standing in right now—well, there are two copies of it. It's been sort of split in half. Portals are what let folks like us cross between them."

"There can be two of a world?"

"The world is as many things as people need it to be. The concept that we all live in the same world—that's all in our heads. Surely you knew?" The explanation sounded reasonable enough, but Riku had the feeling Joshua wasn't telling him everything. It didn't really account for why the world would have split.

"I'll tell you what, Riku. I've got a little errand for you."

"Sorry. I don't trust you." Riku turned his back on Joshua and started to walk away. He didn't care much for how the boy was talking down to him, both literally and figuratively. He had to find Sora quickly.

But Joshua wasn't done. "Aw, at least hear me out! I'm looking for a girl named Rhyme. She's the key to the Portal. And on the other side, who knows who we'll find? Maybe even your friend Sora."

Riku looked back with a sharp inhale. Joshua had said the name as if it were nothing. "You know Sora?" he asked.

Joshua was trying to hide his smile. "Now I have your attention," he said, then finally leaped down from the arch. "But unfortunately, I don't know where he is. If he's not in this version of the world, I can only assume he has to be in the other one. Simple logic."

Riku wanted to know why he knew Sora's name and what he meant by a "version of the world," but Joshua probably wouldn't answer if he asked him straight out. He mulled it over a moment and eyed Joshua carefully. "Okay, you wanna find Rhyme? You got it. Let's go."

This was a trade, and now that Sora was part of the deal, Riku had no choice but to play along. He walked over toward Joshua.

Just then, monsters appeared around the two of them. Riku readied his Keyblade.

"…These must be the Dream Eaters!"

Yen Sid had already filled him in on the creatures that inhabited the Sleeping Worlds. There were Spirits and Nightmares—and since these Dream Eaters were hostile, they must be the latter type.

And yet Joshua was still smiling without a care in the world beside him.

"You should run," Riku said. "I'll take care of them." *These guys would be the perfect warm-up for the exam.*

"Well, I don't really need to run, but I'm happy to leave the fighting in your capable hands." With that, Joshua perched himself on the lip of the fountain.

Riku worried that he might not be able to keep the boy safe if things got bad, but Joshua seemed completely unbothered. Maybe he knew something Riku didn't...? Riku turned away from him to face the Dream Eaters.

"Here goes!"

Riku sprang upward and right into the middle of the Nightmares. He'd given himself an extra assignment during this exam: keeping the darkness lurking in his heart in check during his battles. Was he truly worthy of bearing a Keyblade?

That was when Riku noticed something. Not a single one of the Dream Eaters was going after Joshua. The creatures were only attacking Riku, as if the boy observing the battle from the fountain didn't exist.

What's going on here...? Is he with them?

"Whoa!" During Riku's brief moment of distraction, a Dream Eater leaped at him and left him with a small scratch on the cheek. "I deserved that one," Riku muttered to himself with a rueful smirk. After rubbing the wound on his cheek, he finished off the Dream Eater in one hit. Either way, he wasn't going anywhere unless he got rid of these guys first. Swinging his Keyblade and casting spells, Riku wiped out the group in no time at all.

"Nicely done." Behind him, Joshua offered a round of applause.

Riku turned around, catching his breath. "Joshua, why don't they ever attack you?" he asked, watching him sternly.

Depending on how he answered, Riku was considering calling off the whole deal. But Joshua got to his feet with a soft smile.

"'They' being Dream Eaters? They won't go after you unless you're a dreamer. Which is funny, because I've got plenty of dreams."

Joshua's smile never wavered, so maybe Riku had just imagined the hint of melancholy behind his words. There was something else that bothered him, too. *My dream...*

"But they're definitely attacking me. So...you think I'm a dreamer?"

"Every human being is a dreamer. I had a friend once who said he never dreamed of anything, but it turned out that his were the most powerful dreams of all. You sort of remind me of him."

Riku had never given any thought to dreams. And Joshua wasn't a dreamer? What was that all about?

"Why don't we give your dreams shape?" Joshua suggested. "In this world, they take form as Dream Eaters, which can become great allies." He scooped up a small, shining fragment of something that had been left behind after the battle.

"What's that?"

"This is a Dream Piece. They're what Dream Eaters are made of."

Riku picked up another tiny fragment from the ground.

"Here. You'll need a recipe, too."

Riku combined the pieces according to the recipe Joshua gave him. The small glow of the fragments came together into a bright light, and within it appeared—

"A bat...?"

A flying Dream Eater with the big ears and wings of a bat fluttered around Riku happily. This was Komory Bat.

"I think you two will get along just fine. Now then, shall we?"

Riku followed after Joshua, and Komory Bat weaved circles through the air behind him.

"Hey, there," Riku said to the little creature.

"Squee." Komory Bat gave a small cry.

"The Second District is just ahead, but I'm sure you already know that," remarked Joshua as he opened the door. Stepping into the streets of the Second District, Joshua seemed eager to hurry ahead.

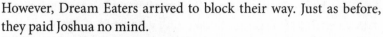

However, Dream Eaters arrived to block their way. Just as before, they paid Joshua no mind.

Because he didn't have dreams.

"Dreams, huh…?" Riku said softly as he tightened his grip on his Keyblade. "Hey, Spirits are the good Dream Eaters who like eating nightmares, right?" Riku directed his gaze up toward Komory Bat, his new friend. "Does that mean you're gonna help me out?"

Komory Bat answered by flying straight into the pack and immediately began fighting the Dream Eaters with its wings and ultrasonic waves. Riku followed the Spirit's lead and hurled himself into the fray with his Keyblade. Komory Bat had the makings of a good partner, he could tell.

Once all the Dream Eaters were gone, Riku stepped into the plaza of the Second District where Joshua was waiting.

"I think you two have got it covered."

"Yeah." Riku nodded, and Komory Bat landed on Riku's head.

"Huh. That's a good look for you," Joshua said with a chuckle.

Just then, an angry shout filled the plaza. "I gotchu now, Joshua! Once I take you down, yo, me and Rhyme is goin' back where we belong!" cried a boy wearing a beanie with a skull on it and white running gear. He was charging toward them with a finger pointed.

However, Joshua didn't seem troubled at all. He simply shrugged and shook his head.

"Beat, how many times do we have to go over this? You've been tricked by that rogue in the black coat."

Riku glanced at Joshua, startled by his remark. A black coat— someone from Organization XIII?

"I'm telling you you've made a friend of our enemy."

"Just can it, a'ight? Your inverse psychiatry ain't gonna work! Let's go, Dream Eaters!" The boy called Beat ignored Joshua's attempt to reason with him and held up his hand. Dream Eaters arrived, but as always, they only moved toward Riku, not Joshua.

"What? Man, not cool!" Beat complained.

Joshua chuckled in amusement. He really wasn't worried at all.

Riku brought his Keyblade into position and faced the Dream Eaters. Defeating them shouldn't be an issue with Komory Bat's help.

After Riku had made short work of them, Beat plopped down on the spot with a frown. "You know what? Forget it. This is stale, yo."

Joshua ambled over toward Beat. "Playing the tough guy twenty-four seven? I'd be worn out, too."

"I just…wanna protect the one person who matters," said Beat, clenching his fist with his back still toward Joshua.

I know the feeling…

The faces of Sora and Kairi appeared in Riku's mind.

But then, a strange sensation came over him—

"Why am I suddenly…so sleepy?"

An intense drowsiness overwhelmed Riku, and he collapsed to the ground asleep.

Long ago, in the age of fairy tales, the world was filled with light—a gift, many believed, from an unseen power known as "Kingdom Hearts." You see, Kingdom Hearts was protected by its counterpart, the "χ-Blade," so that none could ever lay hands on its mysteries.

But in time, the world was overrun by legions who wanted the light all for themselves, and the first shadows were cast upon the land. These warriors crafted "Keyblades" in the image of the original χ-Blade, and waged a great war over Kingdom Hearts. We call this the Keyblade War.

But though the war extinguished all light from the world, the darkness could not reach the brightness inside every child's heart. With that light, the world was remade as we know it today, with countless smaller worlds shining like stars in the sky.

As for the real χ-Blade, it did not survive the battle. The two elements that created it, one of darkness and one of light, shattered into twenty pieces—seven of light, thirteen of darkness.

And as for the source of all light—the one true Kingdom Hearts—it was swallowed by the darkness, never to be seen again. As long as it remains there, even the brightest world will have its dark corners. After all, light begets darkness, and darkness is drawn to light.

For this reason, some decided to use the Keyblade—a weapon designed to conquer the light—to defend the light instead. These were the first heroes of the Keyblade.

Was that a dream just now? Did I fall asleep?

Riku could feel his consciousness gradually returning from the darkness. That wasn't a dream; it was what Yen Sid had told them before setting out. *Right, he told us about the Keyblade War, the seven lights and thirteen darknesses, and the heroes of the Keyblade.* He'd always thought of Sora as the Keyblade's chosen one, but maybe there were others out there. *Anyway, why did I get so sleepy all of a sudden...?*

Riku shook his head as he climbed slowly to his feet, then looked for Joshua and Beat. There was no trace of either of them.

Suddenly, someone else came running by. "Hey, do you mind?" she shouted, hurrying into the First District with a pack of Dream Eaters hot on her heels.

Riku couldn't just stand by and do nothing. He headed toward the First District with Komory Bat and opened the door.

The Dream Eaters had her cornered against a wall, and Riku jumped into the fray, placing himself between them and the girl. "Stay back," he warned her.

He didn't have time to even see what the girl behind him looked like, as Komory Bat had already recognized the Nightmares and started firing off its ultrasonic blasts.

"You beat me to it."

Smiling at the Spirit's bravery, Riku brought down his Keyblade on the attacking Dream Eaters.

He always felt better fighting when he had someone to protect. He hated losing, so he'd always wanted to be strong—but that desire always brought with it a hint of guilt.

Riku took a breath once the Dream Eaters were wiped out. He didn't have time to hang around here. He had to find Joshua and Beat—

"Seriously, thanks," the girl said from behind him. "I'm Shiki, how 'bout you?"

"Riku." He turned around toward her. She was smiling at him and holding a black cat plushie in her hands.

"Thanks, Riku."

"Sure." With a nod, Riku started to walk away.

"Hey! That's it? You chat up a girl and then just say, 'Sure,' and walk off?"

This was unexpected. He stopped and looked back at Shiki. "I'm bad at this. Sorry. Look, it's not safe here. You should go home."

"If it's dangerous, how can you just leave me here? Aren't you my knight in shining armor?" Shiki held up the cat in her hands, then hugged it tight. "Well?" she said with a wink.

"Kn-knight?" he stuttered, taking an instinctive step back. "You've got the wrong idea." *A knight?!*

"Omigosh, I was so just kidding," the girl mumbled to herself in disbelief. "You get out much?"

He honestly had no idea how to reply to that.

"You remind me of this guy I know. Well, good thing we met."

Riku finally gave up. "Yeah, great. Just…do whatever," he said, then turned and began to walk away. She was going to follow him no matter what he said; he could tell that much, at least. But he still felt a bit off his game.

Where am I even supposed to go?

"I bet it's this way, Riku!" Shiki marched ahead, and now it was Riku who was following her.

"Hey! We should stick together!"

But Shiki rushed on ahead, through a door that led somewhere Riku had never been before. Shortly after, he heard her scream from the other side. "Eek!"

Riku broke into a sprint and found her surrounded by Dream Eaters, as he suspected.

"This is why I said we should stick together…" Annoyed, he readied his Keyblade.

"Well, which is it? A second ago, you were telling me to do whatever."

"…Just get behind me, okay?"

Riku leaped forward into the mob of monsters. He'd never met a girl like Shiki before, so he really had no clue how to interact with her. Fighting Dream Eaters was way easier than dealing with her.

"Good work!" Shiki called out from behind him, clapping her hands once the creatures were defeated. Riku had a sneaking suspicion she was making fun of him. Now that he thought about it, some of Joshua's comments had made him feel the same way.

Riku turned toward Shiki and gave her another long look.

"Hey, no staring!" She laughed and struck a pose.

"…"

But Riku kept watching her anyway. *Her clothes remind me of Joshua's, like they could've come from the same world. Are they connected somehow?*

"Ugh, what's with all the monsters? I can't wait to get back home!"

"Is that your dream?" Riku asked, remembering Joshua's words. Dream Eaters didn't attack anyone who wasn't a dreamer, meaning Shiki was someone who harbored dreams of her own.

"Well, obviously I wanna get back home, but I have another dream, too."

"Uh-huh."

"Sheesh, Riku, you ask some weird questions. Let's get going already!" Shiki dashed off. Maybe she didn't want to elaborate.

"Would you stop running off?" Riku hurried after her, rushing through an alleyway and arriving at a plaza with a big fountain. This was the Fourth District, a vibrant area lit with chains of lamps across the streets. Riku and Shiki descended some stairs and passed by a large, domed building.

Shiki just kept pressing on, almost as if she knew where she was going. When they reached the large doors farther in the Fourth District, the two of them went into the Fifth District together and started onto the small bridge by the entrance.

"Over there!" Shiki bounded over the bridge and up some steps that led behind a building on the other side of the pool.

"It's too dangerous to go off on your own!" Riku called out to her as she disappeared around the corner, and immediately after, there was a scream.

"Eeek!"

"Perfect." Frustrated, Riku crossed the pool after Shiki and started up the stairs. "You can't expect me to..."

The one waiting for him wasn't the girl but a figure in a black coat. At the stranger's feet lay Mr. Mew, the black cat plushie Shiki had carried.

"Shiki! No way...," Riku murmured.

The person in black stomped on Mr. Mew, then kicked the doll away. "How did *you* get here?" the stranger asked. The voice belonged to a man.

Mr. Mew collided with Riku's chest and fell at his feet.

"Who are you?" Riku asked.

"By choice or chance? You cannot control what you're not aware of. This wakeless sleep will be your prison to wander...forever."

The man slowly descended the steps as he spoke, and Riku edged back. *Do I know him...? Yeah, I get the feeling I do.*

"What do you mean?" Riku looked down and clenched his fist over his chest. *A wakeless sleep—what is he talking about...?*

Just then, he heard a loud, familiar voice shouting at him.

"Riku, don'chu listen to that punk!" It was Beat. When Riku looked up, he spotted the hotheaded boy alongside Shiki on the bridge. "Shiki's gonna be fine!"

Shiki looked down.

What's going on here...?

"She told me whassup. Hoodie here set this whole thing up, yo. He promised to send Shiki back to our world, and you was the cost of travel." Beat jabbed a finger at the man in the black coat. "Yo, this is seriously one half-baked excuse for a mission. Betchu you ain't even a Reaper."

As Beat laid out the facts, the man slowly removed his hood. Beneath it was a young man with silver hair.

"All right. Who are you?" Though Riku had never seen the man before, his heart seemed to be warning him that he knew this guy. It was the same feeling he had the moment he first heard his voice. As Riku tried to figure out what exactly was making him so uneasy, the youth raised his hands skyward.

A black light began to gather over his head and eventually transformed into a giant Dream Eater, a monkey with no lower body. Riku had never seen one this big. The colossal Nightmare, called Hockomonkey, flew through the air and into a building in the center of the Fifth District.

After it was gone, the young man in the black coat vanished into a swirling mass of darkness that resembled a gateway to the corridors.

"Wait!" Riku immediately tried to catch him, but he wasn't quick enough.

"I'm really sorry, Riku." Shiki apologized in a small voice. Her gaze was firmly fixed on the bridge where she stood.

"It's all right." Riku picked up Mr. Mew and tossed it to her. "Beat, watch her."

"I gots this, yo!" Beat called heartily.

Nodding to him, Riku pursued Hockomonkey into the garden in the building.

The instant he stepped inside, the Dream Eater was shooting fire at him. Riku batted the flames away with his Keyblade, then closed the distance. Although they were indoors, Hockomonkey's speed and ability to fly was making it hard to catch.

Komory Bat fluttered in a circle around Riku.

"Wanna give me a hand, Komory Bat?"

"Squee-wee!"

As the Spirit landed on Riku's head, he felt power welling up inside him with a blinding burst of light.

"...Huh?"

Feeling a strange sensation on his back, Riku turned to check behind him and saw a new pair of bat's wings. Komory Bat was nowhere in sight, but he could sense the presence of his companion within him. So Komory Bat could merge with Riku, allowing him to borrow its powers.

"Okay, let's get to work."

Riku jumped up and soared in the air. Now that he could fly, pinning down Hockomonkey was actually possible. He flew right into its face and beat it with his wings.

"Gwaaaargh!" It bellowed in pain, leaving itself wide open.

"Time to end this!"

Never one to waste a good opportunity, Riku dove in and brought the battle to a conclusion with his Keyblade.

As he did, Komory Bat emerged from his body. "Squeep!" it chirped, circling around Riku while Hockomonkey's glowing form rose up through the roof of the garden.

Riku hurriedly dashed from the building and rejoined Beat and Shiki on the bridge, where they watched the Dream Eater's body burst into a shower of light.

Then the twinkling shards drifting downward projected four figures in front of them: Sora, Joshua, and another boy and girl Riku didn't recognize.

"Hey, what's this?" Shiki asked in wonderment, walking toward the image of the boy.

Riku took a step toward Sora, too. He couldn't touch him, but he could feel his friend's presence. "What are we...seeing?"

Beside Riku, Beat had fallen to his knees in front of the unfamiliar girl, rubbing his eyes.

"This is so messed up, man! She's right here in front of me and...I can't reach her!"

He was reaching out, desperately trying to hold on to her, but his hands passed right through her, unable to make contact.

"If your hearts are connected," Riku told him, "you'll reach her."

Riku then looked at Sora. *I'm sure we'll see each other again—just not right now.*

"Rhyme..." Beat looked intently at the girl.

"Neku...," Shiki said to the boy.

"Sora..." Riku turned to the friend beyond his reach and said his name, too.

But soon after, Shiki, Beat, and the boy and the girl on the other side vanished into a flash of light.

Did that mean that the four of them had made it home? Sora and Joshua were the only ones left. Joshua began to speak to Sora, their gestures giving every indication that they knew Riku was there. Riku hadn't been able to hear anyone from the other side, but for some reason, Joshua's words reached him now.

"In their world, something happened that brought their existence to an end. To keep them from fading altogether, I gathered up the very last remnants of their dreams and looked for a place to give them refuge."

Joshua started walking away from Riku and Sora. *Their existence was brought to an end? Is that why Shiki wanted to go home so badly? Maybe she needed to go back for her dream to come true,* Riku thought.

"It was then this world appeared to answer my call, and Rhyme's dreams allowed us to reach it. Here, I thought they might have a chance—that the pieces of their dreams could make them whole again." Joshua turned back around toward Riku and Sora. "Imagine my surprise when I realized dreams take bodily form in this world. It struck me—by linking their dream pieces back together, maybe I could make them exist again. Maybe I could give them another chance."

"It can't be that simple," Riku said to Joshua in the other world. Apparently, Joshua really could sense and hear him.

Sora couldn't hear Riku, but Joshua's presence in both worlds meant they were connected. It let him know Sora was safe, at least.

"Well, why can't it?" Joshua said in reply. "By ourselves, we're no one. It's when other people look at us and see someone—that's the moment we each start to exist. All they needed was for someone to see them, to connect with them. And the two of you were a big part of making it happen."

"Joshua, just...who are you?" Riku asked. He had to be pretty special to be able to pass from one side to the other—was it okay to let him be?

An easy smile rose to Joshua's lips. "Let's say...a friend," he replied, and a pair of white, angelic wings appeared from his back. With a few powerful flaps, Joshua quickly ascended into the heavens, and just like that, he was gone.

"...Joshua," Riku murmured, and a Keyhole appeared before the two boys.

Riku looked at his friend a world apart. Sora was looking back.

The two shared a nod, then held their respective Keyblades up to the Keyhole. The light from their keys opened the door of slumber.

Riku took one last look at Sora. With another nod, his friend disappeared.

He and Sora might not cross paths during this exam, but he'd never be sure of his own strength if he didn't go it alone. It was the same for Sora—this was a journey for him to discover his own capabilities, too.

"—Guess it's time to go."

With that, Riku departed for the next world.

CHAPTER
2

La Cité des Cloches

RIKU ARRIVED IN A CITY LINED WITH ROWS OF BRICK houses. He seemed to be in a backstreet somewhere; there wasn't much light. The streets were paved with stone. A ways ahead, he could see a bright area that looked like a plaza.

"Squee."

Riku looked up and saw that Komory Bat was still with him. He also heard another noise from down by his feet.

"Mrarf."

"Wha—? Who're you?!"

A Dream Eater that looked like some kind of doggish-cat thing was standing there, wagging its tail at him. It didn't seem to be a Nightmare.

"Are you tagging along, too?"

"Mewf." Meow Wow rubbed against Riku's legs.

Does this mean Dream Eaters besides the ones I made can join me? Or maybe he's the Spirit of someone else in the same position as me.

"Don't tell me you're Sora's?"

"Prrrarf."

Meow Wow rolled over and showed Riku its belly, all but asking for a rub. Riku knelt down and complied. *Guess I should just be happy to have the extra help.*

"Okay, let's go."

As soon as Riku started off for the plaza, a man came running up to him.

"You there!" The golden-haired man was wearing armor, and he had a neatly trimmed beard on his chin. "Have you seen a gypsy woman?"

"Gypsy"? What's a gypsy? "Nope," replied Riku. "Sorry."

"All right. Thanks."

The man turned around and hurried back toward the plaza. From the look of it, he was in trouble with an older man dressed in black-and-purple robes.

"I'm terribly sorry, sir," said the man in armor. "We've lost her." He bowed his head.

"Slippery vermin!" The older man clenched his fist so hard it was trembling with fury, then glowered at the younger man. "I am beginning to question having summoned you back from the wars, Captain Phoebus."

This Phoebus person just kept his head down until the man in the robe began to walk away, then hurried out of sight after him.

Riku didn't know what was going on, but it couldn't be anything good.

Behind him, a woman with rich black hair and dark skin stepped out of hiding.

"Thank you. You stood up for me. I'm Esmeralda."

"Riku. And it's not like I know what a 'gypsy' is," he replied honestly.

He hadn't gone out of his way to help her, really; he just couldn't say he'd seen something when he didn't know what it was. That said, Esmeralda didn't seem like the kind of person who would be hurting anyone.

"Why are they chasing you?" Riku asked.

"Judge Frollo has been hunting us for years. We gypsies are guilty of nothing but loving our freedom, yet Frollo hates whatever he can't control."

Someone who wants to hunt gypsies and take away their freedom? That guy in the robes must have been Frollo, then.

"Now he's even brought in fresh blood to torment us," she continued. "I'd hate to know what darkness drives that man."

Riku frowned. So he used the darkness, and that same darkness drove him forward. Darkness was a part of everyone's hearts, but an obsession was at once intriguing and disturbing.

"Tell me more. Was he always like this?"

"I don't give Frollo much thought," she snapped, as if just saying his name left a bad taste in her mouth. She could see in his eyes that he had more questions, so she turned behind her, toward the large building in the square. "But if you'd like, you could try Notre Dame. They say it's a place for answers."

"Got it. I'll go there."

Riku set off for the open square with the cathedral, where the sun was free to shine. Unlike the backstreets, the area was filled with several tents and lined with small, decorative flags. Maybe there was a festival going on? When he reached the middle of the plaza, Riku looked up at the cathedral. It was enormous, decorated with statues along the walls to guard it from evil.

Riku climbed the steps and peered inside through the big doors. "Is anybody here?" In the very back of the chapel was a stained glass window, where a few rays of light were shining through. Other than that, the place was empty. Riku stepped into the chapel and started walking toward the back.

Esmeralda had said he might learn something by coming here, but Riku got the feeling he might have been better off trying somewhere else.

Just then—

"Who...who are you?" Someone called out to him from behind.

Riku turned around and saw a short man standing there, his gaze fixed on the ground. "I'm Riku," he replied, introducing himself as he walked over.

"Oh. M-my name's Quasimodo. I'm very sorry, but the archdeacon is away."

With nothing more to say, Quasimodo turned away and started walking back into the cathedral. There was something awkward about his hunched gait.

"Actually, I'm looking for a man named Frollo," Riku pressed. "Do you know where he is?"

Quasimodo looked back. He was far from handsome, in both his face and his build, but he didn't appear to be a bad person.

"My master? He said he had business on the outskirts of the city."

So Frollo's his master? "Do you mean you know him?"

"Oh yes. He's...he's very kind. Master Frollo saved my life," Quasimodo explained, looking at the statue in the back of the chapel. Maybe it represented a god to the people here. "He protects me from the outside world."

If so, then why does he sound so sad?

"He 'protects' you from it?" Riku asked. Given the melancholy tone of Quasimodo's voice, he doubted there was much protecting going on here at all.

"The people out there would be cruel to me. I'm a monster, you know."

Quasimodo opened his hands and stared at them intently for a moment before covering his misshapen face. *Sure, he doesn't look like everyone else. But still—*

"Is that what Frollo told you?"

Quasimodo raised his head.

"Trust me, looks can be deceiving."

Riku remembered how Kairi had been able to sense his heart, even when his appearance had changed. She'd seen the face of Ansem and still called him Riku instantly.

"A good friend sees you for who you are, no matter what face you wear. You should go out there—find some friends who understand you."

"Oh no…" Quasimodo turned away. "My master forbids it. I'm not to set foot outside."

"Are you sure that's what's stopping you? Because I think something else is holding you back."

Despite Riku's continued suggestions, Quasimodo started to walk off, all but dismissing the idea.

Back when Riku had been in Ansem's form, he'd felt like he wasn't himself anymore—so much so that he couldn't stand to use his own name. He'd even believed staying in that form forever would be all right, as long as he could keep Sora and Kairi safe from a distance. But he knew now that he was wrong.

"Ask your heart, Quasimodo."

The man stopped.

I know how much it hurts to lie to yourself and keep your heart locked away, Riku thought. *There's so many things you can only learn by stepping out into the light. Maybe I don't have the right to tell you what to do until I can take my own advice—but I don't know if there's anyone else who can.*

"I'll check the edge of town. Thanks," Riku said to Quasimodo's back, then left the church behind.

He hoped with all his heart Quasimodo would find it in himself to step out into the sun someday.

Riku proceeded through the plaza in front of the cathedral and made his way to the outskirts. This city was fairly large.

Riku sensed a strange presence around him. "Dream Eaters!"

He brought his Keyblade up and held it at the ready. Komory Bat flapped around Riku's head, happy to help him in the fight, and then flew straight into the pack of monsters with Meow Wow close behind. Between Meow Wow's ramming attacks and Komory Bat's disorienting ultrasonic waves, they made for a good team.

"...Nice work, guys."

One Dream Eater snapped at him, but Riku whacked it with his Keyblade and hurled himself into the fray. He made his way toward the edge of town, scattering the successive waves of creatures that appeared.

Finally, he stepped through the large gate and found a long bridge just as an enormous shadow whipped by overhead. Riku looked up instinctively and swallowed.

"A Dream Eater! And a big one!"

There was a massive beast flying through air. This Dream Eater, called Wargoyle, had a rainbow-colored body, large wings, and a menacing aura around it that reminded him of Hockomonkey in Traverse Town.

Once the Nightmare reached the middle of the bridge, it circled back around and opened its jaws wide.

"What?"

The flames from its mouth ignited the pile of cargo directly behind Riku, and the next volley cut off the way back to the city.

Retreat seemed like the best option here. Riku took off running, trying to escape the inferno closing in behind him.

Each burst of fire kindled more of the boxes piled here and there along the bridge, but Riku could sense Komory Bat and Meow Wow doing their best to keep up behind him. As far as he could tell, they were managing to avoid the flames.

"Stay safe, guys," Riku muttered under his breath as he ran desperately, hurdling over the unburned goods in his way.

Around that same time, Frollo and Phoebus were having a stand-off in front of a small house on the outskirts of town.

"Stand aside, Captain Phoebus."

"I will not! What have these people done wrong?" Phoebus stood in front of the modest home, shielding it from the judge. His sword was drawn, and its tip was directed toward Frollo. There were small children inside the house.

"I have proof this family gave harbor to gypsies!" Frollo spat icily.

"That's not a crime."

Not only was Frollo convinced the gypsies were sinners, now even helping them was a sin? Phoebus was starting to believe the only explanation was that Frollo was out of his mind. In fact, he didn't even understand why the gypsies were so maligned to begin with. Frollo claimed they had turned their backs on the divine, but what had they actually done? The girl was the one he was really after—what was she guilty of?

"I can think of few crimes that are greater," Frollo replied.

Without warning, a giant monster swooped in from the direction of the city and hovered behind the judge as if it served his will.

"What demon is this?" Phoebus cried, just as Riku came running up.

"Oh, you are mistaken, Captain Phoebus," said Frollo. "This is no demon. It is righteous judgment! I have been granted this power so that I may smite all gypsies now and forever!"

Frollo slowly approached Wargoyle and then looked back. A sinister black aura emanated from around him.

"This is all wrong!" Phoebus brought his sword back into position, and Riku brandished his Keyblade next to him.

A normal person probably wouldn't be able to go toe to toe with this Dream Eater. "He won't listen," Riku warned the captain. "Once you've fallen that far, there's almost no coming back."

"How dare you. I am a virtuous man. Good and evil shall be made plain once the gypsies face the fires of judgment," Frollo declared confidently, although his displeasure was plain.

"!" Phoebus took a sharp breath.

With a small "hmph," Frollo began to walk away, and Wargoyle made to follow him.

"No, you don't!" Phoebus jumped in their path, but the Dream Eater swatted him aside with its sharp talons. "Agh…!"

"You all right?" Riku rushed over to Phoebus and saw a wound on his arm.

"Well, I can't say you didn't warn me."

"You should take it easy. I'll deal with Frollo," Riku said, looking toward the city where Wargoyle had gone.

"Thanks. I gotta tell you, this is embarrassing—having to rely on a kid," Phoebus told him with chagrin.

"You wouldn't be the first. Sorry," Riku replied with a little smile.

The captain followed his lead, grinning back. "I'll admit, you look more capable than me right now. All right, be careful. It looks like that creature is heading for the cathedral."

"Okay. Got it." Riku took off running for the city just as his two Spirit companions finally caught up to him. "Hey, we're heading back."

The Spirits slammed on the brakes, skidded to a halt, and did a U-turn back toward the city. Riku ran after them.

The plaza in front of the cathedral was ablaze, and tendrils of fire were rising from the tents. Riku spotted a silhouette in the conflagration and hurried over to it. It was Quasimodo, with Esmeralda in his arms.

"Is she going to be all right?"

"I'm fine, thanks to Quasimodo," Esmeralda answered from Quasimodo's arms. The young man was watching her with concern.

"Quasimodo, where did the creature go?"

"It's…it's up there."

When Riku looked up at the cathedral with Quasimodo, he saw Wargoyle circling above them, waiting.

"Right."

I have to take it down.

Riku started running to the cathedral, but then Quasimodo cried out desperately after him. "W-wait. Wait, I'll go with you!"

"Thanks, but stay with her."

Quasimodo had already won his battle—escaping the cathedral to save Esmeralda.

"Quasimodo. Did your heart have the answer?" Riku stopped and turned around.

The young man nodded with a smile.

Riku responded in kind, then plunged into the cathedral barely in time to see some unfamiliar Dream Eaters getting stamped out of existence.

The trio responsible were statues like the ones around the cathedral.

"Well! I guess…you three got this covered," Riku commented.

The three little statues hopped around contentedly.

"It was a walk in the park!" one of them crowed.

"How would you know? You don't have any legs," retorted another.

"Yeah, but— Aw, gimme a break! It's just a figure of speech."

More Dream Eaters appeared behind the statues as they bickered.

"Both of you, pipe down," scolded the third. "And get ready! 'Cause here come some more!"

"Yee-haw!"

As the gargoyles got ready for another battle, Riku decided to leave it to them and dashed up the stairs to the roof.

"Ha-ha-ha-ha-ha...!" Frollo surveyed the flames consuming the plaza below, a sword in his hand. "Yes! Let it burn. The flames will consume everything! You see? This is the power that has been granted to me!"

The darkness was like a shroud over him, and he seemed nothing short of insane.

"I see a sad old man with a dark heart," Riku shouted toward his back.

Frollo spun around to face him. "Again, you are wrong! Now you will be judged, like the rest!" he intoned with terrible malice, just as Wargoyle shot upward behind him.

The gust stirred up a burst of embers—and Frollo lost his footing. The hem of his robe fluttering in the air, he tumbled to his doom.

"Judgment is mine!" he screamed, plunging into the inferno.

As he witnessed the miserable end of the road to darkness, Riku didn't notice that he was biting his lip.

That was when someone else walked up to the sword Frollo had dropped.

Someone he recognized.

"You're Ansem!" It was none other than the one who had once taken over Riku's body and tried to keep it for good. "Why are you here?" he shouted.

Another silhouette emerged—the silver-haired boy he had encountered in Traverse Town.

"Your best friend is never far." Beside the silver-haired boy, Ansem picked up Frollo's blade and looked it over. "So sad. The cost of yielding to the darkness."

"You could write a book about that," Riku yelled. *You and Frollo aren't all that different. And neither was I. Back then, I could have fallen onto that same path and met the same fate.*

But not anymore.

"But I embraced the darkness—and unless you hurry up and learn to do the same, your story will end just like his." Ansem pointed the sword at Riku.

"I walk the road to dawn!" Riku answered, summoning his Keyblade to his hand. *I've chosen my path, so why do I still get so upset? I've decided to walk toward daybreak, to find the light beyond the darkness. The middle road isn't the road to nightfall. It's the road to dawn.*

And yet, the boy with silver hair fixed Riku with a quiet look. "Still afraid of the dark, I see."

Riku felt his whole body going cold with sweat. *I'm not afraid of the darkness—and yet I have to keep reminding myself of that. What if it isn't really true?*

The boy turned away from Riku and disappeared into the Corridor of Darkness that opened behind him, and Ansem started after him.

"Wait!" Riku called.

Ansem stopped and shot him a glance. He almost seemed to be smiling. It made Riku angry.

I—I'm not scared of the darkness. No way... Am I?

No, I still have a Keyblade in my hand. It's trying to guide me toward the light.

"Groaaaaar!" Wargoyle swept in front of Riku and bellowed.

Shaking off his hesitation, Riku tightened his grip on his Keyblade and sprang into the air.

"Help me out here!"

Komory Bat landed on his back and lent him its wings with a flash.

Riku took the battle to Wargoyle in midair. "I'm not going to lose. This is just one more step toward the light."

Closing the distance between himself and Wargoyle in the blink of an eye, Riku hit its massive, fire-breathing jaw with an upward slash. The flames spewed into the air, and the Dream Eater let out a screech, soaring upward in an attempt to make an airborne escape.

Riku hurriedly flew after it, but Wargoyle was ready to get back in the fight. It spread its own wings, and then fired off a volley of projectiles with a great flap.

"Urgh—!"

He managed to keep himself safe for the most part with his Keyblade, but several of the shots still found their mark.

When Riku briefly landed on the roof, he felt a gentle wave wash over him. Meow Wow had cast a healing spell on him.

"Thanks."

Riku stood up and glared at the hovering beast. He wouldn't be able to borrow Komory Bat's power for much longer.

"Here goes!"

With a bound, Riku flew into the sky and hurtled directly into Wargoyle with incredible speed.

"This is it for you!"

He lashed out with a mighty blow to the center of its chest.

"Guhah…"

As Wargoyle went still, Riku swung his Keyblade and knocked away the creature's huge wings. One of the wings came loose and fell to the ground. Thrown off-balance, Wargoyle began to fall like a stone.

"Did that do it? Whoa!"

Komory Bat had separated from Riku, and it just barely managed to catch hold of his back before he fell. Meow Wow was wagging its tail at Riku on the roof.

Wargoyle's other wing came off as it plummeted down into the same inferno that had claimed Frollo.

"Looks like we got him…" Riku touched down on the roof and petted both Komory Bat and Meow Wow. "Thanks guys, I owe you one."

The Spirits rubbed up against Riku with happy noises.

"Put out those fires!" he could hear Phoebus calling down below. True to his title, the captain of the guard would take care of getting the blaze under control. With a smile, Riku left the roof.

By the time he reached the plaza, the conflagration had been extinguished. It hadn't spread to the rest of the city.

"R-Riku...!"

Quasimodo came running up to him. Phoebus and Esmeralda were with him.

"Master Frollo—he made me live inside the bell tower, but the real walls were the ones I built around my heart. You helped me see that, Riku," Quasimodo told him with a grin.

Riku shook his head quietly. "I was...speaking from...personal experience."

It's like Quasimodo said: I'm the one building these walls around myself. Whether I stay in this prison of darkness or move into the light is up to me.

"You still keep a lot locked inside, don't you?" Quasimodo asked.

Riku lowered his gaze.

He knew by now that keeping his heart under lock and key was the same as letting the darkness control it. And the one who had stained it with darkness was him. Riku was painfully aware of that now. Frollo was the same. The judge hadn't been especially weak of heart; darkness lurks within everyone.

"We all do that sometimes. There are just some things we need to keep separate from the world at large, at least until we have time to figure them out," Esmeralda warmly said after a few moments of silence. He nodded at her gentle smile, but the doubts he had about himself were still there inside.

Where is my heart destined for?

Will I find the answer by opening the doors of sleep and stepping through? When my Mark of Mastery exam is over, will I have my answer?

I want to hurry ahead, but there's some small part of me that's still hesitating. Am I afraid?

Or is it...something else?

CHAPTER
3

Prankster's Paradise

SOMEWHERE IN AN AMUSEMENT PARK BY THE SEA, A
large birdcage was hanging with a puppet trapped inside—except it
wasn't truly a puppet at all, but a boy.

A cricket dressed as a gentleman in a tuxedo and top hat with
an umbrella in hand peered into the cage and scolded the wooden
puppet who had been given life. "Shame on you, Pinocchio, playin'
hooky and…goofin' off in a place like this!"

"I'm sorry, Jiminy. I was going to school till I met somebody. Yeah!
Uh, two big monsters with big green eyes!" As Pinocchio tried to
demonstrate just how big the monsters were with his hands, his nose
grew a tiny bit longer.

"Oh, you don't say. And then what happened?"

"They, uh, they tied me in a big sack!"

As the boy gestured, his nose grew even more. It was pretty long
by now.

"Sounds like you were horsin' around."

"But I snuck off when they weren't lookin'."

This time, Pinocchio's nose shot all the way out of the cage and
started blossoming.

"My nose! What's happened?"

"There! Ya see where those tall tales will get ya?" Jiminy said from
atop the flowering branch.

Just then, a star glimmered in the night sky.

"Hey, look at that!" Pinocchio cried.

"That star again. The Blue Fairy!"

The brilliantly twinkling star seemed to draw closer until its light
took the form of a fairy dressed in blue.

"Why, Pinocchio. What has happened to your nose?"

"Oh, um…"

"Perhaps you haven't been telling the truth, Pinocchio." The Blue
Fairy gently chided the speechless boy. "Sir Jiminy?"

"Well, ya see, um, Your Honor, um, Miss Fairy…"

The fairy's gaze made the cricket nervous. He had been instructed to give the boy a good heart, and this present state of affairs didn't reflect very well on his performance.

"Oh, please help me," Pinocchio pleaded with her. "I'm awful sorry."

"You see, Pinocchio? A lie keeps growing and growing, until it's as plain as the nose on your face," she admonished, still soft and gentle.

"I'll never lie again—honest I won't."

"I'll forgive you this once. But remember—a boy who won't be good might just as well be made of wood."

"We'll be good! Won't we?" said Jiminy, turning back to Pinocchio as the boy started to say the same thing.

"Very well. But this is the last time I can help you."

With a wave of her wand, the Blue Fairy returned Pinocchio's nose to its normal size at last.

Riku instantly recognized the place where he landed.

"This is—"

The ceiling was ribbed with what looked like bones, and water had collected on the floor. In the pool were the scattered remnants of a small boat, scraps of wood, barrels, and other broken pieces of flotsam that must have washed in from somewhere.

"Pinocchio! Son! Where have you run off to?" an old man shouted. Riku knew that voice, too—it was Geppetto's.

That settled it. Riku was inside Monstro's mouth.

Spotting Geppetto on the deck of the wrecked boat, Riku called out to him. "What's the matter?"

The old man with a white mustache and bifocals was holding his head in his hands.

"Huh?" he asked, looking up. "Goodness, who are you?"

"Riku."

"Oh, Riku. You poor lad. Seems you were swallowed up by Monstro just like the rest of us. My name is Geppetto, and I'm looking for my son, Pinocchio," the elderly gent stated sadly.

"Pinocchio's gone missing?"

"I'm afraid so. After all my searching, I found him here in the whale. But then he ran off again to who knows where."

Riku thought back, remembering what had happened here inside Monstro. He had kidnapped Pinocchio, a puppet with a heart, thinking he could use him to find a way to get back Kairi's heart...

Is this world in the past? Or...what?

He didn't know how things worked in the Sleeping Worlds. If this was like before, though, he would have to save Pinocchio this time. "Mr. Geppetto, let me go look for your son," Riku offered.

"You would do that? Thank you. Are you sure?"

"Yeah. Leave it to me," Riku replied, ready to go. That was when he heard another voice he knew.

"Did ya say you were really going to help us find Pinocchio?"

"Jiminy?"

That voice was Jiminy's, no question. The cricket looked quizzically up at Riku.

"Huh? That's right—name's Jiminy! Jiminy Cricket. But shucks, have we met?"

"No—you know, never mind."

Jiminy seemed confused when Riku brushed off his question, but he didn't press the matter. "Hmm, if you say so. Anyway, Pinocchio comes first."

"Right. Any idea where he went?"

Jiminy would probably know something.

"Well, I'm almost certain he wandered off with a stranger."

"Can you describe him?"

"Hmm...I remember he was dressed in a black coat."

Riku's expression darkened. On this journey, he'd started to associate the black coat with one person: the boy with the silver hair.

"Thanks." When Riku turned to leave, Jiminy hopped onto his shoulder. "Huh?"

"Well, I'm goin' with ya. Pinocchio's gonna need his conscience, and that's where I come in."

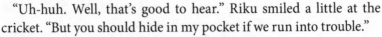

"Uh-huh. Well, that's good to hear." Riku smiled a little at the cricket. "But you should hide in my pocket if we run into trouble."

"If you insist!" Jiminy dove into Riku's pocket.

With that, Riku proceeded from Monstro's mouth to his gullet. Komory Bat and Meow Wow were with him.

The undulating, brightly colored walls inside the whale also brought back memories. The Dream Eaters were still showing up, but Riku dispatched them as he hurried along.

Next came the stomach. Unlike before, the whale's belly was like a strange green swamp.

"Ow!"

When Riku stepped into the liquid, he felt a jolt of stinging pain. This was probably Monstro's digestive fluid.

"Wanna give me a hand?"

"Squee-squee!" Komory Bat replied. Riku took hold of the Spirit's legs and crossed over the acid, while Meow Wow deftly hopped across the bog below.

"He's a helpful little fella, isn't he?" Jiminy poked his head out from Riku's pocket.

"Careful. You *really* don't want to fall."

As small as little Jiminy was, that swamp would swallow him up whole, and that would be the end of his story.

"Whoa, that was a close one!" The cricket clamped his top hat down and burrowed back into the pocket.

Once he'd reached the other side with a hand (leg?) from Komory Bat, Riku continued even deeper inside. Suddenly, Jiminy leaped down from Riku's pocket and let out a shout even before Riku could.

"Pinocchio!"

The boy was following the young man in the black coat. "Jiminy!" he shouted over his shoulder.

"Let him go now!" Riku shouted. The young man nudged Pinocchio's back with a hand, urging him forward.

The boy and Jiminy ran to each other.

"Thank goodness," Jiminy sighed. "Are you all right? Riku and I looked for ya everywhere."

"Uh-huh. I'm just fine." Pinocchio's face fell. "Sorry, Jiminy. I messed up real bad. You and Father must have been so worried about me."

Jiminy smiled at the sincere apology. "Why, Pinocchio, I think ya just might be finally startin' to learn." His eyes were welling with joyful tears.

Satisfied that both of them were safe, Riku approached the person in the black coat. "Who are you?"

Instead of replying, the stranger removed his hood.

"Me?"

The face beneath the hood was none other than his own. The Riku in the black coat opened a Corridor of Darkness behind him and vanished into it.

Riku tried to chase him down, but he knew he wouldn't make it in time. He watched his hand reach out after him and hover in the air for a moment.

"As I live and breathe…," Jiminy exclaimed nervously. He'd seen the whole thing.

"That was my…my dark side. I gave in to the darkness once. And ever since, it's chased me around in one form or another. The Seeker of Darkness who stole my body…a puppet replica of the shadows in my heart…and now I'm facing me."

Riku recalled the other version of himself he had met on a previous journey.

Have I really conquered the darkness within me…?

"Your dark side?" Jiminy asked.

Pinocchio came alongside him and looked up. "Gee, Riku, don't you have a Jiminy like I do? He's my conscience. He's taught me all kinds of important stuff. Maybe you just need somebody to show you what's right and wrong."

Jiminy hopped onto Pinocchio's shoulder as he looked into Riku's face. "Sure. You can't shoulder all your problems alone, ya know. You must have somebody—a friend you can talk to?"

The cricket's question made Riku think of Sora. Of course, Riku couldn't tell him everything, but Sora was still a friend with a special place in his heart.

"Yeah...actually, I do." Riku closed his eyes and imagined Sora's face for a moment, then looked at Pinocchio and Jiminy. "That stupid grin he's always wearing—he's the best teacher I could ever have."

"Gee whiz... I wish I had lots of good friends," Pinocchio said with envy.

"You will, Pinocchio. More than you can count," Jiminy reassured him as he twirled his umbrella.

At that moment, the world shook with what sounded like a howl.

"What now?" Something was on the loose farther in. "Pinocchio, Jiminy, you should head back. I'll see what's shaking things up."

"Okay!"

"Okay!" they both cried together.

Riku made sure they were headed toward Monstro's mouth before he set out in the opposite direction.

The moment he made it into what was probably the whale's intestines, the giant Dream Eater in front of him attacked as if it had been waiting for his arrival.

"...Whoa!"

Riku dodged out of the way, sliding past the huge creature and bringing himself back into a fighting stance with his Keyblade ready.

This colossal Dream Eater shaped like a crayfish was Char Clawbster. At the ends of its arms were propeller-like appendages that shot fire at him.

Riku leaped into the air, closing the gap between them and slamming his Keyblade onto the monster's back. But its shell was too tough; the blow hardly did any damage.

Riku hopped off its back and onto the ground again.

Meow Wow came running up to him while Komory Bat was distracting Char Clawbster with magic spells from its wings.

"You're here to help me out?"

"Mruff!"

With a burst of bright light, Meow Wow lent Riku its strength.

"Here we go!" Riku could feel the power flowing through him, even if he wasn't as fast as he was with Komory Bat.

As Char Clawbster furiously pursued Komory Bat with both propellers upraised, Riku found an opening and slid beneath it.

Once he was there, he swung up with his Keyblade in a flash.

Just as he thought—the Nightmare's underbelly was much softer than its back.

With Char Clawbster stunned, Riku went after its head with blow after blow.

The Dream Eater leaped upward in an attempt to escape the onslaught and clung to the ceiling.

"Urgh…!"

That was when Riku's link with Meow Wow ran out. Exhausted, the Spirit lay down flat on the floor and rested.

"Thanks."

As if it had been waiting for its big moment, Komory Bat fluttered in circles around Riku's head. When it had Riku's attention, it flew off to a strange protrusion and began to weave circles in the air around it.

Avoiding the fiery assault Char Clawbster blasted down from overhead, Riku rushed over to the protrusion and struck it with his Keyblade.

And the world flipped upside down.

Meow Wow fell toward what had been the ceiling, bouncing slightly as it landed. "Meyipe!"

Komory Bat and Riku were fine, one having wings and the other landing deftly.

So that protrusion was a switch for flipping what was up and down.

"Squee-wee!" A pleased Komory Bat did a circuit of Riku's head, then flew off to cast more magic at Char Clawbster.

"Take a breather," Riku told the tuckered-out Meow Wow and then dashed after Komory Bat toward the monster.

Then, with a great jump, he brought his Keyblade down on Char Clawbster's head. Riku could feel a sound impact in his arms. The Dream Eater then fell still and faded away.

"That should do it...!"

Riku landed and watched until the Char Clawbster had vanished entirely.

"Are Pinocchio and the others safe?" he murmured, then ran toward Monstro's mouth.

Pinocchio rushed over to Geppetto. The old man spread his arms and took the boy in an embrace, both of them overjoyed.

Had Pinocchio actually been reunited with Geppetto back then? Riku and Sora had crossed paths in this world during their first journey, only to separate again.

This world was reborn as a dream, and it's like the past is coming to life again, too. I feel like I've atoned for the awful things I did back then, but that's just a dream of my own. My guilt hasn't been erased. He remembered what Yen Sid had said.

"The world was freed from darkness but has yet to wake from it."

Meaning this world was trapped within a never-ending dream. Were those wishes that hadn't come true before now being granted here with this dream...?

Just then, the Keyhole leading to the next world rose up before Riku.

He held up his Keyblade, opened the door, and proceeded to the realm that lay beyond.

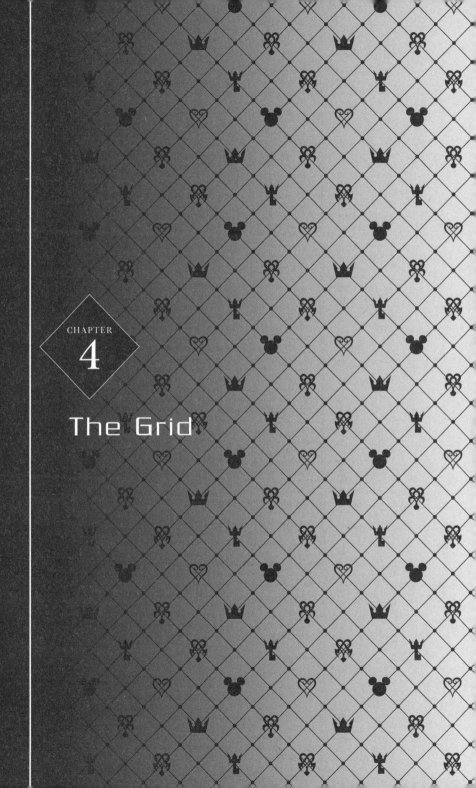

CHAPTER
4

The Grid

RIKU SURVEYED THE NEXT WORLD WHERE HE FOUND himself.

This time, his destination was nothing like anywhere he'd ever been before.

Even the air felt somehow different. There was no natural light like the sun or the moon to illuminate his way, only the pale white-blue glow from the buildings and pathways.

Riku then noticed that his own clothes were different, too.

"Is this world special?" he muttered, looking at the skintight, bodysuit-like getup. It had lines of the same pale light running along it. He was even wearing a helmet.

A light shown down on him from above, and when Riku instinctively looked up to see what it was, there was a large, bridge-shaped transport ship—a Recognizer—floating overhead with a searchlight focused on him.

It was a strange machine in an even stranger world, and Riku eyed it with extreme caution. A lift descended from the Recognizer, and two men wearing black suits with orange accents stepped out.

Before he knew it, there were two more men in the same suits wielding staves behind him, making four altogether. All of them wore black helmets that hid their faces.

"Another stray," said a man—a Black Guard—in an odd, muffled voice.

Riku suspected it would be wiser to go with them than to resist at the moment.

Though the Black Guards took hold of his arms, Riku shook off their grip and boarded the lift of the Recognizer himself.

Once they were on board, the vessel rose into the air and flew off toward somewhere. Another young man in a suit similar to Riku's was beside him. He had brown hair and an intense look on his face—he seemed very different from the Black Guards.

"Are you a prisoner?" he asked.

"Yeah. It looks that way," Riku replied, and the man's expression softened a bit.

Everything visible from the Recognizer was dim and bathed in a pale light.

"Name's Sam." The man introduced himself.

"I'm Riku," he replied before then asking a question of his own. "Where are we, Sam?"

"We're on the Grid," Sam told him.

The Grid—Riku had never heard of this world before.

The Recognizer passed between buildings during this exchange and came to a halt. Only Riku was brought down from the ship; apparently, Sam was being taken to another location.

Riku and Sam shared a glance, and Riku nodded before he watched the Recognizer fly away.

Before him lay a wide road—almost like a racetrack.

"You're in luck. Only a precious few are granted Light Cycle battle privileges," someone said.

When Riku turned to face whoever it was, he saw a man in a black suit with glowing orange lines—CLU—standing there. His lines were longer and more distinct than those of the Black Guards. He wasn't wearing a helmet like them, either, so the cruelty in his face was clearly visible.

One of the Black Guards beside him then approached Riku and handed him a sticklike object.

"You gonna explain why it's so lucky?" he asked dubiously.

"I'll show you."

Two machines—Light Cycles—raced past Riku, and Riku noticed they had a stick on the front like the one in his hand.

"How hard can it be?"

Riku broke into a run and split the stick into two handles—and a Light Cycle appeared around them. As Riku hopped aboard, the cycle accelerated with perfect timing and began speeding along the circuit. In front of him were Light Cycles with Black Guards aboard.

He gave his own vehicle a sudden burst of speed and fired off a shot. Once he had grown accustomed to the speed of his Light Cycle relative to the others, as well as the trajectory of his projectile weapons, Riku landed hits on both of the cycles, which sent them crashing in spectacular fashion.

There was a wall up ahead.

"I think I've had enough entertainment for one day."

This time Riku fired on the barrier, destroying it and escaping from the designated path. Beyond the wall stretched a road that was smaller than the racetrack yet still fairly wide.

"Riku!" someone called out to him.

It was Sam. *Looks like he was able to make a break for it, too.*

"You made it. You escaped from the games."

"Yeah." Riku answered, climbing off the Light Cycle.

"I know a way off the Grid," said Sam. "Wanna come with?"

Does that mean Sam isn't from this world, either?

"No. You go ahead." Riku still had something he needed to do here. He was glad Sam felt that way, but he couldn't go with him. Actually, he was worried about whether Sam even knew how to escape at all. "Wait, what's the way out?"

"Through the Portal."

"Portal?"

Riku reacted to the word. Joshua had also mentioned a "Portal" back in Traverse Town—they connected worlds. Did something similar exist here?

"Yeah, it's like a gate that opened when I came here. Once I'm back in the real world, I can delete CLU. And then…then my dad will be able to come home."

"Your dad?" Sam was getting more and more heated, and Riku needed him to explain.

"He vanished—twenty years ago when he came here to the Grid. But because he needed to protect his disc from CLU, he went into hiding. He's been trapped there ever since. But I'm gonna change that."

Though Riku was concerned for Sam and his mission to save his father, it was the Portal that piqued his interest most right then.

"I see... Sam, you mind if I go with you after all? To the Portal?"

"Sure. I'll take what help I can get. But first there's someone I need to meet. He's in the city," Sam said with a slight smile, looking toward the rows of buildings.

"Got it," Riku replied, then took off with Sam. They rushed through a major throughway and arrived at the city before too long, when Sam came to a stop.

"Kill some time till I get back," he told Riku, then went off to who knows where.

Though his behavior was a bit worrying, Riku decided to roll with it for now.

But as if they had been waiting until he was alone, Dream Eaters arrived. In the same instant, Meow Wow and Komory Bat revealed themselves to protect him.

"Glad I get to fight more than boredom."

Riku summoned his Keyblade and rushed into the battle.

Right around that time, Sam was nervously watching a woman lying on the ground—Quorra.

She was completely motionless with her eyes open, like an automaton that had fallen still. A man wearing a brown robe stood in front of Sam.

"Your disc... Dad, it's gone."

The disc and its priceless data had vanished from the back of the man in the robe—Sam's father, Kevin.

"It is." Unlike his son, Kevin replied with gentle calm as he walked over to the immobile Quorra. "She's stable." With that, Kevin stepped away from the girl and looked off into the distance.

"We have to go back," Sam pleaded. "CLU will use it to reach the outside world. I can stop him from destroying it if you'd just let me do this!"

"You've done enough already!" Kevin barked.

Sam looked down nervously, then asked the question he had been wondering about. "So what do we do now?"

"I don't know. Nothing. We do nothing. Be still. Wait."

You think we can just wait? thought Sam. However, he wasn't sure what to do in this strange world.

"We can hop a Solar Sailer. A full-on sprint to the Portal. We can beat CLU there!" Kevin said, rethinking, then looked at Sam. "Let's get her out of here."

Kevin began to walk off as if his mind were made up, while Sam picked up Quorra as ordered.

After Riku finished off the Dream Eaters, he heard a strange noise coming from the direction where Sam had gone.

"What?"

He ran toward the sound and found Sam carrying a woman in his arms, with another man beside him.

"Sam!" he called.

But the newcomer, Kevin, was the one who answered. "Who's this?"

"I'm Riku. Sam and I were on our way to the Portal."

Kevin shot Sam a glance to ask if Riku was telling the truth. When Sam nodded, Kevin seemed to understand everything. "Come with us," he said to Riku.

"Where we headed?"

"The Portal, but we need a Solar Sailer. There's one in the underground docks."

With that, Kevin set off with Sam and Riku in tow.

Once Riku and the others were safely aboard the Solar Sailer, they caught their breath as it departed the underground docks. Sam put Quorra down, and a hologram shaped like a human face appeared from her chest.

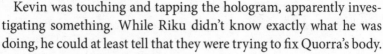

Kevin was touching and tapping the hologram, apparently investigating something. While Riku didn't know exactly what he was doing, he could at least tell that they were trying to fix Quorra's body.

"Is she gonna make it?" Sam asked worriedly.

"I don't know."

"But didn't you write her code?"

Was Quorra a program, then? Did that mean Kevin was Quorra's maker?

"Some of it. But...the rest is just...beyond me."

"She's an ISO."

"ISO?" Riku considered this unfamiliar term.

"A whole new life-form. Quorra is the last ISO."

"And you created them?"

"They manifested, like a flame. They weren't really...really from anywhere. The conditions were right, and they came into being. For centuries, we've dreamed of a pure existence beyond our own. I found them in here, like flowers in a wasteland. They were spectacular. Everything I'd hoped to find in the system—control, order, perfection—none of it meant a thing. The ISOs—they were gonna be my gift to the world," Kevin explained reverently as he manipulated the hologram.

Riku found the idea intriguing—"a pure existence beyond our own."

"There, good as new. It's gonna take a while for her system to reboot."

The hologram vanished back into Quorra.

But Riku still had questions. "So what happened...to your gift?" he asked Kevin.

"CLU. CLU happened. He was built to create the perfect system. But endless potential can never, ever be fully realized. CLU saw the ISOs as an imperfection, so he destroyed them."

"He screwed up." Sam shook his head.

"No, he's me. I screwed it up. Chasing after perfection—chasing after what was right in front of me. Right in front of me."

It was possible that what Kevin meant were Sam and Quorra. In his pursuit of perfection, he had lost something important—what mattered more than anything else. *Look too hard for one thing and you miss everything else. And then the people around you get hurt in the process. Ansem the Wise was the same. His single-minded desire to learn more about the heart unleashed so much darkness on the world. We all have a little of that curiosity in us... So if we're not careful, that darkness could come from anyone.*

Riku looked up at the gloomy sky only to spy a Recognizer chasing them down, its searchlight trained on the Solar Sailer.

"Great. They found us," Riku said.

Sam and Kevin looked up.

"We've been put on a new course," said Kevin. It seemed the Solar Sailer had been stopped somewhere other than its original destination.

"...Where...?"

Quorra, who had just regained consciousness, shook her head and got to her feet.

"Don't worry about that. We're getting out of here...!"

Riku and the others hurried down from the Solar Sailer together.

Unfortunately, a lone man in a black suit was observing the area. He wasn't quite the same as the other guards—this one was Rinzler.

Quorra suddenly removed the disc from her back.

"Good-bye." With that, she handed the disc to Kevin and suddenly darted away.

"Quorra. Quorra!"

"No, wait!"

Kevin stopped Sam before he could go after her, and Rinzler caught Quorra almost as soon as she rushed out of hiding.

"She's removing herself from the equation," Kevin said.

Sam turned toward him. "We can't just let her go," he replied firmly.

"Yeah." Riku agreed as well.

But Kevin stopped them. "No. Hold on, Sam. What about getting you to the Portal? You shut them down from the outside."

"But Quorra comes first! And we still have to get back your disc."

"Sam. If you chase two rabbits, you won't catch either."

They definitely weren't on the same page.

Still, Kevin handling things on his own didn't seem like as much of an issue. Riku spoke up.

"If this is a father-son thing, I won't butt in, but we should probably get that disc back at least—before CLU uses it to destroy the outside world. Come on, Sam."

Sam hesitated for a moment, but then—

"Right. Meet me on the flight deck and get us some wheels," he eventually answered. It sounded like he had an idea.

"Wheels? What's your plan?" Kevin asked uncertainly.

"I'm a user. I'll improvise," Sam replied, and he hurried away with Riku. "Riku, I gotta save Quorra, too."

"I know. We will."

Riku nodded as Sam told him what he intended to do. Despite what he'd said, Riku couldn't just leave Quorra to her fate after she had made a diversion for them.

"The disc should be somewhere on the Throneship. I saw it dock here earlier. Over there!"

A small vessel, the Throneship, was docked where Sam pointed.

"All right," Riku replied, and they dashed down the path leading to the ship and into the vessel. Sam walked up to the disc within, where it was affixed in the center of the deck. Unfortunately, an alarm went off the moment he touched it.

The ship's doors opened, and Rinzler arrived, bringing Quorra with him.

"Sam. Go!" she yelled, only for Rinzler to push her out of the way. He charged at Sam and Riku while removing the discs from his back.

In the same moment, Sam brought Kevin's disc up, ready to fight, and he hurled it toward Rinzler at terrific speed.

Rinzler dodged and suddenly bounded into the air, but Riku's Keyblade slashed out and knocked their foe through the door.

"What are you doing here?" Quorra asked angrily, but Sam just told her where to go.

"To the flight deck!"

"But CLU will be here any minute. We'll never make it."

"Don't worry. Riku's here to help," Sam answered before picking up the disc and heading to the flight deck. The remaining two followed.

"Hurry!"

On the flight deck, Kevin was ready and waiting with a Light Jet. Once everyone was aboard, he launched the craft without further ado. They were going to the Portal.

The Portal resembled a circular stage in the air, glowing blue. After passing through the entrance, three of the group stepped onto the path leading to the Portal itself.

However, CLU awaited them in the middle of the walkway.

"This is mine." Kevin stepped forward along the narrow path toward the Portal, high in the air. One fall from here and that would be the end of it. "Had a feeling you'd be here!" he said to CLU.

"You! You promised that we would change the world…together! You broke your promise!" CLU shouted.

That was when Riku realized something. Though there were some discrepancies like their ages and facial hair, they looked exactly alike—in other words, Kevin was CLU, and CLU was Kevin.

"I took the system to its maximum potential. And now you see the applications at my disposal!"

As CLU grinned, a gigantic Dream Eater emerged behind him. The creature, which had arms like large scythes and a giant disc around its legs, was called Commantis.

In the darkness and gloom, the Dream Eater shone out bright as if to remind them that it wasn't part of this world.

"You can leave this one to me." Raising his Keyblade toward Commantis, Riku charged.

Meow Wow and Komory Bat chose that moment to make their entrance. Meow Wow bounded a step ahead of Riku and then turned around toward him, tail wagging.

"Are you telling me to get on?"

Riku hopped into the air and then, using Meow Wow's back as a platform, made another leap and swung down at Commantis's head with his Keyblade. The blow struck home, and he followed it with a blast of magic.

When the Dream Eater let out a shriek and tried to cover its face with its scythes, Komory Bat attacked from behind with some ultrasonic waves.

Riku wasn't able to deal much damage thanks to the distance between him and the airborne creature. When he considered that there wasn't much space to work with, either, accepting a helping hand appeared to be the best option.

"Komory Bat!" At Riku's summons, the Spirit made a beeline to a point directly overhead. "Help me out here!" Riku extended his hand, and light burst from Komory Bat, fusing with him and becoming his wings.

Riku kicked off the ground once more, this time soaring into the air and delivering a series of attacks to Commantis in one go. Hovering, he watched the Dream Eater fall still.

"Is that…is that it?"

The power within Riku suddenly drained, and he sensed Komory Bat separating from him. Almost as soon as he hit the ground, Commantis faded away in a flash of light.

"Gaaahhh!!" CLU roared after losing Commantis. "I created the perfect system!" the program shouted imploringly at his creator.

"The thing about perfection is that it's unknowable. It's impossible, but it's also…right in front of us all the time. You wouldn't know that because I didn't when I created you. I'm sorry, CLU. I'm sorry."

CLU's eyes narrowed for moment when Kevin apologized, but they soon filled with rage as he dealt the older man a kick. He raised his leg again, but Sam tackled him to stop him. CLU hurled Sam down the path, closer to the Portal.

Quorra took that moment to hurry over to Kevin. "Go," Kevin ordered her in a quiet, gentle voice. Though she hesitated for a moment, she quickly leaped into the air and landed near Sam by the Portal.

Riku planted himself in CLU's path when the program tried to go after them. CLU came to a halt and glared at Riku.

"CLU! Remember what you came for," Kevin shouted.

CLU turned back and walked toward him as the pathway behind him began to crumble. There was no way to save Kevin now.

CLU knelt down and pulled the disc off the injured Kevin on the ground. Gloating in his victory, he watched the data rising from the disc.

"No..."

But then his eyes went wide, and he let out a shout.

Kevin had switched the data on the disc.

"No... Why?"

"He's my son."

CLU threw down the disc at this answer, then turned back and ran at Quorra and Sam. He leaped over the missing pathway.

"Go!" Kevin shouted, and Sam reacted.

"Dad!"

CLU just barely managed to catch hold of the edge of the crumbled path.

"Sam! It's time!" Kevin called out as he got to his feet.

"No!"

"Sam, it's what he wants," Quorra told the young man as she held him back and removed her disc.

"I'm not leaving you!" Sam shouted again as Quorra handed him the disc.

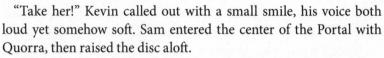

"Take her!" Kevin called out with a small smile, his voice both loud yet somehow soft. Sam entered the center of the Portal with Quorra, then raised the disc aloft.

Light washed over Sam and Quorra, and then they were gone.

"Yes! Good-bye, kiddo," Kevin said quietly. Were they able to hear his voice?

CLU clambered up onto the path and dashed for the Portal. Riku stepped into his way with Keyblade in hand. "Don't even think about it."

Just then, he saw Kevin place his hand on the ground on the other side of the severed pathway, and a circle of light rippled out from his body.

In the blink of an eye, the light pulled CLU toward it and drew him into Kevin. For a moment, the air was thick with an indescribable tension as CLU returned to Kevin. The next, radiance engulfed everything around them.

And then Kevin, Quorra, and Sam were all gone. The light had disappeared from the Portal. In those brilliant, blinding few seconds, fate had separated a father and son forever.

The Portal is gone. These gates that connect worlds—maybe when we pass through them, we're challenged and changed. And it's not over. There are more trials ahead we have to overcome.

"But we'll be ready, Sora."

Riku addressed his friend who wasn't here, then held out his Keyblade to the Keyhole floating in the air.

No matter what trials waited beyond the gate, the only way was forward.

And Riku ventured into the next world.

CHAPTER
5

Again

RIKU HAD BEEN EXPECTING TO ARRIVE IN A NEW world, but instead, he found himself in one he had already visited on this journey.

"Traverse Town? Why am I back?" Riku muttered as he looked around.

Nothing had changed at all. He had supposedly opened the door of this world, so maybe there was still something wrong here?

Riku heard soft footsteps behind him and turned around. "Joshua."

"Nice of you to join us," the boy said in his usual easygoing way.

"What happened?"

"Trouble happened. I was hoping one of you could help."

Joshua may have been subdued and calm, but if he was seeking their help, this world must be having an especially hard time.

"When did Sora get here?" Riku asked Joshua about the other version of this world. He couldn't do that in the other worlds, but Joshua was special, and plus, he knew his friend.

Joshua laughed at the question. "Bravo, Riku. Why can't he be this quick on the uptake?"

"Yeah, well, Sora's a little…"

While he didn't know exactly what had been said on the other side, Riku had a pretty good idea, and just imagining it brought a smile to his face.

Joshua did the same and began to laugh out loud, but his expression quickly turned solemn and grave. "Now, let's get down to the problem. We've got a nasty Dream Eater on our hands. It keeps jumping between worlds. Not only that, it knows how to summon creatures like it."

What kind of power or inherent traits would allow a Dream Eater to cross between both versions of the world? Far as I know, only Joshua can pull off that particular feat. If a Dream Eater can make the jump, too… That's hard to believe, even coming from Joshua.

Riku mulled it over for a moment as the other boy continued.

"Pretty powerful ones, too. The others are on a mission to stop it, but they need help."

"The others? You mean Shiki and her friends?" Riku remembered the two he'd met before, Shiki and Beat.

"That's right. They all found their Game partners, and Shiki is over fighting in the other Traverse Town. In fact, Sora is helping them out."

"Good to hear. So what can I do?"

If they were with Sora, there wasn't much cause for concern. As long as they worked together on both sides, not even a Dream Eater that moved between worlds should be a problem to defeat.

"Actually, the Dream Eater just reappeared in the Fountain Plaza. I sent Beat and his partner to face it."

"I'm on it." *If I'm going to help, then the earlier the better.*

Riku set off to take care of it straightaway, but Joshua called out to stop him. "Riku. There's something else you need to know."

"Hmm?" Riku glanced back and noticed that Joshua looked fairly serious.

"These two Traverse Towns separated by the Portal… I was under the impression they were parallel worlds, but it looks like I was wrong."

"Wrong how?" Riku came to a halt. *Does he mean to say the two sides only look connected, but they actually aren't?*

"That's where it gets tricky. After you and Sora left, Shiki crossed the Portal to join her Game partner. Did you notice Players have a mission timer inscribed on their hands? Well, when she got to the other side, Shiki had more time left on her clock than her partner. And when Beat's partner crossed over to the other side, she had *less* time left."

"So time flows differently here and there? So what? That's true of any two worlds. Their home world would be running on a different time axis, too," Riku replied.

Each world had its own unique passage of time. For instance, it was possible that when Shiki and the other girl went back to their home worlds, no time at all had passed there, meaning they had returned right after the moment they were erased. That was simply how it worked.

"Yes, I understand that. But if these Traverse Towns were parallel worlds, then time would flow the same in both. But it doesn't, ergo they are not parallel worlds."

"You mean...there's a past and a future." *If the worlds are connected but not parallel, does that mean Sora and I touched down in different times?*

Joshua had more to say, though. "No. Impossible. The worlds are clearly separate—it's not just that time sets them apart. As you yourself noted, every world flows at its own pace, which tells me that for all their similarities, these are two distinct worlds."

"Distinct worlds?"

Riku fell into thought, unsure of the implication of what Joshua had said. *Two nearly identical worlds that are completely separate—and yet tied to each other...?*

"Yes...but this is all conjecture. It's like the same world imagined by two people. What does that tell you? That we're in..."

"A dream..." Riku offered the solution that popped into his mind. It wouldn't be far-fetched to imagine time flowing differently in a dream. Master Yen Sid had already explained to them that these worlds were sleeping. *But then who's the one doing the dreaming? Is it me? Sora? The world itself?*

"Yes. Bravo again, Riku. In which case none of this may matter one bit to me or my friends. But to you and Sora, I think it might be a vital clue."

"Right... Thanks. So you need me in the plaza?"

"Wow. I'm running out of 'bravos.'"

Riku was grateful to Joshua for filling him in. That sounded pretty important. As he turned to walk away, though, Joshua stopped him once again.

"Huh…?"

"What's up?"

"Your little friend here…" The boy was looking at Meow Wow with his arms crossed.

"Something wrong?"

"You only had one Spirit when you left, if I recall."

It was true. Komory Bat was the only Dream Eater Joshua had taught Riku how to create.

"Yeah. He just kinda showed up and started tagging along."

"Hmm…" Joshua contemplated the matter.

"No, really, is something wrong?"

"It's nothing," Joshua said, giving the smile of one who knew more than he was saying. "Well, I'm counting on you."

Tilting his head in puzzlement, Riku left for the Fountain Plaza.

When he arrived, Riku found Beat battling the Dream Eater alongside the tomboyish girl he'd seen on Sora's side the last time he visited this world. Their foe was Spellican, a Dream Eater resembling a giant bird hovering in the air and wielding a staff.

"Beat!" Riku dashed into the plaza and placed himself in front of Spellican to shield Beat and his partner.

"About time, yo!"

"Oh, here we go again. Five seconds ago, it was, 'Where's Riku?'— and now the act?" The tomboy, wearing a big beanie and baggy T-shirt, rolled her eyes next to Beat.

"Bwaaah! Don't tell *him* that!" Beat grabbed his head melodramatically.

Chuckling at her partner's antics, the girl turned to Riku again. "It's so nice to meet you. I'm Rhyme. Riku, right? Sorry my partner's acting like a doofus." She bobbed her head.

"I am not!" Beat shouted. "Ya always gotta go around and…and garnish my reputation!"

"Since when? You burned that bridge all by yourself. 'Nobody raises his reputation by lowering others,'" Rhyme shot back.

Riku had to fight back a smile as he watched them go.

"Yo, Riku. You gonna sit here and let her get in my grill?" Beat asked angrily.

He had to swallow his laughter. "Sorry, it's just...you two are cut from the same cloth."

"I ain't made of cloth!" Beat snapped.

"I know!" answered Rhyme at the same time. "Beat looks and talks like a punk, but there's a heart of gold in there somewhere."

"Yeah. He's come through for me, so I know what you mean." Riku agreed wholeheartedly with Rhyme's honest appraisal of his good points. Of course, he also agreed with her less flattering comment, too.

"There, see? I'm a—," Beat started to say with pride, only to tilt his head in confusion. "Rhyme! Did you just call me a punk again?"

"Skwaaaaaaa!!" Spellican finally screeched, apparently unable to bear any more of this conversation.

The trio turned toward the Dream Eater and readied themselves. "All right, now we ruffled its feathers," said Riku. "Ready to do this?"

"Yeah!" Beat and Rhyme both bravely called.

Meanwhile, Spellican waved its staff and created several magical circles on the ground. As Dream Eaters emerged from them, Spellican flew high into the sky out of reach.

"Me and Rhyme'll handle things here."

"You go after that thing!"

"Right!" Exactly as they suggested, Riku chased after Spellican.

The first stop after the Fountain Plaza was a back alley. The bird conjured more circles as it escaped, which in turn brought forth more Dream Eaters.

"Quantity versus quality, huh?"

Riku took down the monsters alongside Komory Bat and Meow Wow, but the Dream Eaters just kept coming one after the other.

"There's no end to them!"

Spellican was going to get away at this rate.

That was when Riku heard a voice call out to him—Joshua's voice.

"Riku, the Third District! We're going to pin it between both worlds!"

"Okay!" Riku shouted, then wove his way through the Dream Eaters and hurried to the Third District.

Riku made it into the Third District just as Spellican was flying toward the door to the First District.

He sprinted ahead and planted himself in its path. "I got you now!"

This time, the Dream Eater tried to double back for the Second District, but that was when Beat and Rhyme caught up.

"This is my street, yo!"

"You gotta play by the rules."

Though it seemed momentarily nonplussed, Spellican quickly summoned a suspicious-looking orb—a Portal. With a screeching cackle, the Dream Eater glided into the gateway.

"Oh no!"

"Hey!"

Beat and Rhyme were both frustrated, but Riku knew they had nothing to worry about.

"Sora, you got this," he said with soft certainty, watching the Portal fade.

"This is so tired, yo. Every time we chase him down…"

"I know. But we've got an ally on the other side. Don't worry." Riku walked over toward Beat with a smile.

"Yeah, well, I still don't like it," the boy grumbled.

Joshua drifted slowly down from above in front of him. "You know, you are such a good listener, Beat. You're like a sponge, really," he said with a meaningful grin.

"Me? I'm not a sponge. I'm just me."

"You mean Daisukenojo Bito?"

"Don't use my full name!"

So that's his real name: Daisukenojo Bito. Riku had been all over

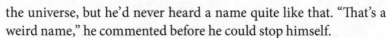

the universe, but he'd never heard a name quite like that. "That's a weird name," he commented before he could stop himself.

"Hey!" Beat snapped, while Rhyme and Joshua laughed at the two of them.

Up ahead, the Keyhole to the next world appeared and grabbed their attention.

"Well, it's time to go," Riku said before raising his Keyblade.

"Hey, Riku—thanks," called Rhyme.

"Yeah, stay cool," added Beat. "We'll catch up with you soon."

"Mm-hmm, say hi to Sora."

Rhyme and Beat sounded reluctant to part ways, but they also seemed confident that they would meet again.

"Sure," Riku replied with a smile.

On the other hand, Joshua was still a little concerned. "Riku. Remember what I said. Be careful. If this really is a dream, it's going to lie to you to try and make you think it's real."

"I got it." Riku nodded. The line between dream and reality would blur in these worlds—if the world itself was lying to him, discerning the truth could prove difficult.

"What? I don't got it." Beat cocked his head to the side, totally confused.

"You and Sora would break your heads on this one," Joshua quipped.

"Bwaaah?" Beat protested, prompting the four of them to break out in laughter again.

I bet Sora's already made short work of that thing on the other side.

Riku raised his Keyblade to the Keyhole and moved on to the next world.

CHAPTER
6

Country
of the Musketeers

THE FIRST THING HE SAW WAS A BUILDING OF STONE, brightly illuminated against a dark night sky.

In front of it was an expansive garden, and the whole place reminded him of a large mansion. As Riku landed among the shrubs and flowers, he spotted a familiar figure entering the building. He frowned.

That was Pete, although this one had a red outfit and peg leg, unlike the one he knew. He was even wearing a crown.

"What kind of world did I end up in this time?" Riku muttered to himself as he thought things over. *Pete's here, so does that mean this place is connected to Disney Castle? But I don't think the castle is asleep—so is this some other world?*

Still, wherever this was, Riku couldn't just ignore Pete, knowing his history of wreaking havoc.

Komory Bat and Meow Wow were by his side, too. "Shall we?" Riku said to the two Dream Eaters, then followed Pete into the building.

The floors were covered in crimson carpeting, and the interior proved to be as opulent as the outside.

Now, where did he go? Riku proceeded farther in and came to a huge auditorium.

So this place was a theater, and Riku had entered from stage left. Over on stage right, there were three people carrying what looked like wooden panels. Riku swiftly ducked behind the curtain.

What were they about to do?

The trio in brown hoods were the Beagle Boys, each toting a wooden board shaped like a person—Mickey, Donald, and Goofy on closer inspection. It seemed the three of them were together in this world, too. Riku smiled at the possibility of running into Mickey.

The Beagle Boys arranged the panels of Mickey and his friends on the stage.

Behind them, Pete was standing on a prop shaped like a boat, surveying the stage like a director.

He smirked, and then a big crate plummeted down from a scaffold above the arranged panels. Mickey and the others were smashed to pieces.

Hold on, is he planning to—?

"Wait!" Riku rushed onto the stage, trying to catch Pete before he vanished.

But Pete had already jumped down from the boat and disappeared backstage along with his henchmen.

Riku took another look at the scattered splinters of Mickey and his friends. *Looks like Pete and his goons are setting a trap for those three, and this was a test run. I have to stop them.*

He stepped through the door the Beagle Boys had come from when they brought the panels and found himself backstage.

The moment he stepped into the dim, dusty room, Komory Bat flew off ahead of him with Meow Wow close behind.

"You found something?"

Riku went after them and discovered a large locked chest—and it was moving.

Komory Bat circled the chest once and flapped its wings beckoningly at Riku.

"What is it?"

Riku hurried over to the chest and held his Keyblade up to the keyhole. The lock clicked, and the lid opened to reveal the one trapped inside.

"Minnie!"

Minnie, who wore a pink dress and a crown, lay on her side within the chest.

"Are you all right?" Riku lent her a hand as she climbed out.

"Oh, thank you for saving me!"

Minnie curtsied politely to Riku, then quickly turned away and started to leave.

"Where are you going?" Riku hurried to ask.

Minnie stopped. "I have to help the Musketeers."

"What happened? Tell me what I can do."

Riku wasn't quite sure what "Musketeers" referred to, but he could infer from Minnie's panic that it probably had something to do with Mickey and his friends.

"Who are you?" she asked.

"Riku. Mickey's my friend," he replied. Riku wasn't confident he actually knew the Mickey of this world, but Minnie would probably get the picture.

She smiled with a bit of relief, then began to explain.

"Oh, Riku, the stage has been rigged with a machine to lure Mickey and the others into a terrible trap. If we could only find something to control the device from here…"

As she filled him in, a suspicious figure was hard at work behind Minnie—one of the Beagle Boys who had been hauling over the wooden silhouettes earlier.

"Lucky I remembered. Look what I nearly forgot!" the Beagle Boy muttered to himself as he removed the wheel from a device. When he finally turned around, he noticed Minnie and cocked his head in confusion. "Eh? Why's the box sans mouse?"

That was when the remaining Beagle Boys showed up.

"Oy, quit messin' around."

"The boss is losin' his patience!"

When they finished scolding their comrade, the other Beagle Boys spotted Riku and Minnie, too.

Minnie was the first to raise her voice. "There it is! That's the gadget we need to retrieve!"

"I'm on it." Riku rushed toward them, and the Beagle Boys fled all at once.

"Run for it!"

The Beagle Boys had darted into a costume room. Komory Bat and Meow Wow would be especially helpful here, just as they had been when they found Minnie earlier.

"Take it away, guys."

"Squeep."

Komory Bat fluttered around happily, then hovered in front of one of the many clothing shelves and flapped its wings.

"Gotcha!" Riku swept the clothes aside, and just as he thought, there was one of the Beagle Boys hiding with his head in his hand.

"Eep!"

Before he could get away again, Riku grabbed him by the collar and knocked him out. "Two more to go!"

"Mrarf."

Not one to be outdone, Meow Wow trotted up to a wood door farther in the room.

"Over there now, huh?" Riku smashed the door with a swing of his Keyblade.

"Ack!"

Riku easily rendered this Beagle Boy unconscious as well. That made two.

Only one more left.

Meow Wow and Komory Bat moved farther backstage into the dark substage, where all the machines were for the sets.

"So the last one is here…"

Unfortunately, it seemed neither Komory Bat nor Meow Wow were up to the task of tracking down the final Beagle Boy. Riku proceeded carefully, inspecting every inch of the area.

After a moment, Komory Bat flapped up into the air around a pile of lumber between some pillars.

"Something fishy there?"

Riku scattered the mountain of boards with his Keyblade to reveal a small room—but there was nothing inside but a few small posts. No Beagle Boy.

"…Nobody's here, you know," he told Komory Bat.

"Squeewee."

Komory Bat flew even higher, and a look upward revealed a garret-like space overhead. Riku couldn't find a way to get to it, though. This time, it was Meow Wow's turn to circle a small pillar.

"You telling me to spin this?" Riku slowly began to rotate the spindle-like apparatus, and a purple curtain slid down between the columns. At the same time, a small lift descended a short ways away.

"There you are!"

"Wa-wa-wah!"

As the Beagle Boy desperately tried to flee, Riku smacked him on the head.

That was all of them, and yet, he still hadn't found the wheel.

"Did they hide it somewhere?" He started to hurry back the way he had come, when a big mole-like Dream Eater, Holey Moley, suddenly crawled out of the ground at Riku's feet.

The monster swatted Riku and Meow Wow away, then disappeared back into the floor. Riku quickly readied his Keyblade, but he couldn't get a bead on it.

"Where did it go…?"

Next, it came from behind, and the blow to his shoulders sent Riku to his knees. By the time he looked back, the Dream Eater was gone.

After that, it popped out of the wall.

As its name would suggest, this Dream Eater was like a mole tunneling through space.

"They just never want to make this easy, do they?"

Riku leaped forward and whacked Holey Moley on the snout. It was a good hit, but the creature burrowed back into the wall.

"Now where…?" As Riku looked and listened, Komory Bat flapped over to the other side of a screen. "There it is!"

Beyond the screen, a paw appeared. The rest of the Nightmare was hiding, but Riku still attacked it with a series of solid blows.

As the paw disappeared in defeat, Riku heard Meow Wow yelp.

"Hold on!"

Riku climbed a stack of crates and brought his Keyblade down on Holey Moley from overhead while it was busy squaring off with Meow Wow.

The surprise attack was more than enough to stun the Dream Eater.

"Time to finish this!" Riku shouted. As if awaiting those very words, Meow Wow hurtled toward his chest. The Spirit's body and power became light that merged with Riku. "Here we go!"

With the extra power from Meow Wow, Riku hit Holey Moley dead on the nose.

"Did that do it?"

The Dream Eater clutched its head in pain, then went still and vanished in a flash of light.

"Riku, hurry! The machine!" Minnie shouted as she emerged from her hiding place.

Riku looked closely and saw the wheel laying where Holey Moley had vanished. He picked it up and went over to the device on the wall. Once the wheel was back on the shaft, he spun it slowly. "How do you like that?"

The machine went into motion, and the gears started rotating.

"Impossible!" they heard Pete bellow from the stage.

"Looks like I was right in the nick of time...Sora," Riku whispered, then smiled. Sora was fighting in the other world, and he had called on him for help.

I bet Sora's helping Mickey out right about now. Riku was sure of it.

"Oh, thank goodness. You truly saved the day, Riku. I see you're as brave as a Royal Musketeer," Minnie told him joyfully.

"'Musketeer'? What is that anyway?" he asked.

Minnie beckoned Riku closer. She seemed to have a secret to share with him.

What she told him surprised him. "They...they actually say that?" he asked.

"Of course. Every Musketeer is taught those words. It's a very important motto and a solemn pledge that brings us all together."

A pledge that brings us together... And it reminds me of myself. Riku got to his feet and let out a small sigh. "You're right. And it does fit the moment."

He raised his Keyblade toward the sky.

"All for one…and one for all."

He was positive that Sora, Mickey, Donald, and Goofy had all said the same thing on the other side. After all, they were connected.

With their bond in his heart, Riku set forth for the next world.

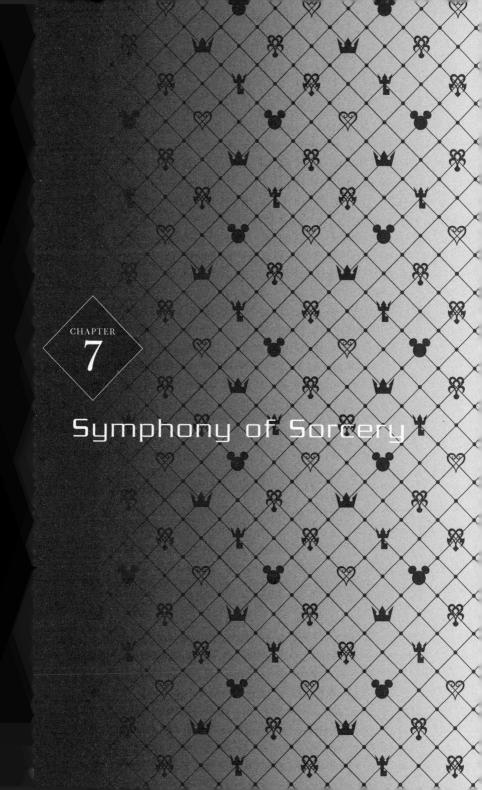

CHAPTER

7

Symphony of Sorcery

WATER WAS FLOWING DOWN A FLIGHT OF STAIRS, enough to soak into Riku's shoes. It was like standing in a river.

This looked pretty much the same as the first floor of Master Yen Sid's tower—except for all the water. It was apparently coming from upstairs.

Riku began climbing the steps. The stairs and the rooms along the way were almost identical to those of the Mysterious Tower.

When Riku opened the door on the top floor where Yen Sid usually was, he found Mickey sitting at a desk in the middle of the flooded chamber.

"Mickey!" Riku ran over to his friend, but Mickey's eyes remained closed and his expression intense as he waved his arms like a conductor.

There was an ominous aura in the air, especially around the music stand to Mickey's rear.

"It's this musical score. It has him trapped."

Riku approached the stand and summoned his Keyblade, but then he heard a voice.

"You won't be able to defeat that darkness with brute force. I'm Mickey, the sorcerer's apprentice. Who are you?"

It belonged to Mickey.

Riku didn't know where the voice was coming from, but he could definitely hear it somewhere in the room.

Should he respond to the mouse with his eyes shut and hands waving, or should he direct his answer somewhere else?

"Riku."

Unsure of what to do, Riku decided to just speak into the air, then asked a question of his own. "If brute force won't work, tell me what will."

"Do ya really mean you're gonna try and help me?"

"Yes." Of course. Not helping Mickey wasn't an option in Riku's book.

"Gosh, Riku, something tells me you and I are gonna be good friends, and we'll help each other out a lot someday."

Riku couldn't help a little smile.

"Inside this music is a Sound Idea powerful enough to dispel the darkness. Can ya find it?"

As Mickey spoke, another musical score appeared in the air and descended to the flooded floor.

"I'll try. Leave it to me."

Riku accepted the task gladly, then walked over to the second music stand and raised his Keyblade. Light and sound welled from the score, pulling Riku inside.

He landed deep in a forest bathed in moonlight.

Behind him, Komory Bat and Meow Wow followed along—and in front of him, a group of Dream Eaters appeared.

"Here we go!" Riku called out to his Spirits, then leaped into the battle. He swung his Keyblade the way he always did, but—

"Hey, what's going on?"

Normally, whenever Riku's blows landed, he would hear and feel the impact—but this time, each strike created a beautiful tone, almost like he was playing an instrument.

"Let's try that again!"

When he performed a series of attacks, the notes became a melody playing over the sounds of the world around him, joining together to create their own sort of symphony.

Just then, some white flowers opened nearby.

"Hmm…?"

Their big petals were arranged like steps, allowing access to a place he couldn't reach before.

"Well, I guess that works…," Riku muttered, then climbed the floral staircase and made his way deeper into the woods, where the trees reminded him of fall.

Like before, Riku struck the Dream Eaters with a nice tempo. Komory Bat and Meow Wow's attacks produced melodies, too.

As soon as the symphony came together, some withered brown

leaves rose up to create yet another set of platforms leading Riku farther into the forest, where snow had started piling up.

The snow crunched under his feet with each step. When Riku played his melody of attacks here, platforms shaped like snowflakes formed over a frozen pond, and at the top of the hill on the far side was a gleaming musical score.

"This must be the Sound Idea..."

When Riku lifted his Keyblade, the score turned into light and flew into his chest.

But immediately afterward, he felt the ground suddenly dropping away beneath him.

"What...?!"

And Riku tumbled headfirst into the darkness.

Riku awoke on one of several bleak mountaintops, nothing like the forest from before. He was on a crag near the summit, where red lava burst from the crater with a wave of intense heat.

The young man with silver hair was standing right beside the lip of the volcano.

"You waiting for me?" Riku asked, looking up from the stone.

"Yes. The boy chosen by the Keyblade—Riku."

"What?"

Whatever he'd been expecting to hear, it wasn't that. He'd always believed Sora was the Keyblade's hero, not him. But this guy was saying that Riku was the chosen one.

"It was yours first, wasn't it? But you succumbed to the darkness you could not control, and your prize—the Keyblade—passed on to Sora instead. Your mistakes always end up being other people's problems."

To Riku, the accusation was a painful truth. Still, he lifted his head with a smile on his lips. "Maybe so. But I'm here to change all that."

"Once again you performed predictably, although on a grander scale than I imagined."

"If you're feeling so chatty, let's skip to where you reveal what this is all about." Nothing anyone could say would make him falter. Not anymore.

He just smiled back at the young man, indomitable.

Behind the youth, lava erupted from the crater, casting its red light over the both of them.

"I don't know how you did it, but you really have found a way to trap darkness inside your heart. And a boy who's immune to darkness is of no use to us."

"Well, there's some good news." Riku wasn't sure anyone could ever be truly immune to the darkness, but maybe he'd found the next best thing—belief and clarity of purpose. He would never fall prey to the darkness again.

"Your abyss awaits."

As if on cue, lava shot from the volcano all at once, filling the area with black smoke.

What climbed from the crater was Chernabog, a horned fiend with large black wings like those of a bat.

The monster rose into the air along with the lava spewing from the mountain.

"Help me out?"

At his call, Komory Bat circled Riku's head once and merged with him in a flash of light. Bat wings sprouted from his back—and now he could chase the fiend down.

Riku leaped away from the ground to confront Chernabog in mid-air. The fiend flapped its wings, unleashing balls of fire toward him.

Riku deflected the attack with his Keyblade, then immediately closed the distance between them and dealt Chernabog an upward blow from chest to chin.

"Graah!" The great creature clutched its head and hid its body behind its wings.

"Now! Blizzaga!" The moment Chernabog opened its wings again, Riku seized the opening to cast a spell.

The demon spit out a fireball at nearly the same instant, but Riku's icy magic obliterated Chernabog's flames and scored a direct hit on the creature.

"I think that did it!"

Chernabog went limp and slumped over the mouth of the volcano. And darkness swallowed the realm again.

The next thing he knew, Riku was back in front of the music stand in the room with Mickey.

"Thank you, Riku. Say, can we try out Sound Idea?"

At Mickey's suggestion, Riku began to wave his Keyblade like a conductor with a baton.

When he did, light emanated from his Keyblade, creating a mysterious and wonderful sound. Yet it seemed incomplete somehow.

It transformed into light and flew to the musical score behind Mickey, but the dark presence around it wasn't dispelled yet. And no sooner had Riku realized it than a new sheet of music arrived.

A harmony started to flow from the new Sound Idea, filling the chamber. The swell of music and light poured into the score, and the darkness was no more.

The light grew and grew, until it swallowed the whole room in brilliant white.

"That was amazing! What happened?"

The flood receded, and Mickey rose from his chair, now awake and looking around in confusion.

"Sora." Riku told him the name of his friend who had found the other Sound Idea. Sora was a world away and yet right by his side.

"Sora? Funny... Just hearing that name kinda makes me wanna smile," Mickey said warmly.

Riku responded with a smile of his own. "Yeah. That's how he is."

Just hearing his name is enough to make you smile. Yeah, that's Sora all right.

"Whaddaya know... Riku and Sora. The Sound Ideas you two

set free joined together. And when they did, they made a great and powerful harmony."

Their two melodies had combined to make a song, which in turn became power—and when people joined forces, they were stronger for it.

"Sora can find the brightest part of anything and pull off miracles like there's nothing to it. It's pretty hard not to smile around him."

I can't bring happiness to other people the way Sora can, but I hope I can at least help him in some way, Riku thought.

"Wow! No wonder the music sounded like so much fun. But I bet he's got you to thank for that. Having such a good friend means he could really enjoy it."

"Huh?" Riku was startled to hear that.

"It's like each of you is holding on to a little part of the other. Your hearts are always in tune, so they're free to sing. Gosh, I hope I can be part of the team someday."

"Someday"? Mickey, you've already helped us both more times than we can count. Maybe you haven't yet in this world, but I know you'll get your wish.

"You will. Trust me." Riku hugged Mickey's shoulders.

Then Mickey hopped into the air as if he had just remembered something.

"Oh no! I've got to hurry or I'll be in trouble!" he cried. He dashed from the room, giving Riku one last smile before he left.

Once he was alone, a Keyhole floated up before Riku. This was the final Keyhole—maybe.

He couldn't stop thinking about the "abyss" supposedly awaiting him. What did that mean?

Their worlds appeared parallel, but they weren't at all. What was Sora doing?

Whatever the answer was, he would find it beyond this door.

Mickey & Lea's Side

Quite some time had passed since Sora and Riku's departure.

Mickey was inspecting a bookshelf in Yen Sid's chamber. Maybe there was a book that would prove useful in the journey and battle to come. He wanted to gain even the tiniest bit more knowledge of the worlds while he had the chance.

Sora and Riku were busy with their Mark of Mastery exam, and Mickey was positive they would pass it and become true Masters. That was why he had to be sure his mind was sharp for the upcoming conflict.

Behind him, Donald was gazing at the sky through a star-shaped window. "Gee, I hope Sora's okay," he said, worried.

"He'll be just fine as long as Riku's with him," replied Goofy, but Donald didn't seem convinced. He and Goofy had traveled alongside Sora a long time; maybe they knew to be worried about something Mickey wasn't aware of.

"Hmm…" Donald had his head to one side.

Mickey recalled something from his previous trials.

This Mark of Mastery exam was an exam in name only, since it was actually an important battle to awaken people who were sleeping in the darkness of sorrow.

They had to free the Sleeping Worlds that had not been completely restored and rouse the three Keyblade wielders—Terra, Aqua, and Ven. Mickey had once fought alongside them. The trio's power would be essential in putting a stop to the designs of Master Xehanort, who was at the root of all the conflict that had come before.

When he thought of it that way, it was easy to see why Donald was so nervous. Master Xehanort had set traps within traps for them in the past: Ansem the Wise and the false Ansem, as well as

Organization XIII, Xemnas, Xehanort, and then there was Master Xehanort himself.

His convoluted mess of connections and schemes had caused them grief more than a few times.

What if... Mickey turned to face Yen Sid and started to voice his suspicions. "You don't think...?"

What if they had already fallen into the evil master's snare?

Why are the Sleeping Worlds asleep at all? Why weren't they freed back then? Could it be because...?

"Master Yen Sid!"

Just as Mickey cried out, a lone bird flew in through the moon-shaped window.

"Look, it's a raven!" Goofy seemed confused why it was here.

Mickey instinctively swallowed. He knew that raven. "Uh-oh!"

"That raven is Maleficent's," Yen Sid murmured.

Something similar had happened once before. Mickey remembered the report from the three good fairies, Flora, Fauna, and Merryweather. Right before their second run-in with Organization XIII, a raven from Maleficent had arrived at the tower after a newly awakened Sora had come to prepare for his fight.

"What's it got?" Donald squawked.

The raven dropped Minnie's tiara and a letter on Yen Sid's desk before flying away.

His heart racing, Mickey picked up the letter.

"Well?"

"Gawrsh, what's it say?"

Donald and Goofy approached with trepidation.

The letter was from Maleficent, and what it said left Mickey filled with despair.

Once he had finished looking it over, his face grim, he said, "It's from Maleficent. She's kidnapped Minnie."

"She took Queen Minnie?" Donald and Goofy exclaimed in unison.

Maleficent had chosen the middle of the Mark of Mastery exam to make her move. Was it coincidence? Or...was she was in cahoots with Master Xehanort?

"The letter says for me to return to Disney Castle...or else," Mickey told them.

Yen Sid closed his large eyes and replied straightaway, "Mickey, there is no time to waste."

It was possible that he had foreseen this very development.

"Okay," Mickey replied, then looked at the worried Donald and Goofy. "You fellas stay here."

"King Mickey, we're going with you!"

As soon as he told them to stay behind, the duo cut him off with a pair of salutes.

They were concerned for Minnie, too—of course they were.

Mickey's stern expression softened a bit. "Gosh...I guess you're right, pals," he said. "We friends need to stick together."

Donald and Goofy shared a look and smiled.

"Master Yen Sid, we'll be back!" Mickey called to the sorcerer before running from the room. Donald and Goofy weren't far behind.

Once they had gone, Yen Sid let out a long sigh. "The timing is too perfect, too calculated. Maleficent must sense a change in the forces of darkness," he said softly.

His misgivings were exactly the same as Mickey's, as was the first culprit to come to mind.

"A change...like Xehanort."

The sorcerer crossed his arms and closed his eyes as he pondered what lay in store for the heroes.

Axel strode swiftly through the Corridors of Darkness. Now that he was human, traveling this way didn't feel too great. There was no telling when the darkness might devour him.

Even Nobodies feared the darkness slowly taking them over, but he'd never thought his black coat would come in handy. Now he would have at least a little protection.

Yes, Axel was now truly flesh and blood, which meant that the idea of losing himself to the darkness frightened him. He broke into a smile—what a human thing to feel.

Still, he needed the power of darkness to open these corridors. Without it, he wouldn't be able to travel from Radiant Garden to other worlds. The darkness in his heart gave him that power, and he had at least enough for this.

Was any human truly free of darkness in their heart? Wasn't that the nature of sadness and regret? At the same time, he also harbored doubts about the claim that Nobodies didn't have hearts.

That's what he had been told many times, and he used to believe that was just the way it was.

But was a heart something that could be truly lost? He had felt sadness and loneliness, he knew—but didn't you need a heart for that? Or was it just the imitation of one provided by his memories?

There was a fleeting ache deep in Axel's chest.

Hadn't he felt this same pain as a Nobody, too?

You made us a promise.

Axel suddenly got the sense that he'd heard Roxas's voice, and he stopped.

That you'd always be there...to bring us back.

That's right, he had promised. That he'd always be there to bring them back. Axel then realized something.

"Us"...? Didn't I just promise to bring Roxas back? Was there someone else? Not...Isa?

No, that can't be it. It's not Isa. But who else would I have made that promise to? My memories are a mess.

Wait, have they been altered? Maybe even erased? But what would anyone have to gain by that?

Was I trying to bring back someone whose name I can't remember? Someone besides Roxas?

"Sheesh... So much for getting it memorized," he muttered, scratching his head furiously.

He did make the promise; that much was certain. He had no doubt that he had sworn to bring Roxas back—and when he finally did, he would learn the identity of the one he couldn't remember.

And even if I don't, I hope it'll give me a place to start. I'm sure it will. That's why I left Radiant Garden.

I can't do anything on my own. I need help—and I know just who to ask.

I'll help them however I can, too. Both for their sakes and for Roxas.

Axel resumed walking through the Corridor of Darkness.

Back at Disney Castle, Mickey burst into the royal hall to confront Pete and Maleficent. Pete had Minnie in his grip.

"Pete, you big thug!" Donald shouted.

"'Thug' works for me. We all got a role to play, right?" Pete responded with a grin.

"Gawrsh, at least he's honest, in a dishonest way," Goofy commented.

With Minnie captive, Pete had the advantage, and he knew it.

"Silence! No underling of mine shall be insulted so. I have great plans for dear Pete and for all the worlds...once I have taken them for my own," Maleficent proclaimed.

"Then I've got bad news for you—that day's never gonna come," Mickey told the evil fairy.

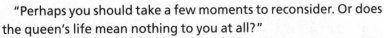

"Perhaps you should take a few moments to reconsider. Or does the queen's life mean nothing to you at all?"

Maleficent's reply made their position clear. They could do nothing as long as Minnie was a hostage.

As Mickey and his comrades racked their brains over what to do, Minnie shouted, "Mickey! Don't you listen to her! You can't let Maleficent have her—"

But Pete covered her mouth before she could finish.

"No! Minnie!" Mickey took a step forward as he cried the name of his beloved queen. He glared at Maleficent, clenching his fists for a moment to calm the fury in his heart. "All right, Maleficent. Tell us what you want."

She smirked and stroked her chin. "Let me see... Shall I begin with this world? I much preferred it in its darker, more ominous permutation."

"You said it. This place needs some lights-out time!" Pete added.

But Mickey didn't believe for a moment that that was enough reason for her to come all this way.

"You're lying, Maleficent. Not even you would go through this much trouble just for that. What is it you're really after?" he pressed.

The fairy regarded him coldly. "Very perceptive. I presume you are familiar with Xehanort, the man who led me to discover worlds outside my own?"

At that name, Mickey and everyone else with him gasped.

"You know him?" Mickey asked, his voice tight.

"As do you, I see." Maleficent chuckled before continuing. "Yes, he shared everything with me—how to go about winning a heart over to the darkness and, most gloriously, about the seven hearts of pure light—the ones that would grant me the power I need to conquer all worlds."

Maleficent had once led several other villains in a quest to take over every world.

So Xehanort even had a hand in Sora's first battle against her?!

"However, the worlds were too complex, too much for even me to contain. It seemed I had miscalculated. Then it came to me— Of course! I could go about conquering other worlds in my own manner. You do have the 'data' for all the worlds, do you not? And now you will hand it over to me."

"What do ya mean?" Mickey asked back. "Data for all the worlds"—was she talking about the datascape?

"Don't you bozos pretend you don't remember. Me and Maleficent was trapped inside it. Now cough it up!" Pete hollered.

Not so long ago, Mickey and his friends had watched over Data-Sora's adventures in the datascape and even joined him. As for the datascape itself, it was made from Jiminy's journals, the records of their travels up to this point.

But what would that have to do with Maleficent's intentions?

"Why do you want the data?" Mickey demanded.

"I'm afraid that is no concern of yours," she told him icily.

Mickey was ready to fight her if he had to, and he took a step forward, fixing her with a hard look.

"Ah-ah-ah... Wouldn't want Her Royal Minnie Mousiness to get a boo-boo, now would we?"

But Pete's warning brought him to a halt.

"I see you have failed to recognize the futility of your situation. Very well... Face your doom!"

With that, Maleficent unleashed her magic. But when the spell was about to hit Mickey and his friends, something deflected it.

What? How...?

Mickey noticed a pair of round, disc-shaped weapons—chakrams— at the edge of his vision.

That couldn't be—?

But there was no time to check who threw them. He couldn't let this moment go to waste!

"What?!" As Pete staggered back, Minnie seized the opening to cast a spell of her own.

"Light!" It was enough to free her from his clutches, and she ran for it. "Oh, Mickey!"

The king rushed over to her, and they took each other's hands.

"Minnie!" Then quickly putting Minnie safely behind him, Mickey brandished his Keyblade. "Maleficent...you lose!"

Victory was certain at this point. Mickey glared at the witch and her cohort.

"Say, uh, milady, I think the pip-squeak's right. We better hit the road," Pete said, so meekly that it was hard to believe he had been so arrogant before.

"I now know what I seek lies within these walls. Trust that I will eliminate you in good time." Still confident, Maleficent opened a Corridor of Darkness beside her and stepped into it with a swirl of her cape.

"Hey! Wait for me! Maleficent?" Panicking, Pete hurried after her, and the two of them disappeared.

Meanwhile, another dark portal had opened in the room.

Mickey looked over at it and called out, "You used the darkness to get here? That was reckless."

A man in a black coat slowly emerged and yanked the spikes of his chakrams free of the floor.

Though Mickey had lowered his Keyblade, Donald and Goofy still had their respective weapons at the ready.

"But gosh, I didn't expect you to save us...Axel."

The man he had called Axel smirked and replied with a smile. "Axel didn't. My name is Lea." Axel—no, Lea put a finger to his temple. "Got it memorized?"

"No way—you're human again?" Mickey exclaimed in surprise.

"Looks that way," Lea said and smiled with a shrug.

"But what happened?" Mickey asked.

Lea looked intently at him. "Well, like you said, I'm human again. That probably gives you the general idea, right?"

Mickey gulped.

"Anyway, I don't think I could've timed that much better. I was just coming here to ask where you guys were—and look what I find." Lea popped his neck, then bent down closer to Mickey's face.

"Thanks. But why did you want to know where we were?"

"King Mickey! Don't tell me you trust a member of the Organization?" Donald shouted, his staff raised.

Mickey remembered that Axel had once betrayed the Organization and worked alongside "Ansem"—Riku in Xehanort's form—but Lea apparently wasn't going to tell that to Donald and Goofy.

"Hey, hey, is that any way to talk to the guy who saved your life?" Lea chided, and Donald fell silent.

Donald didn't know that Axel had saved Sora at one point even further in the past, too.

"You helped me once before...right?" said Goofy, putting away his shield at last. After he'd been knocked unconscious in Hollow Bastion, Axel was the one who had roused him.

"Did I? Don't recall. Anyway, I need a favor," Lea said with a solemn look.

"What is it?" the king asked, looking up, and Lea held his gaze. Slowly, he began to explain.

"He saved us."

While Mickey gave Yen Sid a brief report in front of the sorcerer's usual seat, Lea stood quietly off to the side, looking at the ground.

The whole flight back to the Mysterious Tower in the Realm Between, Donald hadn't taken his eyes off Lea.

"What is this favor you ask?" Yen Sid inquired.

Lea looked the sorcerer dead in the eye and told him. "Teach me how to wield a Keyblade."

"WHAT?!" Mickey, Donald, and Goofy all shouted at once, and Donald continued with a loud "Absolutely not!"

Unlike the flustered trio, Yen Sid just let out a long breath and replied, "I sensed something was amiss nearly the moment Sora and Riku departed. Xehanort must have known what we were attempting even before we began."

Donald and Goofy shared a worried glance.

"But you do know where they are?" Goofy lowered his head, as if he found the question hard to voice.

Yen Sid gazed for a moment at the fist on his knee, then stroked his long beard and started to speak. "You must understand, this examination is in no way how the Mark of Mastery is usually found. However, in light of what they must do next... it was a necessity. If Sora and Riku complete their test by finding the seven doors corresponding to the seven pure lights, they will return home with a new power. At that point, they will both be true masters. However, the dangers make this more trial than test." Yen Sid's voice was grave as he explained Sora and Riku's exam.

Lea crossed his arms, his right foot tapping impatiently, and Yen Sid fell silent.

"But are they safe now?" Mickey pressed.

"Considering their ability, I would like to believe that they are. However, all my attempts to locate Sora and Riku end... questionably. Xehanort is a devious tactician. There is nothing we can do that he will not, to some extent, be able to predict."

Donald sighed, unable to hide his concern.

"As you can see, the Organization's members are complete people again. Xehanort will be no different. We cannot afford another moment's hesitation. We must consider any strategy to outwit Xehanort and catch him off guard."

The sorcerer examined Lea for a silent moment, then said, "I must warn you again—the road will not be easy."

"Fine. Let's jump right in," Lea replied firmly, arms still crossed.

Yen Sid beckoned him into the inner chamber, and inside, Lea was met by three brightly smiling old fairies.

"Welcome!"

"Uh, what?"

Lea was confused. No one had ever seemed so happy to see him, at least not since he became a Nobody.

"Let's see, and you are...?"

"Lea."

The fairies were each wearing robes and hats of a different color: blue, red, and green.

"I'm Merryweather."

"I'm Flora."

"And I'm Fauna."

The trio introduced themselves together. The fairy in blue was Merryweather, the one in red was Flora, and the one in green was Fauna.

"Oh my, what a dreary black coat."

"But we weren't asked to give him a new outfit."

"Such a shame."

The fairies chattered away as they fluttered around him.

"Now then, deary, we're going to take you somewhere special."

"Somewhere special?" Lea asked.

"Yes, a very special place," Merryweather replied.

"Well then, let's be off!"

The three fairies all waved their wands toward him.

Startled, Lea noticed the twinkles of light surrounding him—and a moment later, he vanished.

After Lea was gone, the mood in Yen Sid's chamber turned somber.

If Master Xehanort had laid a trap in Sora and Riku's Mark of Mastery exam, then the two boys were in danger.

Not only that, but the sorcerer was indeed "considering any strategy" to outwit him, and the one they had just chosen was another source of worry.

"Master Yen Sid. Gosh, do ya think he'll be able to do it?" Mickey asked, unable to take the oppressive atmosphere any longer.

"It's clear you cannot teach a cat to bark. But Merlin and the three good fairies are aiding him in a place that's more...temporally flexible. My hope is that he can at least learn to wield it. He certainly has fire, so I suppose now it depends on how strongly it burns."

How strongly his fire burns...

If Axel's behavior was anything to go by, Lea's determination was strong. Mickey had seen it himself. But what about his physical abilities? Regardless of how strong Lea was, Mickey could imagine how strenuous the training must be.

All he could do for now, though, was have faith in him.

"Oh... But what about Sora and Riku?" Mickey asked next.

Yen Sid let out a deep breath. "Well, if we are running on the assumption Xehanort knew what we were planning, then he still would need to have been there—back in the very place and time when the Destiny Islands were lost to darkness. Otherwise, Sora and Riku would have been beyond his reach."

"Gee, do you really think it's possible Xehanort could have planned things that far in advance?"

"No, as a matter of fact, I do not."

Mickey patted his chest in relief at those words. The exam had begun in the place Sora and Riku had once left behind so long ago—the Destiny Islands.

"One dream is connected to another, which is why we must choose in which 'Sleeping World' you will begin. I will return you to the Destiny Islands just before they were swallowed by the darkness and plunged into sleep."

It had also been a world of memory.

Because of that, Xehanort couldn't possibly have interfered in the exam unless he was there himself. Not even a man like him had that much power.

"But what if he did the same thing as Sora and Riku did, and he jumped through time?"

Goofy cocked his head to one side questioningly.

"For that to work, a version of himself would have had to exist at both source and destination. Not even Xehanort can transport his whole body across vast reaches of time."

Aside from a few exceptions, Mickey had never heard of anyone traveling through time.

Something bothered him, though. Mickey recalled something Jiminy had written in his journal about their first adventure.

When did Ansem—Xehanort's Heartless take control of Riku?

He had manipulated the boy by worming his way into the darkness within Riku's heart, which must have happened in the midst of battle. Or had it…?

No, Riku was already in the darkness's thrall at the onset of their journey.

Why had it been necessary for Xehanort to take control of Riku as a Heartless and not as Xehanort himself?

"Oh!" Mickey exclaimed as he realized something. "Oh… Oh no." After thinking for a moment, he looked at Yen Sid. "I remember—Xehanort did give up his body. It was a version of him that was possessing Riku."

It had been necessary for Xehanort to discard his own body to seize control of Riku's heart. Did that mean he had planned everything from the very beginning…?

Yen Sid's eyes went wide. "No! It cannot be. Could he be that cunning, possess that kind of foresight?"

Donald and Goofy looked at each other nervously.

His expression grim, Mickey looked up at the sorcerer. "If it's all right with you, can I go help Sora and Riku out?"

He wanted to go, more than anything. *I'm the only one who can save the two of them now.*

"How? You cannot enter the world of a dream. Where will you go?" Yen Sid admonished him.

Mickey replied with confidence, "If Xehanort really is behind all this, then they won't stay in the dream worlds forever. Eventually, they're gonna reappear somewhere that we can go reach 'em. And we can even probably guess the place. Follow the hearts, and you'll find the way. That's something Master Aqua told me once."

"We'll never be apart no matter where we are.
Because we're connected."

Mickey recalled what Aqua had said.
Everything's going to be fine. Nothing can tear us apart.

"Aqua, never forget, we'll always be friends."

Mickey's promise to Aqua had bound their hearts together, and Sora and Riku were connected to him in the same way.

Yen Sid nodded deeply at Mickey's reply. Now that he was ready to go, Donald and Goofy approached the king anxiously.

"King Mickey…"

But before they could say any more, Mickey shook his head. "Aw, fellas, you're my best pals. But this time, I really do need to go it alone." He smiled at them. "The dangers are greater than anything we've ever faced before. If something were to happen to Sora and Riku and me—why, you'll be the only ones left to keep this world safe."

Donald and Goofy deflated at Mickey's words.

"Mickey, I was not able to locate Sora, but I sense Riku's presence in the Realm Between. Trust your heart, and I know you will find him," Yen Sid told Mickey.

"Thank you. I promise I'll bring them both back safe and sound," Mickey assured him, his hand clenched in a determined fist.

Lea had thought he was ready for this, but he hadn't imagined it would be this hard.

He gazed directly ahead as he took a few deep breaths. Fighting Roxas was nothing compared to this. That battle had been tougher than anything else he'd ever faced, but not because of his opponent's skill. No, it was the animosity in his best friend's eyes.

And back then, he hadn't known what would befall them when he did bring Roxas back to the Organization.

Things were different now, though. Lea knew exactly what to do. There was no telling how it would all shake out, but at least his course was set.

He would bring Roxas back, and then he would return the other one his friend had mentioned back to normal.

He didn't know if "back to normal" was the right way of putting it. Maybe he was trying to restore things that were beyond fixing.

But I can't just call it quits when I don't have the whole story. I won't give up, not when I promised you. I'm coming. Wait for me.

I made that promise on the clocktower, watching the sunset, and I won't stop until I've kept it.

I've got it memorized. I won't forget.

"I'll always be there to bring you back…," Lea muttered with a grin as he panted.

It was a wish—an oath, a promise.

I'll bring you back as many times as it takes. I'll always be there. For my sake and for both of yours.

"It's because you two are my best friends."

Who taught me that?

Best friends?

We were in Twilight Town—on the clocktower, the same place as always. We had all been eating some cold, salty ice cream. Me and Roxas and…who else?

I can't remember—but that doesn't matter. All I know is that you both are coming back.

Not just Roxas but the other person, too. That's why I'm going to get a Keyblade.

Sure, it's gonna be rough going, and I know I'm doing something crazy. But it'll take more than this to bring me down.

I'm strong, after all.

CHAPTER

8

The World
That Never Was

AFTER OPENING THE SEVENTH DOOR, RIKU ARRIVED IN
a place he knew.

A world of white and gray.

*Isn't this the headquarters of Organization XIII? What am I doing
here? How do I get back home?*

"Your abyss awaits."

Riku reflected on what the silver-haired young man had said.
*What did he mean by "abyss"? Well, only one way to find out. Let's
keep moving.*

Komory Bat was overhead, and Meow Wow was at his feet. At
least he wasn't truly alone; the fact gave Riku courage.

"Let's go." With a call to the Spirits, Riku broke into a run.

And as he suspected, this world was rotten with Nightmares, too.
They were stronger than any of the ones he'd met before, and they
just kept attacking.

He wasn't about to lose, though. Sora was probably fighting right
about now, too.

Riku did away with the Dream Eaters as he raced down a seemingly endless corridor with the Nobody emblem here and there
along the walls. No doubt about it, this was definitely the home base
of Organization XIII.

*Seriously, what is going on? If opening the seven Keyholes brought
me here, does that mean this is a Sleeping World, too? No, that doesn't
sound right.*

Meaning, someone led me here...?

If indeed he had been led here, then in all likelihood this was some
kind of trap. Was this a dream, or was this reality? Riku didn't even
know that much. Either way, his only option was to keep going forward.

Riku arrived at what he guessed was the outer wall of a castle, and
in the distance, he could see a circular plaza surrounded by giant
columns. The floor was marked with the Nobody emblem as well.

And as he made his way over to it, Riku spotted someone there in the center.

"Sora!" he cried. It was his friend, floating over the white surface and caught in the grip of an inky darkness.

Riku ran to Sora and looked up at him. Sora was completely motionless, and his eyes were closed in a deep sleep.

"Sora! Don't! You've gotta wake up! Sora!"

Riku reached up and tugged his friend's hand, but Sora still didn't awaken.

The dark haze around Sora began to flow out, swirling around Riku and gathering in a single location.

And then—the darkness became a person in a black coat. But this coat wasn't a sheer black; there were purple emblems on the sleeves and hem. Glowing red eyes peered out from within the hood.

"Are you what's trapping him in that nightmare?" Standing with Sora behind him, Riku raised his Keyblade toward the Anti Black Coat. "'Cause if you are, I'm what nightmares fear!" he yelled as he lunged forward and closed the gap between them.

However, Anti Black Coat slid backward and vanished.

"What?!" Riku didn't even have a moment to think before the Nightmare's black claws caught him from behind and sent him flying through the air.

"Urgh—!"

Riku barely managed to recover and land on his feet instead of his face, but in the next instant, Anti Black Coat melted into the darkness again and reappeared some distance away. Fighting this guy up close was going to be too much trouble.

Riku caught his breath, then prepared a spell. Calculating the space between them, he suddenly cast Dark Firaga.

Anti Black Coat was stunned by the spell, and without giving his foe a moment to recover, Riku closed in and sent it sprawling.

"Is it over?"

It wasn't. Anti Black Coat floated through the air and regained its balance, then watched Riku from overhead.

His opponent was completely silent, even when Riku's hits landed. It was creepy.

All at once, the Dream Eater fired off several bolts of darkness. Riku swiftly batted them away and pounced once more.

Meow Wow jumped forward, and Riku sprang off its back to jump even higher and unleash another blast of Dark Firaga from the air.

This time, Anti Black Coat went still, and not long after, it turned to darkness and faded away so completely that its very existence was like a dream.

But Riku didn't stick around to watch the Nightmare's demise and hurried straight back to Sora.

His friend was still asleep inside what looked like a sphere of light.

"Sora, don't chase the dreams," Riku said to him. "They'll lead you nowhere, just to an abyss you'll never be able to wake up from."

The radiant orb enclosing Sora rippled—no, Sora himself was distorting.

Within the warping image, Riku could see something that looked like the entrance to the World That Never Was—the place where he had taken Ansem's form to fight Roxas.

"What? What's going on in Sora's world?"

As if on cue, the world around Riku began to waver as well, and yet Sora still wouldn't wake up.

"Why won't he open his eyes? Is he still in the nightmare?" Riku shouted angrily before hearing a voice.

That is right.

He knew this voice. "Ansem!" he yelled, but there was no sign of its owner. The world rippled again, but it was beginning to return to normal.

Sora can no longer wake up. No matter how many nightmares you consume, you cannot wake up someone who has fallen into the chasm of dreams.

"What?"

Now a black fog was stealing across the world around him.

Dreams hold our memories. Sleep holds our dreams. And darkness—it holds our sleep. Sora's heart belongs to the darkness now.

Though Riku could hear his voice clearly, he couldn't find the source. *Maybe...I'm hearing Ansem from within.* The thought frightened him.

Still, be that as it may, he had to bring Sora back from his nightmare.

"Sora would never give in to the darkness!" Riku shouted back at Ansem, wherever he was. The darkness could never take him, not the Sora he knew.

But you feel it, don't you? This world, the nightmare, the abyss. Why haven't you returned to the reality whence you came?

"No. This is a..."

Was he saying that this was still a nightmare, not the real world? But the doors of sleep had been opened—how was this place still around? Where was he?

Dream of a dream. A twofold nightmare. This whole journey, you have been inside Sora's dreams. And now darkness within darkness awaits you.

A pool of darkness immediately spread beneath Riku's feet.

"What?" There was nowhere to run as the dark mire clung to his legs and pulled him down. "No. I can't get loose!"

Though he desperately struggled to pull his legs free, it was no use. "Ungh—!"

And Riku disappeared beneath the surface.

His eyes closed, Riku floated within the pitch-black space.

There was no sound or light here.

And before Riku hovered the very Ansem he had been confronting.

"At the start of your test, when you struck out from that tiny island, you saw me there dressed in a robe," Ansem explained, his voice measured and unhurried. "Immediately, you knew something was wrong, so without even knowing it, you dove into Sora's dream.

And you became exactly what that sigil on your back represents—a Dream Eater to protect Sora from nightmares."

"Me? I'm a Dream Eater?" Riku opened his eyes and asked. He hadn't exactly been looking at his back over the course of this exam. *The sigil was there the whole time? Really?*

"Correct. But you failed to protect him. After all your efforts to command the darkness and protect those you cherish, it is a shame you locked that power away in the end."

Riku had no regrets about shutting away what he'd gained by drawing upon Ansem's power—the power of darkness.

I wanted to protect the people I cared about, but I let the darkness in to do it. That "power" was my weakness. I don't need it now.

"Except…it's not over. I can still save Sora."

"So you understand what to do. Set the darkness in you free, and you can rescue your friend."

I've traveled through the worlds more than once, and I've learned plenty along the way.

Light and darkness aren't separate; they're two sides of the same coin. Those negative emotions like fear, sadness, doubt—they're part of the darkness in my heart. What's made me stronger was keeping that sadness contained, locking it away—no, by embracing it and carrying it with me.

"Ansem," Riku said to him. "Or…Xehanort. You used to be a Keyblade wielder. But darkness stole your heart and the Keyblade with it. Don't you see? That's half the reason I'm even on this journey. After allowing darkness into my heart, am I still fit to wield the Keyblade? Even after locking you away, here you are, haunting me again. So I get it now. There's no point in trying to hold the darkness back."

"At last, you see clearly."

The deeper the darkness, the brighter the light shining within it—and the greater the sorrows I've endured, the stronger I've become.

"You know…when I look at you…there's this memory that flashes back. A secret I said I'd keep when I was little. The main reason I kept dreaming about the outside world…was 'cause of him."

Riku reflected on that childhood memory—and the promise he had made.

"Strength for what?"

How did I answer back then? I've forgotten all this time.
Why...did I want to be strong?
To protect what matters more than anything to me. That's just as true now as it was back then.

"My journey begins here and now. I'm going back to the real world and then to Sora's side."

"That...is your answer?"

Yes. That's my answer. "I know the way. Consume the darkness, return it to light." Riku summoned his Keyblade to his hand, then fixed Ansem with an angry look.

"You can try," Ansem hissed, and the darkness around them came away and swirled into a vortex.

Their bodies drifted slowly downward, until they reached a surface made of dry, heavy branches.

Komory Bat and Meow Wow aren't here. Guess I'm on my own this time.

"Ansem! You're part of my heart now. Part of the light!"

When Riku overcame Ansem, the darkness that lurked within him, he would open the path to light. No, maybe he already had.

He would never fall to his inner darkness again.

"Ever the fool, boy. And forever a pawn of the darkness!"

Darkness flowed from Ansem's form and congealed into a gigantic black figure behind him that roared threateningly.

"Bring it on!" Riku yelled as he lay in wait for his charging foe.

They were locked together in intense, close-quarters combat. Riku would knock Ansem away, and his foe would come barreling forward just as before.

Finally, Riku dodged and cast a spell, but Ansem came at him yet again as if it were nothing. The figure behind Ansem reached out and sent Riku flying with a punch.

"Ngh—!"

Riku dropped to his knees as he tried to pull himself together.

The shadow wasn't through yet, though, as it pounded the ground with its fist and sent a shock wave into Riku. It was a direct hit, and as soon as Riku hit the ground, Ansem was coming for him again.

Riku scrambled to his feet and blocked the attack.

They separated again, and this time it was Riku who closed the distance, swinging with his Keyblade as soon as he was within reach.

"Foolish boy..."

"Speak for yourself, Ansem!"

Stepping back for a moment, Riku got his Keyblade into position and caught his breath.

An indomitable will was coursing through him.

"Impossible...!"

"I will carry my darkness with me—and reach the dawn!" Riku shouted as he charged. This was his final attack.

He jumped into the air in front of Ansem, then brought his Keyblade down onto the shadow behind him from overhead. The powerful follow-through brought the Keyblade all the way down to Ansem himself.

His opponent fell still and seemed to fade into the shadowy figure behind him. Riku could tell that Ansem was spent.

"Is it over...?"

The black shade reached out for him, and Riku instinctively raised the hand holding his Keyblade.

When he did, the creature froze for only a moment before toppling over backward and melting away into the gloom.

Riku stared at his hand around his Keyblade.

Just now, that was—

"Strength for what?"

*   *   *

He recalled that question that had come back to him just before the battle.

I wanted to be strong so I could protect what I care about more than anything.

"So long as you have the makings...
"And you will find me, friend—no ocean will contain you then..."

Ansem was once the darkness in my heart, but I've defeated him now. I've finally found it.

"Strength to protect what matters," Riku said to himself. He lowered his Keyblade.

The world wavered again.

Riku stood with his eyes closed and found himself in the World That Never Was.

He was in the place where he had fought Roxas as Ansem back then. He'd seen this place in Sora's dream, but it was possible that this was the real world.

He had escaped from the dream realm.

It was all part of Ansem's—of Xehanort's plan that he had been separated from Sora from the outset. They had been unknowingly led astray from the Mark of Mastery exam and fallen right into his clutches.

Sora's gotta be here somewhere.

Riku began to walk toward the castle—the real headquarters of the Organization.

But then he came to a halt. "Hey, wait..."

There was no path. Only a precipice with the Organization's keep floating off in the distance.

"Squeekwee!"

Suddenly Komory Bat circled above Riku's head, chattering furiously.

He may be back in the real world, but he could still borrow the Dream Eater's strength. Which meant Sora still wasn't awake.

"Mrarf!"

He heard another cry, this time from far away.

Across the chasm, Meow Wow was watching him from atop the Organization's castle, apparently calling him over.

Is that where Sora is...?

Komory Bat landed on his shoulder. "Squeep," it said as it rubbed against his cheek.

"I get it. You wanna lend me a wing, huh?"

Riku petted the Dream Eater. He had never been alone, so he could be confident they would be together from here on, too.

"Squee-kee!"

Komory Bat took hold of Riku by the back and lifted him up, then flew toward Meow Wow.

"Thanks."

"Squeee."

Once they had landed safely at the castle, Komory Bat rubbed against Riku's cheek once more and flew into the air. Meow Wow brushed up against his legs.

"And thank you, too."

Riku scratched the Spirit's belly, prompting it to roll over happily.

He gave the building a hard look, took a deep breath, and stepped inside.

Within were thirteen tall chairs arranged in a white, circular room. They were all empty and all high overhead—except for one.

Sitting in the chair closest to the ground was—

"Sora!"

Riku started to run over to his sleeping friend, but before he could reach him, a dark portal formed right in front of him. The person within it knocked him away.

"Ngh!" Riku crashed to the ground, and the silver-haired boy he had encountered more than once stood over him.

"Hands off my new vessel."

"'Vessel'?" Riku asked as he raised his head.

"Yes. We originally had our sights set on you. But you developed a certain...resistance to darkness. So we did what the Keyblade did and moved down the list. Roxas... Now, there was a worthy candidate. But unfortunately, he became too aware of himself and returned to Sora."

Riku got to his feet, glaring angrily at the silver-haired youth.

"Organization XIII's true goal is to divide Xehanort's heart among thirteen vessels. Thanks to you and Sora, we learned not all our candidates were fit for the task. But we managed to make up the difference. And now, Sora, the thirteenth vessel, is within our grasp."

"Thirteen...Xehanorts?" Riku whispered. What did that even mean?

Columns of darkness began to appear over the empty chairs, each one leaving a seat occupied by someone in a black coat.

However, the tallest one remained vacant.

"The real Organization XIII."

Meaning the Organization XIII from before was just a sham?

"I am Xehanort from the most distant past. My future self gave me a task—to visit the splintered versions of myself in many worlds and ensure they gathered here today," said the young man. *What does he mean, from the "distant past"?* Riku recalled the names of all the ones he knew with some direct connection to Xehanort. *There's the Xehanort who called himself Ansem, Xemnas, and the Xehanort here in front of me.*

And one more.

Master Xehanort, the one he only knew by name from Yen Sid.

"There are restrictions to movement through time. First, you must leave your body behind to do it. Then there must be a version of you waiting at the destination. Upon arrival, you can only move forward as per the laws of time. And you cannot rewrite the events that are destined to happen."

So Xehanort was always around in one form or another, is that it?

No, not Xehanort—Master Xehanort.

A shock of anxiety ran down his spine, and Riku was shouting before he could stop himself. "What have you done?"

"My most future self will arrive soon. Then time for all of us will return to normal, and I will go back to my era to live the life fate has in store. He can vouch for that."

Riku lifted his gaze to the highest chair, where a black haze was coalescing into human form.

That was when a beam of light struck down into the center of the chamber with a blinding flash. The impact hurled the silver-haired boy away.

"Stopza!"

And as time froze around them, Riku recognized the voice.

"I'm glad I'm not too late." The light had brought someone with it, and the newcomer turned and grinned at Riku.

"Mickey!" Riku called the name of his dear friend and ran over to him.

"Just grab Sora so we can go! I can't stop them for long."

"Okay!"

But the moment Riku answered, something knocked Mickey away.

"Whoa!!"

"Mickey!!"

The young Xehanort stood shrouded in darkness. "I said, hands off!"

"How can you be moving?"

A Keyblade appeared in the young man's hand.

"Oh no!" Mickey cried. "Are you…?"

The young man's eyes flashed gold. "Begone!"

In the next instant, darkness overtook Riku and Xehanort.

Riku found himself on a platform patterned like a clockface, surrounded by hourglasses and floating gears that resembled the parts of a clock.

The young Xehanort faced off with Riku, Keyblade at the ready.

This is the version of him from the most distant past. So he has the power to manipulate time? How can he use a Keyblade? Because he's an incarnation of Master Xehanort?

As Riku came out of his thoughts, he noticed the two Spirits by his side. "Let's do this!"

Riku immediately merged with Meow Wow to launch an attack.

Their Keyblades met in a bright burst of incredible speed and force. They broke apart for a moment and fired off magic at each other, but they were evenly matched here as well. For a moment, Riku even thought the young Xehanort might actually be stronger.

Either way, I'm not going to lose. I have to win for Sora, for all my friends.

...For myself.

As they came together over and over, burning off stamina, Riku could feel the determination burning brighter and brighter in his heart.

Meow Wow separated from him, and Komory Bat took its place. Time to take this to the air. Using his new set of wings, Riku rained magic down on his foe from above.

You won't defeat me. Because I want to protect what matters to me. I want to protect my friends—but they aren't the only ones I'm fighting for. I have to do this for me.

"This is the end!"

Riku threw everything he had into a downward slash with his Keyblade—and time stopped. Somehow, young Xehanort's body had transformed into the face of a clock.

No—he had merged with time itself.

As time began to flow again, Riku leaped back into the air and unleashed a succession of Firaga Burst spells. The clock split into several copies, all of which fired X-shaped waves of light in his direction, but Riku knocked each one away with his Keyblade before making for the clock again. He could see the hands of the clock turning back a bit each time they were struck.

What is going on here? Either way, I can't let up now.

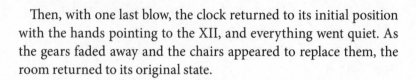

Then, with one last blow, the clock returned to its initial position with the hands pointing to the XII, and everything went quiet. As the gears faded away and the chairs appeared to replace them, the room returned to its original state.

"Are you okay, Riku?"

Mickey came running up to him.

"Yeah. Thanks, Mickey," Riku replied, and Mickey looked up at the tallest chair.

"Master Xehanort!" he shouted. "We were right about you!"

Riku followed Mickey's gaze to the one sitting in the seat. The old man with golden eyes smirked down at them with utter confidence.

This guy must be Master Xehanort!

"All of this was decided. My twelve selves would welcome me here on this day, when I would return a complete person. It is the future which lies beyond my sight."

So everyone here—they're all Xehanort!

Before he knew it, the unknown figures in black hoods had been joined by Master Xehanort, his younger self, Ansem, Xemnas, and Xigbar.

"Why are you doing this?"

Despite Mickey's agitation, Master Xehanort explained at a leisurely pace. "In ancient times, people believed that light was a gift from an unseen land by the name of Kingdom Hearts. But Kingdom Hearts was safeguarded by its counterpart, the χ-Blade. Warriors vied for that precious light, thus beginning the Keyblade War. The violent clash shattered the χ-Blade into twenty pieces—seven of light and thirteen of darkness. And the only real Kingdom Hearts was swallowed by the darkness, never to surface again."

He slowly closed his eyes, reflecting.

"I once tried to create my own pure light and darkness to forge the χ-Blade, but the attempt ended in failure. In my eagerness, I had lost sight of the correct way to achieve my goal. I acted rashly. I can admit that now."

Mickey jabbed a finger at Xehanort. "What you did back then— your mistakes—changed the destinies of three of my friends!" he shouted.

However, the old master's gold eyes were still seeing the past. "Ah, but destiny is never left to chance. I merely guided them to their proper places. The broken boy who failed to be the blade...the misguided master who sacrificed herself for a friend...and the feckless youth who became my new vessel," Master Xehanort said confidently with his legs crossed.

Mickey lowered his gaze. "I couldn't find a way to save 'em. But I wanted to believe that their sacrifice stopped you for good." The king hung his head, but his fists were clenched as he continued. "Why? How was I so blind? I should've seen it, as soon as Maleficent started gathering the Seven Princesses of Heart."

Master Xehanort smiled as he replied. "Yes. They were all my doing. I used the evil fairy to find seven pure lights for me, just as I prepared thirteen vessels to fill with pure darkness."

Finally, Riku stepped forward to stand alongside Mickey and speak to the master himself. "But you failed. Sora stopped you in your tracks on both counts," he contended, with a glance over at his sleeping friend.

"Yes, he did. That dull, ordinary boy—a Keyblade wielder so unlike any I have ever seen. However, I have not abandoned my ambitions—the seven guardians of light and the thirteen seekers of darkness." Xehanort stopped for a moment and sneered again.

"Seven guardians of light? Well, for Keyblade wielders, there's me and Riku and Sora. And my three missing friends, that's six. Then the seventh would be... That means...the thirteen seekers of darkness..."

"Yes, little king. Perceptive. But Sora and another on your list belong to me now. And that puts you three guardians short. But worry not. All of the pieces are destined to appear. Your seven lights just like my thirteen darknesses, whose final clash will beget the prize I seek—"

"The χ-Blade!"

Mickey and Master Xehanort shouted the final words together.

The old master rose from his seat and summoned his Keyblade to his hand. "But first, the thirteen darknesses shall be united. All the seats have been filled. And now the last vessel shall bear my heart like the rest!" he cried, and the chair holding Sora began to slowly rise.

"No!"

"Sora!"

Mickey and Riku exclaimed almost simultaneously.

The king hurried to reach Sora, jumping from chair to chair, but Xemnas leaped up and stopped him in his tracks. Riku had dashed ahead at the same time but found himself held by Ansem.

As Riku and Mickey struggled, Master Xehanort released a black mass from his Keyblade in Sora's direction.

"No!"

But at that very moment, a wall of flames rose to protect their friend, exploding out to burn everything around him. From the fire and sooty smoke, a man in a black coat stepped out with Sora under his arm.

"He made it!" Mickey gasped in relief.

"You!" Xemnas growled, still holding Mickey.

"Axel!" Xigbar yelled as he rose from his chair.

"Axel. Please? The name's Lea. Got it memorized?" he announced to the members of the Organization with a grin.

"You're not supposed to be here!" Xigbar snarled.

"Promises to keep. I'll always be there to get my friends back. What, bad timing? You had your perfect little script, but you kinda forgot to write the sequel. Now, let's find out what happens!" Lea laughed defiantly, holding out his chakram.

"What now, you old coot?" Xigbar demanded, looking up toward Master Xehanort. "Our time is up!"

Just then, one of the figures in the black coats stood up and lunged at Lea with a massive sword—a claymore—in his hand.

Lea parried the attack, but the impact knocked off his attacker's hood to reveal a man with long blue hair and an X-shaped scar on his forehead. Saïx—or rather...

"Isa!"

Lea said the name of his former best friend, glaring at him nearly nose to nose as chakram struggled against claymore.

Realizing he didn't stand a chance while he was holding Sora, Lea spun around and jumped down from the chair.

As he did, Mickey knocked Xemnas aside, while Riku shook off Ansem. The two of them drew their Keyblades to shield Lea and Sora in his arms.

"Why are you here, Axel?" Riku shouted over his shoulder to Lea.

"No, I told you my name's— Agh, whatever, Axel, fine. Now let's get outta here!"

"Right!"

As Mickey nodded his agreement, a black shadow emerged from behind Ansem and flew at Mickey and Riku, snatching the two of them up in its grasp.

"Whoa!"

"Ahh!"

With the two of them caught and Lea unable to act—they were all but doomed. Suddenly, however, they heard a pair of familiar and very distinctive voices.

"Waaaaak!"

"Waaa-hoo-hoo-hooey!"

A light came zigzagging down from above and crashed into the dark creature holding Riku and Mickey. The shock set the two of them loose, and the unexpected blow sent the black shadow back into the darkness.

Now free, Riku and Mickey, as well as Lea, peered into the light to see who had just saved them—and saw a very dizzy-looking Donald and Goofy.

"Were we supposed to do that?"

"I think so."

Riku and Mickey couldn't keep the smiles off their faces as they watched their friends look around, eyes spinning.

"Goofy, Donald! You saved us!"

The air began to tremble, and the members of the true Organization XIII slowly dissolved into darkness.

"We are out of time. Neither the union of light nor darkness has been achieved, and we must all return whence we came. But the gathering of the seven and thirteen is nigh. Let us finish this at the fated place, once your lights and my darknesses have joined together!" Master Xehanort declared—though it wasn't clear if it was meant for the members of the Organization or for Riku and his friends.

The fated place? Maybe Mickey knew where that was.

In that land, a battle had once been fought to determine the destiny of the world, and the seven lights and thirteen darknesses were beginning to come together for the final conflict once again.

But Sora was still asleep.

Mysterious Tower

RIKU AND THE OTHERS HAD RETURNED TO THE MYSTE-
rious Tower floating in the Realm Between.

Sora, still asleep, sat propped against the wall with his legs splayed out. Riku knelt beside him, while Mickey, Donald, and Goofy looked on anxiously. Lea was standing against a wall a short distance away.

"Seven lights, thirteen darknesses... Master Xehanort has been busy," Yen Sid murmured and closed his eyes, once he had received the report.

"Aw, Sora. Don't tell me your heart's sleeping, too," Mickey said to his young friend. He was remembering another boy who had slept in this room—Ventus, one of the three Keyblade wielders who had sought to save the world.

"No, Mickey. This affliction is not the same," the sorcerer said to the king, and Mickey looked over toward him.

"Can we do anything for him?" Riku asked.

Donald, Goofy, and Lea waited anxiously for the reply, too.

"In your Mark of Mastery exam, you were to unlock seven Sleeping Keyholes. By doing so, you would awaken those worlds from their prison of slumber and also acquire the power to free a heart from its sleep." The wizard looked at Riku from his chair. "Riku, you unlocked those Keyholes within Sora's dreams. Therefore, it stands to reason that you now have the power to awaken Sora's heart."

"You want him to dive back into Sora's sleep? But, Master, Sora's heart is down in the darkest abyss," Mickey protested before Riku could answer. His expression was grim. "If Riku's not careful, he might just get trapped down there with him. No... I'll go instead." He couldn't allow his friend to venture somewhere so dangerous.

But Yen Sid disagreed. "And perhaps you may even succeed, Mickey. But there is no denying Riku stands the better chance, having dived into Sora's heart as long as he has," he said, standing to look down at the slumbering boy. Mickey lowered his head, while Donald and Goofy shuffled uncertainly.

Riku studied his sleeping friend's face for a moment and then broke into a gentle smile. "Mickey... I really appreciate it. But...I'll go wake Sora up."

"Riku...," Mickey weakly protested, but Riku just gave him a nod and turned back to Sora.

"Look at his face. Sleeping like nothing's wrong—like there's nothing to even worry about. He's always been like that. The three of us would agree to work on the raft, and then this guy would go take a nap on the beach. You see, it's my job to keep him on his toes. Besides, what kind of Keyblade Master sleeps through his test?"

"Aren't you guys forgetting about me? So I guess I'm the only one working on the raft."

Riku reflected on that conversation on the beach. That was where it all began.

"I'm doing it for me, too. Sora saved me once. And...I heard him call my name. He needs me."

His conviction brought a smile even to Mickey's face. "There's something real strong that binds us to each other. Even in the darkness, you can reach him. All you gotta do is follow that connection!"

"Gee, we're all connected to Sora," Goofy added.

"You said it!" Donald agreed.

At the duo's cheery remarks, Lea joined the conversation, too. "And if the darkness gets ya, I promise I'll bail ya out. Dark Rescue is my middle name."

Riku got to his feet. "Guys, thank you. Sora and I will be back soon," he assured them. After a bow to Yen Sid, he gripped his Keyblade in his hand, raised it up, and held it out at Sora. A Portal appeared. Light radiated from Riku's Keyblade, and the Portal began to shine.

And Riku dove into Sora's sleep.

Darkness was in everything here. Some inky fluid covered the ground, while a black miasma rose toward the sky.

This was the chasm of Sora's dreams…

Riku surveyed his surroundings. The liquid seemed to be massing up ahead, gathering together into the shape of a person.

"What?"

When Riku readied his Keyblade, the humanoid mass turned into a suit of armor he had never seen before. It was about the same height as Riku's current form—himself before he had left the Destiny Islands. And then in the hands of the Armored Ventus Nightmare was a Keyblade of purest jet.

"What are you…?" Riku whispered, but whether or not it heard him, the armor closed the gap between them at incredible speed and went on the offensive. "Urgh…!"

As soon as Riku stopped the blow, the Armored Ventus Nightmare dove into the lightless morass at its feet and disappeared.

"Where'd it go?"

While Riku was distracted, three huge spheres appeared from the darkness and came at Riku. He knocked them away before they could surround him, but the Nightmare abruptly reappeared in front of him with a devastating attack. As he blocked again, Riku noticed something. Aside from the color, the Nightmare's Keyblade was very similar to Sora's.

Don't tell me the one in that armor is—?

His opponent seized Riku's moment of hesitation and landed a chain of blows. This wasn't a foe he could defeat by giving it any less than his all, although the idea wasn't his favorite. His mind made up, Riku parried its attacks. And when he did—it stopped. With an especially powerful blow, Riku knocked the Armored Ventus Nightmare away and thrust his Keyblade at his opponent before he could get back up.

And before Riku knew it, he was grinning.

I won't hold back, and I won't underestimate you. I'll give everything I have to set you free.

I was always jealous of you, Sora. I used to feel it all the time, and

I'd be lying if I said I didn't still. I believed that feeling was darkness, but now I know it's not. The truth is, it gave me strength, and so did having someone to challenge me.

Light and darkness are perfect complements to each other—the shadows are always greatest next to the light, and light shines out brightest in the dark. I know what that means now, truly.

When those dark feelings come over you, only your heart can decide whether to let them sink deeper into the darkness or to bring them out into the light of the sun. Accepting both is what it means to have a heart. It's what gives us strength.

Even wanting to protect those you care about is a form of pride, in a way. I don't think anyone can honestly say it's not. Same with wanting to be stronger.

Joy and sorrow, anger and hatred—whether those feelings become your light or your darkness is for you to decide. The strength of your heart is what allows you to choose.

That's why I choose to let the light shine onto my own darkness.

And Sora, that light is you.

Riku landed a final strike on the Armored Ventus Nightmare, and the armor cracked.

The protective shell shattered with a flash, and Sora appeared from within while the shroud over the world around him began to clear.

But—

"Sora!"

Though Riku grabbed for him, Sora was sinking into the darkness at his feet. He reached out desperately, but he was too late. All that remained was Sora's Keyblade.

"I'll find you, Sora."

Riku picked up his friend's weapon and raised it toward the center of this place—the darkness of sleep—and a Sleeping Keyhole appeared. This was the door leading to the innermost depths of Sora's heart.

Light shot from the Keyblade and into the Keyhole, which glowed brighter and brighter until everything went white.

*   *   *

Riku found himself on a wooden walkway of the isles he called home—the Destiny Islands.

And standing there in the sunset was not Sora but—

"Roxas?" Riku said to the golden-haired boy.

"What is it that you're so afraid of?"

Riku wasn't quite sure how to answer. *What am I afraid of? Well, what scares me more than anything is...*

"Losing something that's important."

At his answer, Roxas disappeared. *Yeah. What I'm most afraid of is losing what I care about.*

Riku began to walk from the bridge to the beach. He remembered playing tag here with Sora countless times.

This time, a boy who looked a lot like Roxas appeared before him.

"Roxas? No, wait..."

Something was different—not only his clothes but something about the way he carried himself.

"What is the one thing you care more about than anything else?"

Again, Riku was unsure. *What I care about the* most?

There was only one answer—what mattered to him more than anything and what terrified him to lose. "My close friends."

Again he answered, and the Roxas look-alike was gone.

He had no idea what was going on here anymore.

Riku suddenly looked up and saw someone sitting on the paopu tree on the islet.

"Sora!"

He hurried over across the bridge, and there he found a dark-haired girl in a black coat, taking in the sunset.

"Who are you?" he asked.

Without even turning his way, the girl asked him a question in return, her eyes still on the sun sinking below the horizon.

"Riku. What do you wish?"

"More questions... All right..."

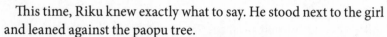

This time, Riku knew exactly what to say. He stood next to the girl and leaned against the paopu tree.

"To recover something important that I lost."

As soon as he gave his response, light engulfed him, and he found himself back on the beach.

A small bottle came drifting in from the sea, painted red by the setting sun.

"What's this?" Riku murmured as he picked it up, and then he heard a voice.

"You were not the visitor I expected." DiZ…no, Ansem the Wise, was walking toward him across the sand.

"What are you doing here?"

Ansem the Wise strode over to the waterline without so much as a glance at Riku. "Perhaps I wanted to atone for events of the past…" He paused for a moment, perhaps considering his next words. "…Even if no apology can undo the harm I have wrought. I felt… that I ought to leave at least something behind. So I digitized myself and my research and hid them within Sora."

Riku looked at the bottle in his hand. "So this is…data?" he asked.

"Yes. A clue, I hope, to finding yourselves or your lost friends in your hour of need."

Little by little, he began to speak.

"The heart has always been quick to grow. Each exposure to light, to the natural world, to other people shapes this most malleable part inside of us. Nobodies are not different from us in that manner. Sora was the only one able to return to his human form without destroying his Nobody. That is a statement to the love in his heart for other people and the bonds that tie them together. Perhaps…he has the power to bring back the hearts and existences of those connected to him—to re-create people we thought were lost to us forever. Our most precious treasures—even an empty puppet—the trees of the forest, and the petals on the wind: There are hearts around us everywhere we look. And it does not take superhuman powers to see them. Surely we remember as children the way our hearts made everything seem so shiny and perfect. Sora has a heart like that—uncorrupted, willing to see the good before the bad. When he sees the heart in something, it then becomes real. When a connection seems broken, he may have the power to mend it."

Silently, Riku just listened.

"He has touched countless hearts, he has accepted them, and he has saved them. And some of those hearts have never left him—whether they fell into darkness or were trapped there, whether they sleep in the darkness of Sora's heart or were welcomed into its warmth. They can be saved. All Sora needs to do is be himself and follow wherever it is that his heart takes him. It is the best and the only way."

Ansem the Wise pointed at Riku's bottle.

"The rest is in there."

"All right. Thanks. Thank you," Riku replied.

The sage looked at Riku. "Of course. Now why are you here?"

"Uh…I kinda need to wake Sora up."

Ansem the Wise smiled faintly at that. "Don't tell me he's gone to sleep again?"

"Yeah. What'll I do with him?" Riku smiled back.

"What, indeed?"

Riku had worked with DiZ in the past, and he had also worked against him. But this time, they simply shared a warm smile.

"Never fear. Sora is safe."

"Huh?" Riku asked instinctively.

"He's not here. You see, by defeating the Nightmare imprisoning Sora, you freed him."

"You mean…the Sora wrapped in that black phantom?"

Ansem nodded gently. Then he said, "Then you came here, and you were questioned by three young people. That was the final key to awaken him. Sora is awake. You can go home now."

So those questions were the key to waking him up—

I knew my answers were right!

"I see. Thank you."

Riku expressed his gratitude again, then held his Keyblade aloft. A Keyhole rose there, and the beam of light lanced into it.

As the boy rose into the air, Ansem the Wise had one final question for him.

"Young man! I do not believe you ever told me your name."

Ansem the Wise had asked him the question once before, back when Riku knew him as DiZ.

"But first, perhaps you could tell me your true name?"

Riku had once answered with another name, but this time, he could hold his head high and say who he really was.

"It's Riku."

He nodded at Ansem the Wise with a smile and vanished into the glow from the Keyhole.

"Is Riku still not back...?"

Sora had awakened with ravenous hunger from his time asleep, and he was stuffing his face with some cake that had been set out on a table.

Beside him, Mickey and Lea, who was sitting backward on his chair, looked over at Riku with concern.

Quite some time had passed since Sora came to, so it was odd that Riku had yet to wake.

Or so they thought, when Riku stirred.

"Riku!" Mickey called.

His eyes flew open, and he sat upright. "Sora!" he shouted—and then he saw his best friend wolfing down cake and tea with Donald and Goofy.

"Hey, Donald! Come on, you're hogging it all!"

"Aw, calm down, Sora, and drink your tea."

"Gawrsh, it sure is yummy!"

The three of them were going at it like usual.

"Hey!"

It was *exactly* like usual, which was why Riku had to interrupt with a good-natured complaint. When Sora turned around, he was in full party mode with a pair of mustache glasses on his face. He looked ridiculous.

Riku suddenly felt very, very tired.

"Riku..." Sora removed the glasses and flung his arms around his friend. "You're safe! Riku!"

As Sora hugged him tight and nearly knocked him into the wall, Riku asked quietly, "Wait, haven't we got this backward?" After a moment, Sora finally let go. "And why are you having a tea party?"

"You're safe, Riku!"

As Sora embraced him again, Riku realized his questions would never be answered. "Ah, never mind. You okay? Feeling all right?"

"Yeah, I've never been better," Sora said, striking a pose for effect. "I was watching what was going on in my dream. And I could hear your voice the whole time. Thanks, Riku!"

Riku nodded, and Sora turned his attention to the rest in the room.

"Thanks, everyone!"

They all shared a look and smiled, while Yen Sid gently observed. Noticing him, Sora asked, "Oh yeah! Did we pass the test?"

"You performed truly admirably, both of you."

As the sorcerer began to speak, Sora and Riku stood and assembled in front of him. Yen Sid cleared his throat slowly, and the cheery atmosphere grew serious. Mickey, Donald, and Goofy all stood beside the desk, while Lea was off by himself against the wall.

"More than anything, I am grateful to have you both back from Xehanort's deception unharmed. And I am grateful to Lea, whose spontaneous actions turned the tides."

He looked over at Lea and nodded. Lea returned the gesture.

"I am also deeply sorry for failing to perceive the danger and throwing you headlong into a perilous test. This experience has revealed many hidden truths, and we must gird ourselves for the great clash with darkness that lies before us. I believe we need a new Keyblade Master, one with a new kind of power."

Riku knew what he was getting at. *Just because you can use a Keyblade doesn't mean you're a master.* Riku felt himself tensing up a little.

"Sora and Riku, you both deserve the honor. However, one of you braved the realm of sleep again to unlock the final Keyhole and save a friend. Riku, I name you our new true Keyblade Master."

Riku was stunned for a moment, not quite sure of what had been said. He was sure both of them would pass as masters, but Yen Sid had named only one of them.

He's not saying...it was just me...?

"Way to go, Riku!"

Sora took his friend by the shoulder, and the reality finally hit him. One person had been named master, and it was Riku.

"Y-yeah?"

"I knew you were gonna pass with flying colors. This is just so awesome!"

Donald and Goofy shared a look at Sora's reaction.

"Gee, Sora, you're kinda acting like it's you that passed."

"I told ya Sora still needed some practice," Donald quipped.

"Hey!" Sora barked.

As they bantered, Riku still couldn't believe it was real. "Really? I'm a Keyblade Master?" he quietly asked, looking over to Sora.

Sora gave him an enthusiastic nod.

"Congratulations, Riku!" Mickey walked up to him and held out a hand.

"Thank you, Mickey." Riku knelt down and clasped hands with the king. "I owe it to my friends." He smiled, full of gratitude.

That was when Lea chimed in, "Ah, I'll catch up with ya in no time flat."

"What? You wanna be Keyblade Master?" Sora asked back in shock.

"Yeah. I mean, I came here to learn how to wield one." Lea stepped away from the wall, puffing out his chest with pride for some reason.

"YOU?!" Sora and Riku exclaimed in shock.

"Hey, thanks for the vote of confidence. You know, I was gonna come swooping in, Keyblade in hand! But I just couldn't get mine to materialize. Must be in the snap of the wrist or something."

As Lea held out his hand in front of him, something flashed into it—

"Oh."

A Keyblade like fire itself.

"WHOA!"

Everyone in the room, aside from Yen Sid and Lea, shouted.

But it wasn't quite over yet.

Sora stood at the entrance to the Mysterious Tower.

"Do ya have to go?" Goofy asked him with worry.

"Well…I did doze off… I just have some stuff to take care of."

"Are you gonna be okay?" Donald was concerned, too.

"Yeah. I won't be long," Sora replied with a grin.

Riku and Mickey looked on from behind Donald and Goofy.

"Be careful," Mickey called.

"*Very* careful," Riku added.

"Right. See you soon."

With that said, Sora held his Keyblade up to the sky. A Sleeping Keyhole appeared in the air, and he vanished in a flash of light.

Sora had arrived in Traverse Town.

"Good, I was hoping this world was still here." But he was all alone. Disappointed, Sora looked around. "But where are they?"

"Mrarf!"

Sora turned around as a familiar cry reached his ears.

"There you are!"

Meow Wow was bounding toward him, overjoyed.

"Did you help Riku?"

"Mrarf."

"Yeah, he told me all about it."

Sora patted the Dream Eater's head as it rubbed against him, then looked up at Komory Bat flying over, too. The Spirits had protected him and Riku.

"Thanks! You're the best."

Sora's new adventure was about to begin.

Right about then, in Castle Oblivion's Chamber of Waking...

A lone boy sat fast asleep.

A peaceful smile rose on his lips, as if he were seeing a pleasant dream.

Then—

CODA

"SORA'S LATE. DO YA THINK HE'S OKAY?"

Goofy watched the sky from the base of the Mysterious Tower. Donald sighed beside him.

"Gawrsh, Lea sure hurried back to Radiant Garden, and now Master Yen Sid's sending Riku away, too, on some mystery errand," Goofy commented, and Donald let out an even longer sigh. "Ya think we'll ever get to do something important?"

Just as Goofy asked his question, someone arrived in front of the Mysterious Tower.

"Wak!" Donald exclaimed as he noticed the newcomer, and Goofy turned to look, too.

"Oh! Welcome back, Riku! Hey, wait…"

Goofy put his head to one side, his surprise turning to a smile as Donald hopped up as well.

Up in Yen Sid's chamber, the sorcerer was speaking to Mickey.

"The Keyblade Wars of yore plunged the true Kingdom Hearts into darkness, and the χ-Blade was shattered. But the light still shining in the hearts of children rebuilt the world that we know today. And the light from the broken χ-Blade was then divided into seven, to protect the number of pure hearts in the world."

"Seven pure lights. They're…the Princesses of Heart," Mickey stated quietly.

"Indeed. Those seven pure hearts form the very source of all light in the world. If they are lost, the world will again give way to shadow. Thus, even if we deliberately avoid finding our seven lights to avert another Keyblade War, Xehanort will still target the Seven Princesses in order to forge the χ-Blade."

As Yen Sid laid out the facts, Mickey grew increasingly uneasy.

"So…there's gonna be a clash between seven lights and thirteen darknesses…and there's nothing we can do to avoid triggering the Keyblade War?"

"To protect the seven pure hearts, we will need seven lights strong enough to stand against the thirteen darknesses."

Seven guardians of light.

With Sora, Riku, and Mickey plus the three that were asleep, they had six. And then Lea made seven.

"But Sora and another on your list belong to me now. And that puts you three guardians short."

Mickey recalled what Master Xehanort had said. They had gotten Sora back, but one of the others—a person lost in sleep—was still in Xehanort's clutches?

If so—they would be down one.

"So we're missing one guardian of light," Mickey mused as the door opened. He turned around. "Riku! You're back!" he greeted his friend.

"That's right," Riku replied, stepping into the room. "Master Yen Sid, I brought you the guest you asked for, but…you never said why."

As Riku spoke, Mickey noticed someone behind him, and when he saw who it was, he yelped in surprise. "Huh? Wow!"

"I have come to learn that you, too, can wield a Keyblade. I am glad you are here."

Yen Sid bade her welcome, and she stepped into the room.

"This time…I'll fight."

Kairi had once said those words as she wielded a Keyblade and faced down evildoers at the end of their second adventure, and now here she was.

And as time marched on, the fated battle drew ever nearer.

"This world is just too small."